NASTY GIRLS

Also by Erick S. Gray

IT'S LIKE CANDY

MONEY POWER RESPECT

GHETTO HEAVEN

BOOTY CALL

NASTY GIRLS

ERICK S. GRAY

ST. MARTIN'S GRIFFIN
NEW YORK

Rest in peace
My beloved cousin
Tarshish "Toot Toot" Massey
Augusst 1974–January 2004
A coward took your life, but he
Didn't take away your love and spirit.
We love you.

Published in the United States by St. Martin's Griffin, an imprint of St. Martin's Publishing Group

www.stmartins.com

The Library of Congress has cataloged the first St. Martin's Griffin edition as follows:

Gray, Erick S.
Nasty girls : an urban novel / Erick S. Gray.—1st ed.
p. cm.
ISBN 0-312-34996-3
EAN 978-0-312-34996-7
1. Female friendship—Fiction. 2. African American women—Fiction. 3. City and town life—Fiction. I. Title.

PS3607.R389N37 2006
813\6—dc22

2006040801

ISBN 978-1-250-80583-6 (trade paperback)

Our books may be purchased in bulk for promotional, educational, or business use. Please contact your local bookseller or the Macmillan Corporate and Premium Sales Department at 1-800-221-7945, extension 5442, or by email at MacmillanSpecialMarkets@macmillan.com.

Second St. Martin's Griffin Edition: 2021

10 9 8 7 6 5 4 3

prologue

1998

"You little bitch! Who the fuck you talkin' to like that!" Mr. Anderson shouted at his fifteen-year-old daughter when he heard Shy scream, "I fuckin' hate you!"

"Don't you know I will come over there and smack the black off your little ass?" Mr. Anderson continued to shout at his daughter, who stood in the corner of their two-bedroom apartment, crying her eyes out. Her father was furious, cursing up a storm. He had a quick temper, especially lately—guys had been calling the apartment asking for Shy at any time of the day or night.

"You got these little knucklehead muthafuckas callin' my home at three o'clock in the fuckin' morning, askin' fo' your fast ass," he shouted. "You out here fuckin' these young boys, Shy? You spreadin' your legs fo' these horny drug dealers?" He turned over a leather chair, his eyes boiling with fury.

"Daddy," Shy managed to say, but fear engulfed her quickly. Her father was up in her face, glaring at her, disapproving of her promiscuous ways and her wardrobe, and ready to kill any nigga that touched or did his daughter wrong. It was a hot July day in the projects, and Shy had on some tight Daisy Duke shorts, a tight tank top, and some ankle socks and Nikes. She had her hair in two long pigtails, and for a fifteen-year-old girl, she had a body well-developed in all the right places, getting her the attention of many young boys in the hood.

Mr. Anderson hated seeing his daughter growing up so fast and dressing like some hoochie on the block. Shy was a beautiful young girl, but she was moving too fast. Mr. Anderson dreaded seeing his baby girl end up like her mother had—in the streets and hooked on drugs, selling her body for a quick high. He wanted his daughter to have something better going for her, and he knew Shy was smart, but he saw in her what he saw in her mother when they first met—they both were attracted to that fast, get-money, flashy lifestyle. Mr. Anderson knew his daughter was enthralled by the bad boys, the thugs, and the drug dealers. Mr. Anderson knew that no decent young man would call a young lady's place at three o'clock in the morning, and sounding straight street. He had picked up the phone, agitated at the late hour, and heard a young thug say, "Ay, yo—is Shy home?"

Mr. Anderson lost it and cursed and threatened the guy, shouting, "You little knucklehead muthafucka! Don't you be callin' here no three o'clock in the fuckin' morning, askin' fo' my daughter. Nigga, is you fuckin' crazy! Come around my daughter and I'll fuck your ass up!" And then he hung up.

Oh, Shy heard her father's mouth the next day, and they both went at it. But with his temper, she knew that if her father had really known anything about the young man who called, he would be at his front door right now, fighting him. Shy didn't disclose the caller's name or location and instead took the verbal abuse from her father.

"You little bitch!" he continued. "I swear, if you come to my home pregnant by one of these drug-dealing niggas, you're gone, Shy. Go ahead—be just like your fuckin' mother, selling pussy in the streets fo' drugs, and end up naked in an alley somewhere with a bullet in your fuckin' head."

Shy didn't want to hear about her mother's death—the pain was still fresh, even though it had happened three years ago.

"Fuck you! Why you gotta talk about Mama like that?"

That smart remark caused her to get a hard right-hand smack across her face.

"You whorin' bitch! You gonna end up just like her, if you keep dealin' wit' these young hardheaded niggas out here," he said.

Shy pushed her father away and ran out of the apartment. She hated how he always brought up her mother's death, trying to scare her into leaving the streets alone.

"Shy, get back here!" Mr. Anderson shouted from the apartment door. "Shy, you get your fast ass back into this apartment, or don't you ever come home again! I swear, Shy, you and your mother are a fuckin' joke sometimes!"

Shy ignored her father's words and ran down the building's pissy staircase with tears streaming down her face. She reached the middle of the steps and noticed two figures sitting at the bottom, their backs to her. She slowed down and stared cautiously at them. One was a lady whose hair was in disarray, and the second was a young man. They were flicking a lighter as they sat closely together, concealing something. To Shy's eyes, it appeared that they were doing drugs—they were hidden away from the public and concealed in the depths of the project staircase, where there was enough privacy to smoke crack. Shy walked down the stairs slowly. When she was up on them, they both turned around and looked up at her.

"Oh . . . ," the woman said. She stared up at Shy, and they recognized each other. "Hey, Shy," the woman said, gripping a long crack pipe in her hand. Her eyes looked drowsy, her movements sluggish.

"Hey, Melanie," Shy said, her voice low.

It was an uncomfortable situation for both of them. Shy had never seen Melanie like this before. Melanie was two years older than Shy, and they had both attended high school. Melanie had been the most popular, best-dressed, most outgoing girl in the school. She had been voted "Most Likely to Succeed." Now, she looked like she didn't have a pot to piss in. Next to Melanie was her boyfriend, Ray. He was holding a lighter and looking around nervously. Ray used to be a cute guy and one of the young dealers on the come up. Shy remembered when Ray used to sell drugs outside her building when she was younger. He had always been dressed in Adidas and big gold chains and had money to burn. Then he got hooked on his own product a year ago and couldn't let go.

"You tryin' to get by, Shy?" Melanie asked, looking impatient.

"Yeah," Shy said.

Melanie and Ray moved against the wall, allowing Shy to pass. As she passed by them, Shy looked Melanie hard in her face and saw the damage crack had done. Melanie turned away quickly, diverting her eyes to the floor, ashamed that Shy had to see her like this. Shy said nothing else. She darted out of the building and into the streets.

Shy wanted to escape her father. She didn't want to go back home, but she was fifteen and had nowhere else to go. She missed her mother dearly, but she also knew that she would never end up like her or like Melanie, sucking hard on that glass dick, and sucking and fucking niggas for crack. Shy always knew that she was too smart for that. She wasn't going to let drugs fuck up her life and screw up her lovely body.

Shy walked down the block to her friend Jade's apartment. Jade was a year older than Shy, and they'd known each other since they were eight. They went to the same schools and had similar taste in boys. They both loved messing with the young drug-dealing bad boys who flaunted their riches and promised them the world.

Shy knocked hard on Jade's door, and her mother answered.

"Hey, baby girl," Mrs. Dunken said, greeting her with a smile. Mrs. Dunken, a petite woman, was in her mid-thirties. She had brown skin and short cropped hair.

"Hey, Mrs. Dunken. Jade here?"

"Yeah, she's in her bedroom," Mrs. Dunken said.

Shy walked into the apartment and down the hall to Jade's bedroom.

"Damn, bitch, you ain't dressed yet?" Shy said teasingly when she saw Jade walking around in her panties and bra.

"Shy, why you at my crib so damn early? You know I don't leave out here till late," Jade told her. Jade was small, like her mother, with beautiful sleek skin and hazel eyes.

Shy sighed. "My fuckin' pops trippin' again. I had to leave. He actin' stupid and shit."

"Damn, what he beefin' about this time?" Jade asked.

"Some nigga called my crib at three in the morning. I think it was Raheem's dumb ass. You know that nigga ain't got no fuckin' sense. Now my pops assumin' I'm fuckin' the nigga."

Jade chuckled. "Bitch, you are."

"He don't know I'm fuckin'," Shy said. "It ain't none of his fuckin' business. He keep thinkin' I'm gonna end up like my mother."

Jade peered into her closet, looking for an outfit to wear for the day. Shy sat on Jade's bed.

"Jade, guess who the fuck I ran into on my way here?" Shy said.

"Who?"

"Melanie. Yo, that bitch was gettin' high wit' her man Ray in my building. I caught her junkie ass smokin' crack in the staircase."

"You know she be suckin' on that glass dick *real* hard," Jade said as she laid a pair of jeans across her bed.

"Yo, I couldn't believe it. I was like shocked and shit. She was lookin' at me and I was lookin' at her. I know that bitch was embarrassed. Yo, fo' real, Jade, I can't never get like that. Bitches be buggin', smokin' that crack. That shit will fuck you up, fo' real."

"I know. Her man Ray got her smokin' that shit. That bitch is stupid," Jade said. "I ain't gonna never let no man do me wrong like that."

"Word," Shy said. "We sistas for life. I got your back, and I know you got mines."

Jade continued to get dressed while Shy flipped through a copy of *Source* magazine.

It was one in the afternoon when both girls left Jade's apartment to roam the streets that hot July day. Both girls wore tight-fitted clothing, Jade in some Guess jeans, and Shy in her Daisy Duke shorts. They both wanted niggas' undivided attention, and that's exactly what they got, making heads turn and cars slow down to a crawl as they strutted through Jamaica housing projects in Queens.

"Yo, Jade, c'mere fo' a minute," Kahlil yelled from across the street. He was hanging in front of the corner bodega with his crew.

Jade and Shy didn't hesitate to cross the street. Kahlil was that fly nigga, making his ends for sure. He was dressed down in a white and blue Phat Farm sweatsuit with a thick gleaming gold chain around his neck. Parked in front, was his white BMW 850 convertible.

Jade and Shy walked over to Kahlil and his peoples, craving their attention. But Jade knew that Kahlil was off-limits because Kahlil had been fucking with her moms for over a year now, and he was loving Mrs. Dunken. To Kahlil, Jade was like his little sista, and nothing more.

Both young ladies were all smiles when they walked up to Kahlil and said, "Hey, Kahlil."

"What up, y'all?" Kahlil said. "Yo, Jade, your moms home?"

"Yeah, she home," Jade said. "Why?"

"I've been callin' your crib and ain't no one been pickin' up."

"She probably in the shower. You know how she be when she be up in the bathroom. Got the radio playin' all loud and shit and can't hear a fuckin' thang," Jade said, wishing he was calling for her.

"A'ight. Ay, yo—y'all comin' to my party tonight, right?" he asked.

"You know it; I ain't tryin' to miss it fo' the world," Shy said.

"You sure your pops gonna let you out, Shy?" Kahlil joked. "That nigga like boot camp and shit . . . got your young ass on lock."

"Fuck him. That nigga don't run me. I'm grown."

Kahlil smiled at her, impressed by her attitude. "Yo, before y'all leave, here's a lil' sumthin' to go shoppin' wit'," Kahlil said, peeling off two hundred-dollar bills from his knot and passing it to Jade and Shy. "Buy sumthin' nice fo' my party tonight."

Both girls were beaming as they accepted the money. "Thanks," they said in unison. Then they walked off giggling and talking about Kahlil.

"Girl, I need a nigga like him," Shy said, stuffing the bill in her pocket. "He would get it every fuckin' night. I would never be stingy wit' the pussy, and he cute. Ummm. I know he got a big dick."

"Bitch, you better stop talkin' about my mother's man like that. You got Raheem, anyway," Jade said jokingly.

"And like it would stop you from fuckin' the nigga," Shy said. "But fo' real, Jade, that's the type of nigga that we need in our life, that get-money, cute, thugged-out, smack a bitch on the ass while he layin' down pipe in a bitch. I'll have his baby."

Jade laughed. "Bitch, you a ho."

"For Kahlil, I'll be whatever ho he wants me to be."

They laughed some more and continued down the block.

The day consisted of flirting with the niggas they liked and hitting up Jamaica Avenue to shop for some skimpy outfits to put on for the party that night.

"Shy, what up, baby girl?" Raheem called out to Shy as he approached her from behind.

Jade and Shy turned around and saw Raheem walking toward them on Jamaica Avenue. Shy caught a slight attitude. "Raheem, what the fuck is wrong wit' you?"

"What you talkin' about, Shy? What you gettin' loud fo'?" Raheem asked.

"My pops trippin' now because you wanna call my crib three o'clock in the fuckin' morning," Shy told him.

Raheem sucked his teeth. "Fuck your pops; tell that nigga to stop sweatin' a nigga. You my girl, and I'm gonna call you when I feel like it."

"Yeah, a'ight. That nigga threatenin' to kick me out," Shy said.

"So, you can come stay wit' me. You know I got you, right?"

"You can't say hi, Raheem?" Jade said with an attitude.

"Hi, Jade," Raheem said shortly.

"Yeah, fuck you too, nigga," Jade said sarcastically.

"Just don't call my crib so late anymore," Shy said.

"A'ight, shorty. Whatever," Raheem said. "What y'all doin' on the Ave anyway?"

"Shoppin' fo' Kahlil's party tonight," Shy said. "You comin', right?"

"Yeah, no doubt," he said.

Raheem put his arm around Shy and walked with her down the Avenue, his pants sagging, wearing a wife-beater and Timbs.

As they walked down the Avenue, Raheem made eye contact with a few young men who passed by them. One of them muttered, "Pussy-ass nigga!" But Raheem just continued to walk down the street with Shy.

"Who them niggas?" Shy asked.

Raheem shrugged it off and said, "Nuthin'. Niggas hatin', that's all."

In the Coliseum Mall, Shy tried on a pair of jeans while Raheem and Jade stood around waiting. Jade noticed Raheem gazing at a certain young female and immediately caught attitude.

"Why you starin' so hard at the bitch?" Jade said, getting loud. Jade knew the girl Raheem was clocking so hard. Her name was Camille, and she was a year or two older than Jade. She seemed like the kind of chick who was out to fuck everybody's man.

"Bitch!" Camille snapped back. "Watch your mouth, little girl." Camille was a pretty girl; five foot eight with a caramel complexion.

"Make me, bitch. You wrong fo' lookin' at Shy's man like that. He don't belong to you!" Jade shouted, causing a scene.

"I wasn't lookin' at the nigga," Camille said.

Shy, hearing the commotion, walked out the dressing room to see her friend Jade getting into a dispute with Camille. Shy never knew Camille like that—she just noticed her around the way sometimes. To her, Camille seemed cool. She thought Camille was the type of woman who minded her business. Why was Jade arguing with her?

"Chill, Jade," Shy said, trying to calm her friend.

"Nah, it ain't right fo' that bitch to be starin' at your man like that!" Jade insisted.

By now, the mall security was on the scene, and Jade and Shy had to continue their shopping outside the mall.

Jade calmed down, and both girls continued their shopping without Raheem and without any more drama.

"Jade, I'm gettin' dress at your crib," Shy said.

"Why?"

"I ain't tryin' to see my pops tonight. I already got my outfit and my shoes. So, I'll just shower up at your crib, get ready, and we can be out."

"Sounds like a plan," Jade said.

Shy spent the remainder of the day over at Jade's crib, listening to music, talking, and getting ready for Kahlil's party.

Shy wore a red and white halter top with the miniskirt, and Jade sported a similar outfit, wearing a white miniskirt and clear sandals. Both ladies were eye candy for sure.

On their way out, Shy asked Jade why she was beefing with Camille. And Jade's reply was, "That bitch be giving me the funny look sometimes. Like she hatin' on me."

Shy said not another word about it. They jumped into the cab they had waiting downstairs.

Kahlil's party was jumping off. It was a house party, with everybody partying in the backyard. The whole hood was out, drinking, dancing, and having a good time, as "Put Your Hands Where My Eyes Could See" by Busta Rhymes blared throughout the DJ's huge speakers.

Shy and Jade walked in like divas. They greeted those they knew and then started to get their dance on. Kahlil hosted the party with a bottle of Moët clutched in his hand, and a woman who was not Jade's moms in his other. But Jade didn't get upset. Kahlil was handing her down too much money to beef about him cheating on her moms. Sometimes she wished he was cheating with *her*.

From the corner of her eye, Jade caught Camille socializing with a few people, and she grimaced at the sight of her. Shy looked around for her boyfriend, Raheem, and smiled when she noticed him coming her way.

"Hey, baby," she greeted, giving him a hug and kiss.

"Let's get out of here fo' a minute," Raheem suggested.

"But I just got here," Shy said.

"Yeah, but I got the keys to my man's whip. He lettin' us use it for a minute. I wanna spend some alone time wit' you. You know what I'm saying," he hinted.

Shy smiled.

"You lookin' good right now, Shy. That skirt is definitely doin' you some justice," Raheem added.

Shy didn't protest. Raheem took her by the hand and walked off with her to the Ford Explorer parked down the block from the party.

Jade remained at the party. Camille noticed the grimy looks Jade had been giving her, and decided to confront her. Camille walked up to Jade and asked, "Bitch, why you got a problem with me?"

Jade caught an attitude and was ready to fight the bitch. "Why you walk around the projects thinkin' you too good? You ain't nobody."

"You a little bitch. You don't fuckin' know me. You don't know shit about my life. So don't come up in my face tryin' to judge me, 'cause I'll fuck your little ass up!" Camille shouted.

"*What?* Bring it then, bitch!" Jade yelled back.

But before the two girls could scrap, Kahlil intervened, saying, "Yo, y'all two chill. Don't be fuckin' up my party wit' y'all beef. Leave that shit on the block."

Both girls glared at each other, knowing not to get Kahlil upset with their problems. So they let their differences be and had peace for the night.

Down the block, a more intimate meeting was taking place. Shy had her miniskirt up around her hips, and her panties on the floor. She straddled Raheem, coming down hard on his eight inches.

"Ahh, fuck me, baby. Ahhh. I missed you," she panted.

With his pants and boxers around his ankles, he thrust himself into her, grabbing her ass, steaming up the windows of the SUV.

Raheem was deep in some pussy. He panted, "Shy, I wanna take care of you. Come stay wit' me. Fuck your pops. You don't need that nigga."

Shy bit down on her bottom lip, feeling Raheem push himself deeper and harder into her. She wrapped her arms around him, hugging him tightly. She was excited about the offer. God knew she wanted to move away from home.

"You feel me, Shy? You feel me, right, baby?" Raheem asked, thrusting himself harder into her.

"Oh, I feel you, baby. Yes, I do . . . ," Shy panted. "You gonna take care of me, right?"

"I promise, baby," Raheem assured her.

"Oooh, baby, I love you. Please, don't ever let me go," Shy said, feeling like she was about to melt in Raheem's arms.

Abruptly, the doors to the Ford Explorer flew open, and three men dragged Raheem out of the car and pushed Shy down on the ground.

"What now, nigga!" one of the men shouted, pushing a .357 in Raheem's face.

"What the fuck!" Raheem screamed. He tried pulling up his pants and at the same time tried protecting himself from the blows that suddenly came down on him.

Shy screamed, looking on in horror as three young men beat her boyfriend down. "Stop it! Leave him alone!" she yelled. Then she tried attacking one of the goons, but caught a closed fist to the side of her jaw, knocking her down on her ass.

Then she heard that terrifying sound she dreaded—two

gunshots ringing out. All of a sudden, everything went still. She looked ahead and saw Raheem sprawled out on the ground. He wasn't moving, and she screamed again, this time in pain.

Camille happened to be nearby and heard the gunshots. Camille had left the party to get away from Jade. She stood a block away from the incident. Then she saw Shy bent over Raheem as his blood spread over the sidewalk. She rushed over to help her. When she saw Raheem, she knew he was dead. Camille placed her arms around Shy and tried calming her down.

"What happened?" Camille asked, concerned.

"They fuckin' shot him! They shot my fuckin' baby!" Shy cried out.

By now a crowd had started to gather. Jade ran out of the party and down the block, fearing the worst. When she ran up on the scene and saw Camille's arms wrapped around Shy, and Raheem bare-assed, dead on the ground, she damn near lost her mind.

"What the fuck!" Jade yelled. She was ready to confront Camille. "Bitch, what did you do?"

Camille looked up at Jade and pleaded with her eyes for her to chill for a moment.

"Jade, they fuckin' shot Raheem. They killed him," Shy said, sobbing.

Jade, putting aside her anger toward Camille for a moment, walked up to her best friend, knelt beside Shy, and put her arms around her.

That night, they all shared Shy's pain.

~ CHAPTER 1 ~

shy

2004

"We gonna do this, baby. I'm gonna make it happen fo' you . . . fo' us," Roscoe promised me.

We were laid up in bed, resting on wrinkled satin sheets, and I just got finished rocking his fucking world. I fucked him so hard that I had him screaming my name. I'm that bitch!

"Watch, Shy, it's gonna be you and me," he said, as I was nestled against his chest, staring at the bedroom walls and listening to his weak promises. But I was used to it. I mean, after a nigga get himself some pussy, he gonna promise you the world while he's up in you, saying shit like, "Baby, I'm gonna buy you that house." Or "Baby, let's get married." Or "Baby, I'm gonna be faithful from now on. I ain't fuckin' wit' no other bitches." Yeah, yeah, yeah, a sista done heard it all before. See, when a nigga is fucking you, that pussy got his mind somewhere else, like warped and shit, and if your pussy is that good, you gonna have a nigga say all kinds of shit and promises to your ass. But after he done came, and got his mind right again, you best believe when you ask about that house, about getting married, that car he promised you, or him leaving other bitches alone, he gonna be like, "Huh? I said that? When?" The nigga get absent-minded and those coochie promises go out the door.

Shit, I know my pussy is good. Every time Roscoe's fucking me, he bragging, "Damn, Shy . . . you got some good pussy, ummm . . . shit, yes, baby . . . ummm, yes . . . I love you! Oooh . . . I love you." Shit, the only time Roscoe will *ever* proclaim his love to me is when the nigga is deep in some pussy. Anytime besides that, it's like, "Yeah, Shy, you know I got love for you, right?"

It's getting so fucking played out. But Roscoe will be Roscoe; I know he ain't changing anytime soon. But I wish he'd try.

I stayed in Roscoe's arms; he felt so good. We didn't say anything else for the moment. We just relished in the good sex and tried to catch our breaths. I looked at the time and saw that it was ten o'clock in the morning, and I felt good because I had the day off and was spending it in bed with my man.

"Shy, you okay?" Roscoe asked.

"Yeah, I'm fine." I replied.

"Why you so quiet?" he asked.

"No reason. I'm just enjoyin' the moment, that's all." I looked up at his handsome face and said, "I love you."

"Yeah, you know I got love for you too, Shy. You my wifey," he said.

I sighed heavily. This nigga. His dick got soft and his mind went "Duh!"

"Say it, Roscoe," I said.

"Say what?" he asked.

"That you love me."

"But I do."

"So why don't you tell me it?"

"Shy, you know how I feel about you. Why you trippin'?"

"Because, we been together fo' a year and a half, and I wanna hear you say it fo' once, wit'out your dick being up in me."

"What?" He chuckled.

I pushed away from him and stared at him. I hate this, because to him, everything is always a fucking joke. I mean, I feel that sometimes he never takes me seriously.

"You love me, right?" I repeated.

"You know I do," he said.

"I want us to settle down and do us, baby. You know I wanna have a baby soon. And I wanna move out of the projects, too."

"Here we go, Shy . . . I told you, shit takes time, a'ight. A brotha ain't made out of money," he stated.

I sighed. Roscoe was full of it. "Roscoe, you tell me that all that hustlin' you doin' out there on them streets, you ain't got no money saved for us?"

"Yeah, I got shit saved," he said on the defensive, like I offended him or some shit. "I ain't stupid," he added.

"So why can't we leave here and get a better place?"

"Because, it ain't time yet. I was born and raised here, Shy. I got business to take care of. Yo, a nigga can't just up and leave like that. You maybe, but not me."

"You're lyin', Roscoe. You just don't wanna leave the projects, admit it. Why are you so scared of change?"

"I ain't scared of shit."

"Whatever!" I muttered. I hopped out of bed and walked into the bathroom naked.

Roscoe was damn near a kingpin in the neighborhood, moving

kilos of that yayo wholesale price here, and to niggas down in the dirty south, and having a tight-knit crew up here in Queens, making crazy paper. I was never too much in his business, but when we met, I knew he was a big-time drug dealer. I was attracted to that type of nigga and that lifestyle. Him and his right-hand man, James—Jade's boyfriend—ran shit in the Jamaica housing projects. And I knew he was making enough money to move a bitch like me out of the projects. I had enough bad memories here with my moms, my pops, and losing Raheem. I just wanted to be somewhere different.

"Shy, why you trippin'? It's too fuckin' early. Damn, we just had a good morning; you know what I'm sayin'. And now you fuckin' it up by arguing over dumb shit!" he shouted.

I came out the bathroom and said to him, "Because, fo' months now, you've been promisin' me this shit and that shit. You gonna move me outta here and shit. We gonna have a baby together. Oh, Shy, you better than here; we need to get you a house, because niggas be wildin' out in these streets. You promised to take care of me, Roscoe, but lately, you ain't been takin' care of shit."

"Shy, you know I take care of your ass," he said coolly. "Didn't I buy you that leather jacket last week? And who bought you those earrings fo' your birthday? I took care of that. Who pay the rent, huh?"

I just looked at this nigga and returned with, "Whatever, nigga!" and closed the bathroom door.

"You know what, Shy? You spoiled, that's what you are. You got one of the flyest cribs in the buildin', your ass stay decked out in Gucci, Donna Karan, diamonds, and shit, and you ain't happy.

Just like a fuckin' woman. Ain't no way in pleasing y'all," he yelled through the bathroom door. "You know what? I'm out!"

I heard that, and I quickly opened the door and yelled, "Where you goin'?"

"Away from here, that's fo' sure. You actin' crazy right now, Shy."

"I thought you were goin' to spend the day wit' me?"

"I was—now I'm not," he said, pulling up his jeans and looking at me like I was crazy.

"You know what, Roscoe, fuck you! I don't need you. You ain't shit, anyway."

"Yeah, page me tonight when you want your back dug out again," he said sarcastically.

I watched this man get dressed and dis me like I wasn't shit. He threw on his Rocawear jacket and headed for the door.

"So you just gonna leave me like that?" I asked with my arms folded across my chest as I glared at him.

"Yo, I'll be back when you cool the fuck off, Shy," he said, and bounced out my apartment so easy.

I swear, niggas ain't shit. He come around last night, lookin' for some pussy, and my dumb ass give him some—yeah, I was horny too, but damn, why he gotta leave out my crib like that? All I asked him was to say he love me, without sex being involved, and move me out the projects, and this nigga just flipped the script on me. You know.

I wasn't gonna cry over that nigga, even though I was hurt. Roscoe promised to spend the day with me, and now he just flew the coop like it was nothing. No, I'm not gonna cry. I'm too old for that—shedding tears over a nigga. I told myself, *Shy, he ain't worth trippin' over. You a big girl.* Yeah, I love Roscoe, but I did have a life before I met him, and I'll have one after him.

Roscoe and I hooked up a year and a half ago in front of a Queens nightclub. It was a year after my bitch-ass father died of cancer. I was chilling wit my girls Jade and Camille, and you know we wasn't paying majority of these clown-ass niggas that tried to holla at us no mind. Majority of them were fake, anyway, and had no game. I mean, this one dude tried to holla at my girl, Camille, because she got the phattest ass out of all of us—but come on, the nigga was ugly wit' crusty, ashy lips—like he brushed his teeth with face powder and shit. And most niggas were staring, but were scared to come over and holla; they ain't had no fucking backbone.

If you like someone, especially a cute female, a brother with confidence would make his presence known in front of her politely, like a gentleman, and say his name and be smooth with his. Don't be shouting out to me, "Yo, ma, let me holla at you for a sec." "Yo, shorty, come here. . . . I wanna talk to you. My nigga wanna holla!"

And then when they don't get their way, and you don't come over, they disrespect you and shout out, "Bitch!" Or "Fuck you! You stuck up, anyway!"

Yeah, whatever, but moments ago, they were longing for your undivided attention. They've already proved to me their type of mentality. And I hate the aggressive males, the ones that pull you by the arm while you're passing by or follow you when it's clear that you don't want to be bothered with them, but they are too stupid or ignorant to back the fuck off.

Like this one nigga followed me for three blocks, calling me out, "Yo, ma—can you stop? I just wanna ask you sumthin', that's all. . . . You look too good to be walking alone and shit. I'll drive you somewhere." Let it be known, I ain't your fucking ma. I ain't your fucking boo. I ain't the one.

God, I hate corny niggas with no type of game to them, especially the ones that drive these nice cars and expect me to stop and give 'em some play because they in a Benz or a new Lexus, and don't even got the respect to stop and get out the car to approach you. They holla at you from the car window. I ain't turning tricks, so I don't know what they be thinking.

But Roscoe, he was different. He's the type of man, when he walks into a room, he gets noticed. All eyes are on him. It's his look and demeanor. When I first met Roscoe, I knew he was a hustler, a product of the streets. It was the way he talked and the wardrobe he was draped in.

It had been 3 a.m., and I was ready to leave because the night was boring and the assholes were out in swarms. I noticed Roscoe in the club, but never gave him a second glance. I just thought he was cute. He had on this navy blue and white pin-striped leather suit, which was looking great on him, with white Timberlands and a long bulky chain that draped down to his abs. He was blinged the fuck out and different from the regular guys that came in with jeans and jerseys and tried their hardest to impress the ladies. But I wasn't the only lady that noticed this fly nigga come into the club; bitches started flocking to that nigga like he was Jay-Z or sumthin'. But I loved the way he would shrug the bitches off and chill with his boys by the bar.

Later that night, I was leaving when I saw Roscoe outside on the corner next to a parked luxurious pearl Escalade, rolling dice with his peoples. I had walked across the street with my girls, when I saw him look up and check me out. He stared at me for a moment, and from that, I knew he was interested.

But I wasn't all that into him—just a little bit. I had just came out of a fucked-up relationship not too long before, and I wasn't trying to mess with some other nigga so soon. I just wanted to do me and chill. I definitely had my share of the thugs and drug dealers at an early age, and when Raheem was killed when I was fifteen, I thought I would never find no other man to replace him. But I was wrong. Roscoe was Raheem three times better.

Roscoe said something to his man, and then he strolled across the street, never taking his eyes off me. Camille and Jade noticed him too, and they smiled. I guess they both thought that he was gonna holla at one of them, or thought he was cute.

"Hey, lovely," he called out, staring hard at me.

I gave him a faint smile as I stood talking to my girls. I started to walk away. Roscoe came up from behind and said, "Beautiful in the denim skirt . . . . I like your walk."

I stopped, turned around, and said, "Excuse me?"

"I like the way you walk. You walk wit' class. I can tell by your presence that you got respect fo' yourself."

"And you know this by watchin' me walk?" I asked, and then let out a sigh. I wanted to play hard to get, but it was hard, because he was so cute and he had so much style to him. But I didn't want this nigga thinking that I was one of these dizzy-ass chickenhead bitches out here that was craving for his attention.

Roscoe came up close and gently grabbed me by my hand, looked me dead in my eyes, and asked, "Can I have a quick moment wit' you? I just wanna talk. I'm not gonna hold you from your girls too long."

I looked at him and knew he was confident with his. He

didn't seem too cocky, and he didn't stutter while he was talking to me. He knew what to say and how to say it. And he wasn't aggressive to the point where I wanted to smack him. The way he grabbed my hand—casually but not scared to touch a sista—said something about him.

I looked over at my girls, and Camille and Jade just looked back at me. Camille shrugged her shoulders and said, "We ain't goin' anywhere, Shy."

So I walked off with Roscoe down the block, where we had a chance to talk privately, away from the loud crowd and the nosy bitches outside the club that were hating on me because I had Roscoe's undivided attention.

When we got to the corner, he said, "Your name Shy, huh?"

"I see you pick up on things," I said.

"I pay attention to a lot of things, especially when I come across a beautiful woman. And you definitely are a beautiful woman. So, is Shy your real name or a nickname?" he asked.

"It's my middle name, given to me by my mother."

"It's nice. I like that . . . Shy. I can get used to sayin' it out loud."

I smiled.

When he talked, he always made eye contact. Not once did his eyes leave mine, which was a positive thing. I hate a man that talks to you, but his eyes are looking everywhere except at you, which either means he's too timid, too weak, or he's devious and you can't trust the muthafucka.

And in return, I stared right back. He was definitely eye candy. He had full lips that were—ummmm. I just wanted to suck that bottom lip so bad! He also had brown eyes and smooth brown skin. Now the bonus was that he was tall. The brotha stood about six-one, rocking cornrows with design parts which looked freshly done. And the clothes! His gear looked spanking new.

"You got beautiful eyes, Shy."

"Thank you," I replied. I ain't gonna front; Roscoe was making me blush. And if a brotha can make me blush, then he was doing his job and was definitely on point with his game.

"I see you're big on eye contact," I said.

"Always. I feel that lookin' in a person's eyes tells you a lot about that person and his or her character. And wit' women, I feel that the eyes tell what the heart is feelin', and the way you're lookin' at me right now tells me a lot."

"Really?" I asked.

"Of course."

"So what are my eyes saying?"

"Truthfully . . . that you're feelin' me somewhat, and I got my foot in the door wit' you. I'm willin' to work on the rest wit' you."

"Are you always this cocky?"

He didn't respond to my question. He just looked at me and smiled. "I definitely wanna take you out sometime. Only you can make it happen. So, will I be leavin' here wit' a smile on my face, or are you gonna have a brotha continuously pursuin'?"

"We can work somethin' out," I told him.

The more he talked, the more he had me open. That shit he said about the eyes, I like. He was smart, and that was another plus.

So I gave him my cell phone and my home numbers, and I rarely give out my home number. But he deserved it. He came correct with his. I gave him his moment, and it paid off.

I went back over to Camille and Jade, and you know they had a bunch of questions to ask a sista. The entire ride home to my place, I thought about Roscoe.

Our first date, Roscoe took me out of town with him to Philadelphia, where he had tickets to a Jay-Z concert, front row and everything. And then afterwards, he had a suite at the Sheraton—you know he had a sista open. I ain't no slut, but I fucked the nigga that night. I mean, who wouldn't? It was worth it.

And as our relationship grew, it was great to know that he didn't have no kids. Oh, God, that was such a bonus, knowing that I didn't have to deal with no jealous bitchy baby mamas. I had no kids, so it was great.

I stood in front of the mirror naked and gazed at myself, like I do every morning. I'm not conceited—well, a little, but a sista like me got it going on. I got a petite figure, with gracefully long black hair that stops at my shoulders. Bitches in the hair salon be hating, because my shit ain't a weave like most fake sistas. My lips are pretty and stay glossed out. To the fellows, I'm known as the chocolate fine honey with the cute butt and curvaceous figure. Roscoe hates it when I walk out on the streets alone, because plenty of brothas be trying to come at me and holla. Most of 'em know that I'm with Roscoe, but they don't care. They be stressing the situation, saying my man ain't gonna find out. But I be loving Roscoe too much to fuck around with these lame-ass wannabe hustlers and gangstas. And I also know you don't shit where you eat. Roscoe do take care of me—I just wish that sometimes he would take care of me a little bit more often.

About an hour done passed since Roscoe left me alone in the apartment. And to be real, I was missing him already. This nigga had my fucking hopes up, thinking I was gonna be with my man all day, and we were going to go out shopping and have dinner at the Olive Garden and just do us all day. Instead he leaves because he claims I got him upset. Yeah, whatever.

Well, I was determined not to spend my entire day off being bored and trapped in this apartment. I was getting into something—I don't care if it was just hanging outside the projects.

I called up Jade, and as soon as she picked up the phone, I heard the drama.

~ CHAPTER 2 ~

jade

"You need to fuck that bitch up, Jade," Camille said to me, looking angrier and more upset than me.

"Fo' real, Jade, that bitch was talkin' mad shit the other night, talkin' about you ain't shit to her and how your man be checkin' her every night. She actin' like he ain't shit to you."

"Where that bitch at right now?" I said. I was heated because I hate when my name is constantly coming out of a bitch's mouth, and the ho don't even know me. And now this ho that Camille is talking about claims to be fucking my man, James, on the regular. Now I know me and James ain't been on smooth terms lately, but for my man to be messing around with some dirty bitch like Tasha—yo, I swear, I'm about to get medieval on someone.

"I heard that bitch be over on Guy Brewer gettin' high and shit wit' her cousin."

"She there now?" I asked.

"She should be; that bitch is a bum. She ain't got no place to be. You need to handle this, Jade. You know I got your back."

It wasn't even noon yet, and here I was, getting into some drama, and Camille ain't no good, because she's a hyper bitch, ready to throw down whenever. She doesn't care with who, male or female. You disrespect her, me, or Shy, and she ready to fuck you up, anyplace and anytime.

And it's funny, because a few years ago, we both had beef with each other, ready to tear each other's hair out, and now we cool like sistas. When Shy's man got killed in '98, Camille stuck around and made sure my homegirl was all right. I gave her props for that. In '98, we both squashed our beef and kept close ties to Shy, who became like our little sista. We all became tight, best friends, damn near sistas, and there wasn't a damn thing that was gonna break us apart.

Now James, we've been together for years, and I know this nigga better respect what he got at home and recognize, because he's walking on thin ice with me. Yeah, he got a big dick, and he's fine as fuck, but a sista can't take but so much. And for him to be fucking around with Tasha, which is the rumor throughout the projects, makes me look bad.

Tasha's a dirty bird-bitch, with no class and no fucking style. She constantly walks around with a scowl on her ugly face, parading around in a dirty blond unkempt weave, thinking she cute. And the brothas be sweating her, because they know she give up easy ass and will suck a nigga's dick for a dime bag and a bowl of Froot Loops. Yeah, she's slim, with a little butt, but come on, it's style, beauty, and grace that counts, and for the brothas that be running up in Tasha, makes me think twice about them. Tasha is like one or two steps from becoming a crackhead and homeless. And if James fucked her, or is fucking her, I swear, that nigga better not bring his dirty dick around me anymore or bring me some nasty disease he got from that dirty bird-bitch!

I looked over at Camille, and she was preparing for battle. She took off her rings and earrings, and had a multicolored scarf tied around her head.

"Jade, c'mon, I don't want that bitch to leave," Camille said.

I threw on a pair of old sweatpants and a blue loose-fitted hoodie. I didn't have to worry about wrapping up my hair, because I sported auburn twists, and it looks so fucking good on me.

Soon as I was about ready to head out the door and go fuck this bitch up, the fucking phone rings. Camille told me not to pick it up, but I was expecting a very important phone call.

"Hello!" I answered loudly.

"Damn, girl, what's wrong wit' you?" Shy asked.

"Nuthin'. Me and Camille 'bout ready to fuck this bitch up," I let her know.

"Who you talkin' about?" she asked.

"That dumb dirty bird-bitch, Tasha."

"Y'all fo' real?"

"Yeah. I'm hearin' about this bitch messin' wit' my man, and you know me and James been together fo' four years now. And I'm hearin' my name keeps comin' out of her fuckin' mouth."

"I'm comin', Jade," Shy said.

"Nah, me and Camille got this," I said to her. I know she was with Roscoe, because all week, she's been boasting about spending some quality time with him and how he was taking her shopping today. "Stay and keep your man company. Don't be leavin' no dick to fight some dirty bitch," I said. Shy's my girl, and the youngest, so sometimes I had to advise her.

"Roscoe ain't even here," she informed me.

"What? Why?" I asked.

"We had an argument, and he bounced. Talkin' about he'll be back when I calm down."

"Why niggas be actin' up?" I asked, rolling my eyes.

"I don't know."

"Jade, c'mon. I don't want this bitch to leave!" Camille shouted.

"Who that? Camille? Tell her ass to calm the fuck down," Shy said, knowing Camille's temper.

I looked at Camille and muttered, "Shy is on the phone."

"So, tell that bitch to come and help beat this bitch down!" Camille exclaimed.

"Jade, I'm coming," Shy said, and then hung up on me.

Shy lived in the building next to mine, and we've been friends since grade school. I'm one year older, and we've both been through everything together, from trifling niggas, to hating-ass bitches, and even getting ourselves locked up a few times in Central Booking for fighting, stealing, and everything else.

Camille, she's like our mother. She's constantly gotta look out for her sistas—especially me, because I'm the shortest, smallest, whatever—being only five foot one, and 110 pounds. But what I lack for in size, I make up for in skills, looks, and my body. What I'm possessing, many brothas be wanting a piece of my sultry and desired look. I'm a bad bitch. I may be small, but I'll fuck a bitch up, quick. I got big titties and a nice little asset from behind, and I always get compliments, especially about my hazel eyes. Niggas be saying that I got them exotic and saucy bedroom eyes. Niggas be shouting out, "Damn, shorty, you got them bedroom eyes. Your little ass. You look like you can work a nigga good in the bedroom. Wassup wit' you, luv?"

But I got James, and I let niggas that stay trying to get into my pants know it too. James been my love for four years now. And if he wanna fuck up and give up this good pussy he's been blessed with for a long time now—oh well, I got plenty of brothas who are willing and ready to take his place.

I headed out the door with Camille right behind me.

The minute we walked out my building, I saw Shy standing on the corner, ready and waiting. That's us, the dynamic trio. Everybody in South Jamaica housing knows we don't play, and we all stick together like white on rice. You fuck with one of us, you fucking with all three of us, and believe me, we'll beat you down.

I greeted Shy quickly, and then we all proceeded toward Guy Brewer Boulevard where Camille was sure that Tasha was hanging.

Of course, I spotted that bird-bitch Tasha chilling in front of the bodega on South Road and Guy Brewer, and just like Camille explained it to me, she was smoking weed with her dyke cousin, Dee—another bird-bitch.

My face tightened up the closer we got, and I clenched my fist, and was about ready to spit fire, I was so fucking mad. Tasha turned around and saw us coming, and of course, she had something smart to say when she saw me approaching her.

"Look at this short bitch here!" she shouted out, standing in front of the bodega in some tattered gray sweats, and an XXL white T-shirt that was clearly too fucking big for her.

"What you say, bitch?" I barked back.

I knew Tasha had to know we came to beat her down. I had Vaseline on, so the bitch won't be able to scratch my face, and Camille had her hair wrapped up tight. We didn't come to talk.

Her dyke cousin stepped in front of Tasha, like she trying to protect her, and said, "What? Y'all bitches think y'all ill?"

The bitch's voice was deep as shit, and she had a mustache above her upper lip, with braids, rocking a gold hoop earring and wearing baggy clothing, looking like a dick swings between her legs.

Camille, that's my girl, and she keeps it gangsta. She said no words and was the first to throw down. She stepped up to Dee, and *pow!* Caught that bitch dead in her fucking face, catching her off guard, making that dyke stumble a little.

I went for Tasha, swinging hard at that bitch. Even though she towered over me at five-seven, I still wild out on her fucking ass. I grabbed a fistful of that fake blond weave with my left hand, trying to pull out her extensions, and bent that bitch over and started pounding on her with my clenched fist, and beat that bitch in her fucking head. Shy jumped in and started kicking and hitting Tasha where there was open space for her to attack.

"Fuck that bitch up! Fuck that bitch up!" I shouted as I kept beating on Tasha.

We both fell onto the ground, and Tasha had somewhat the advantage. She was on top of me and started punching me. I looked up and saw Camille and Dee fighting close by.

By now we were causing a scene, and there was a small crowd gathering around. Some were cheering on our actions, especially niggas.

"Shy, get this bitch off me!" I yelled, trying to get the advantage again. Shy pulled Tasha by her hair, yanking her shit back and pulling out half her dirty fucking weave, and I punched that bitch straight in her fucking jaw. I got up and started wilding out on her, and then I wild out on her cousin too, who was like five-nine, and here was my little ass, jumping on this bitch who was twice my size. With the help of Camille, we busted that bitch's lip, and I scratched the shit outta her face, and ripped open her shirt.

By now, people started to intervene and had the nerve to try and break us up from fighting. This elderly lady—I guess she was in her late forties—grabbed me from behind and shouted, "Y'all cut that out! Get off her!"

I swear I wanted to turn around and punch her in her jaw too. But outta respect, I didn't. I just shouted, "Fuck that bitch! She a dirty fuckin' bitch!"

"Fuck you, bitch!" Tasha yelled back. "You gonna get yours. Watch, bitch! You better watch your fuckin' back!"

"You dirty bitch!" I shouted back, trying to break free from the people that had my little ass clutched in their arms. "You gonna get fucked up again!"

"Fuck those bitches!" her cousin shouted. Some dude had her gripped by the arm, and one of her breasts was exposed. But she didn't care.

I looked over at my girls, and they were all right. Camille's scarf was off her head, and her hair was in disarray, and Shy, she was okay, she had not one scratch, bite, or cut on her.

Before the cops or anybody else came, we went our separate ways. Tasha and Dee went their way, and me and my girls went our way. But I was sure it wasn't over between Tasha and me. I'd handled what I came to do. We don't joke around, and both those bitches knew it too. When we throw down, we fucking throw down. I'll fight like a fucking man; Camille too. Shy, she somewhat all right with the hand skills, but she ain't a true warrior without me and Camille having her back.

Later on that day, we chilled up in my apartment and talked about the dumb bitches. Then ordered some Chinese food and talked about how fucked up men can be. Here I am, fighting this dirty bitch over James. I asked myself, Was it worth it today? Is James truly worth fighting a bitch like Tasha over? I mean, what kind of standards do this nigga got if he's creeping around behind my back with trash like that? How the fuck he gonna go from me, his woman that had his back since the day we met, who cooks, cleans, and fucks him till his dick explodes, to some bitch who niggas know is a fucking nasty ho.

I swear James better come correct with this one. I mean, it was rumored that he was fucking with Tasha, and Camille confirmed it when she told me yesterday that she saw him hugged up on her. And I guess that I was so mad, and believed her, that I had to personally take out my frustration on that bitch. She was at fault just as much as James was. And believe me, when he brings his ass home, he's gonna hear my fucking mouth.

But I couldn't believe James could do that to a sista. I'm too fucking fly for him to be creeping around with something like that. It had me believing that I wasn't pleasing my man right. I know my pussy is good. I know I take care of my man right, so why would this nigga creep around?

Around five that afternoon, Camille and Shy left, leaving me alone to ponder about certain events. All afternoon, my mind was on James. God knows I love that man to death. But if he's fucking around on a sista, especially with Tasha, I swear, I'm leaving this nigga. But first, I gonna beat this nigga in the head with a frying pan, curse his ass out, and then I'm bouncing. And let him be missing a sista. Let him miss all the good loving I've been giving this nigga every night. If he don't respect me, then I'll find a man who will. I know there are plenty of brothers out there who are waiting to step up to bat and get at this, for real.

Around nine that night, I heard keys in the door to the apartment. I remained seated on the plush green couch with Alicia Keys's vocals to her hit song "Diary" softly playing from the speakers. I quickly dried my eyes and got myself ready to confront him.

I had the lights on and sat with my arms folded across my chest and my legs crossed.

James stepped into the room, his manly physique filling the space. He had on a blue Sean John sweatsuit, which he looked really good in, and his shaved brown head glistened like he just came from the barbershop. He looked at me and asked, "Baby, what's wrong?"

I got up, went over to him—and then smacked the shit outta him and shouted out, "You fuckin' that bitch!"

"What?" he returned, looking at me like I done lost my mind.

"Tasha! You fuckin' her, James? You fuckin' that bitch behind my back?"

"I don't know what the fuck you talkin' about! Who tellin' you this shit? Camille? Tell that bitch she need to mind her business!" he stated angrily.

"Don't worry 'bout Camille. I'm hearin' this shit all around. Why you around her fo', James?"

"Jade, why the fuck am I gonna be messin' wit' some bitch up in the projects? You know how nosy people can be. I ain't tryin' to have muthafuckas in my business. You need to tell whoever to stop spreadin' these fuckin' rumors about me. Fo' real, Jade, you gettin' worked up off these silly rumors," he said, glaring at me.

"Silly? I had to fuck that bitch up today, James. I'm tired of this shit."

James sighed, staring at me. "I heard about that. Why the fuck you beefin', Jade? Look at you, and look at her. C'mon Jade, honestly. If I'm gonna cheat on you, you think I'm gonna go for Tasha? You know she ain't my type."

"Whatever, James. I'm tired."

"Jade, listen."

He came closer to me, with me still fuming, and had the nerve to put his arms around me and embrace me. Damn, he smelled so nice, and his touch. I wanted to push him off me. But I didn't.

"Jade, you know how I like my women. Beautiful, assertive, charming, and eloquent. Like the one I'm holdin' in my arms right now." His voice was strong and deep, but also suave and convincing. "Why I'm gonna cheat on you, baby? You always do me right. And I ain't tryin' to lose you over no bullshit rumor about me fuckin' Tasha. C'mon Jade, you know how niggas and these hos out here be hatin' on us. They gonna find any way to break us up, 'cause they know we look too good together. You can't trust them. It's about us, not them, baby."

He looked me in my eyes, and he seemed so sincere. His touch felt so inviting. I thought, *Maybe he's right; maybe I am beefing over some bullshit.* I remembered some of James's ex-girlfriends, and I had to admit myself that he definitely had good taste in woman. I mean, he chose me.

KISS FM continued to play the soft slow jams like the Isley Brothers, Jagged Edge, and Will Downing, and it wasn't making matters better with me trying to be furious with James and getting a straight answer from him.

"Jade, c'mon, let's not fight over this bullshit. We've been together fo' four years now. I love you, baby," he said. Our eyes met. He towered over me and held me softly in his arms.

James is so fine: six feet one, 195 pounds, and ripped with a washboard stomach. He's got smooth brown skin, and his sweet lips are lined with a pencil-thin goatee.

I peered up into his eyes and damn near almost forgot what I was arguing with him about. It's sad to say, but James got that effect on me. We'd argue constantly, but somehow, by the end of the day or night, he got my panties on the floor, my thighs spread apart, and his big dick is fucking the shit out of me.

And of course, tonight was no different. James was so smooth with his that I found myself spread across the carpet, with my legs spread out, having James's face buried in between my thighs and blessing a sista with a little head job.

"You ain't gotta worry 'bout me, baby. I ain't goin' nowhere. I ain't fuckin' around on you," he whispered, lifting his head from the pussy and looking up at me.

"James . . . ," I passionately moaned. A few tears trickled down my face. I wanted to hate him tonight, but he made it so damn hard. "I want you to love me, baby," I said.

"Baby, I do love you. You know that," he said in a gentle

whisper. He was naked, and his body was solid, and his dick was rock hard. He climbed on top of me, putting us in the missionary position, and placed his nine-inch manhood near my goodies.

I reached up and pulled him down on top of me, and felt his long, deep, hard erection slowly enter me. I gasped out as my little ass tried to endure all of the dick he was pushing into me.

"I love you, Jade," he said. "Why am I gonna fuck up this? Your pussy is too good fo' a nigga to be strayin' away from home."

"I love you too, baby," I cried. I wrapped my legs around his gyrating hips as he thrust himself into me, threw my arms around him, and held him close.

I knew that I was in love with him, because if it was anybody else, they would have been out the door.

~ CHAPTER 3 ~

camille

Now this is how a bitch should live. I got my own place, my own ride, and I'm able to take care of myself. I don't stress no fucking nigga. Don't fucking need to.

After that beat down I gave that bitch Dee, and hearing about my girls and they problems, I needed to unwind and do me. I made myself a booty call. I needed to get my shit off. And right now, that booty call was certainly doing its thing. I had no complaints.

"Ahhh . . . shit, baby, eat that pussy . . . ," I moaned, my legs wrapped around my lover's head as I clutched my bedsheets.

I had my boy, Brian McKnight, soft and seductive lyrics playing in the bedroom, with the bass line set just right. The lights were dimmed, and the night seemed so tranquil in the projects, which was unusual, because on a warm night like tonight, usually I would have about six to eight niggas outside my bedroom window gambling, drinking, and being loud and vulgar.

But it was quiet, and I wasn't complaining. I was getting my sex on, and just got finished getting high.

The track to my song, "Anytime," was ending, and I felt myself coming. I clutched the sheets tighter and felt my toes curling, and started panting harder and harder. I closed my eyes and panted out louder, and moaned, "Oooh, ssshhhh—Damn." I had my eyes closed and licked my lips. When I came, my body quivered and then I felt myself collapse. But I wasn't out.

Sierra came out from under the covers. "You like that?" she asked.

"You know I did," I replied.

She came up to me and slowly began to kiss me on my lips. I embraced her, and we continued to do our thing. I rolled Sierra over on her back and told her to spread them. And she did. I kissed her across her belly and then started to slowly finger-pop her sweet, pulsating vagina.

"My turn?" she asked, smiling.

I looked at her and then leaned forward and kissed her Hershey nipples, and started to slowly suck on each one. I heard her moan, and that stimulated me even more. I finger-popped her and sucked on her sugary nipples simultaneously. Sierra clutched my soft white pillow as my lips and tongue went down on her and I tasted a mouthful of pubic hairs and juices. I was gentle. Sierra thrust herself against me and gasped. Several moments passed, and she began to shake, and then she came. I looked up at her, and she had a satisfied grin plastered across her face.

I'm a freak. I admit that. I get my groove on any way possible. I switch back and forth from men and women. I ain't a lesbian like that, because once in a while, I do truly love some dick in me. But sometimes, when I get fed up with these trifling-ass, weak, and small-dick niggas—who sometimes don't know a piece of pussy from an asshole—I switch-hit and call up my girl, Sierra. Sierra, she can make a sista come right. I've been fucking with her for a couple of months now, on some DL shit.

Jade and Shy, they don't know about Sierra—shit, they don't really know that I get down with women like that. That's my business, and I keep it on the low. I don't stress these niggas out here, like my girls do. I get my dick, and after I'm done fucking, I'll tell the nigga to bounce, and call him back up when I want it again. I ain't trying to go through that relationship drama, and worrying about if the nigga is cheating on me or not. Worrying about who he fucking and why he doesn't love me. Shit, I leave that bullshit at the door. I ain't got time for that.

The last boyfriend I had was a year ago. Thomas. He had a big dick, but the nigga couldn't please me right. He tried. I give him that. But I wasn't coming like that, and he got corny and played out. So I dumped the nigga, plain and simple. Thomas wanted love, marriage, kids, house, matching bath towels, picket fences, farms, chickens, and shit. I mean, damn, the nigga was squeezing a bitch into a corner, sweating a sista. I hate it when men get pussy-whipped and they all up on you, wanting to know your business and shit. And God, don't let me have any male friends. The nigga wanted to be all in their business and mine. Thomas would get jealous, and ask, "You fuckin' him?" or "Y'all sure y'all just friends? Where you meet him at?" and my friends, all of 'em are cute, and they have a thang for me. But I keeps it cool and friendly with my male peoples. I fuck who I wanna fuck.

So with Thomas, before shit got even more dramatic with him, I cut him loose. I had to. He was getting on my last nerve. And did you know, that nigga cried? He cried like a bitch, begging for me to take him back. He got down on his knees and said he couldn't live without me. *Damn,* I thought, *pussy got him that strung.* But come on now, I wanted the nigga to have some dignity for himself. Shit, don't be a grown man and cry in front of me, especially if it ain't that serious. I'm gonna dis you and keep it moving. I met Sierra a few months after, and we hooked up, and she know it ain't nothing serious between us, just sex. In fact, she got a husband, and he don't know about her and me. I don't tell, and she don't either.

After sex, I got up off the bed and went into the bathroom. Sierra remained on the bed, watching television.

That dumb bitch Dee, she was a strong ox, but I handled that. That beat down was for my girl, Jade. I don't know how she put up with James. I know he trifling. But knowing them, James came home, she cursed him out, and now they probably fucking each other brains out. He got his way with Jade, and he know it too. Jade be beefing, talking about she leaving James, because he ain't doing her right. Whatever! She's been saying that same old bullshit for a year now. And James still around. Dick must be that good to her. Wouldn't be me.

I went back into the bedroom, and Sierra was getting dressed. She threw on her Guess Jeans and Nikes.

"You out?" I asked.

"I gotta go. It's Danny. You know how he get. It's ten o'clock already. I told him I'd be home by nine."

I sucked my teeth. Bitch rushing home to a nigga. But it ain't nothing. I got what I wanted.

As Sierra was throwing on her jacket, her cell phone went off. She quickly picked up, and seeing her response, I knew it was her husband on the phone. He was probably stressing her whereabouts.

"Yeah, baby . . . yes . . . I'm over at Kim's place. I told you the other night, I'd be over here," Sierra tried to explain.

I just stood there and listened, shaking my head.

"Danny . . . what? It ain't even like that. I'll be home in a half hour. Where are the kids? Okay . . . *Okay!*" she shouted.

She closed her phone and laughed. "Damn, he be trippin'," she said, looking over at me.

I just shrugged. What she telling me for? It ain't my business. Sierra continued to gather her things, and before ten thirty, she was out my apartment and on her way home to her man. They had three kids together. I never asked their ages. I didn't care. I was alone in my apartment, and that's how I like it.

I live in the projects, the South Jamaica Houses area. I moved here after my mother was locked up and my younger brother was killed. My building is down farther, by 110th Avenue. Shy and Jade are closer to South Road, where the more grimy niggas are.

Me, I don't fuck with no nigga up in these projects. They ain't got shit to offer me, and plus, you start dealing with these niggas in South Jamaica, and everybody start knowing your business. I like my business to be discreet. Sierra, she lives out in Long Island with her kids and her husband. I met her in a club one night. And the only time she comes out to Queens is to see me.

Now as for Shy and Jade, both their boyfriends live in South Jamaica housing with them. James and Roscoe, they know each other—fuck, they both hustle together and run the drugs in the projects we stay in. They seemed to be cool with it. Me, personally, I don't really fuck with them niggas like that—well, James, anyway. He's a real fucking asshole. They know who I am, but I keep my social contact with them to a minimum—hi, bye, and that's mostly it.

I threw on my house robe and rolled me up another blunt. A bitch lives in the projects, but my apartment stay hooked up with the fly shit. I got plush green carpeting spread throughout the rooms, imported furniture, a big-screen TV in my living room, my kitchen—shit, cherry cabinets, marble floors, fine appliances—and my closet got nothing but Burberry, Gucci, D&G, Fendi, Louis Vuitton, and Chloé stacked in it.

I live like a queen because I hustle and work for mine. I don't do a nine-to-five, but a bitch does her though. I sell boosted or stolen clothing like Fendi, Gucci, Donna Karan, and Chloé to my clientele in Brooklyn and Long Island. I have a connect who is into B&Es and robberies, and he breaks me off with merchandise to sell for a percentage. I'll keep it at that.

After I got finished rolling up my blunt and sparked it, I flopped down on my sofa, picked up the cordless, and decided to call up Jade and see what went down with her and her man tonight.

After about the umpteenth ring, this bitch finally decided to pick up her phone.

"Hello," she answered, sounding exhausted and shit.

"Bitch, you just got finished fuckin' him, right?" I said.

"Who this? Camille?" Like she didn't know.

"Yeah, bitch. What happened? And why you sound so out of breath?" I asked.

"Um . . . listen, let me call you back, Camille."

"Call me back? Jade, I know you ain't let this nigga off the hook so fuckin' easy like that. Tell me you didn't."

"James . . . he, um . . . we . . . ," Jade stuttered, trying to put the right words together to explain herself.

I had the phone clutched to my ear and waited for her excuse. I took a long pull from the dro and stared at the wall.

"Jade, who that on the phone? Get your ass back on this bed, and let me finish waxin' that sweet ass!" I heard James shout in the background.

"Camille, I'll explain it to you later. But I gotta go. . . . Bye!" this bitch said, and hung up on me.

Now I couldn't believe this shit. We had to beat a bitch down for her man earlier today, 'cause he was cheating on her. And now this bitch let that nigga off the hook so easily. I swear, Jade my girl and all, but she a dumb bitch sometimes. What the fuck was this nigga's excuse, because I was sure I saw that nigga hugged on Tasha on the Boulevard yesterday like they were a couple. So, you know I had to tell my girl this shit. Now we fucked that bitch up and her cousin, and she let James off the hook so easy. That shit got me mad now.

But you know what? It ain't my problem now. From now on, any beef Jade got with her man James, she gonna handle that shit on her own. For real.

I hated her drug-dealing boyfriend, James. He was no good. Roscoe, Shy's man, he sold drugs too, but he was cool with his, and I know he cares about Shy a lot. But James ain't nothing but an abusive, loudmouth, arrogant asshole, who only cares about himself.

Me, I rarely date drug dealers. Thugs, thieves, and bad boys, yes. But drug dealers, I always blamed them for my brother's death and my mother's incarceration. And yes, I know all dealers ain't the same, but I've held a grudge against them since I was nine.

My mother was into drugs when I was young. I hated seeing my moms getting high and not caring if I was around to see and observe. First it was crack, and then she graduated to heroin. That needle stayed deep in my mother's arm almost every fucking night. My little brother, Jamie, was only eighteen months when he was killed. I was eight or nine at the time. We lived in Queens, but at the time, I lived in the Baisley projects on Guy R. Brewer and Foch. The shit still fucks with me today.

I remember it was early afternoon, and Jamie wouldn't stop crying all day, and my mother was in her bedroom, getting high with her boyfriend. Jamie didn't know any better—he was hungry and wet. I tried telling him to be quiet before Mommy got mad, but it was too late. My moms stormed out of her bedroom, high as fuck, and she picked up Jamie and started yelling at him. She shook him back and forth hard. But Jamie never stopped crying. He got louder and louder. I just stood there, tearing up, screaming at my moms to stop before she hurts him. But she didn't listen to me; she kept on with her violent assault against my little brother. And then I heard her threaten, "You little nigga. If you don't stop cryin' right now, I'm gonna throw your ass out the fuckin' window!"

But Jamie continued to cry, and my mother kept good on her threats. She rushed over to the window with Jamie clutched in her arms and dangled him from the sixth floor.

"Stop cryin'. Stop cryin'! Stop your fuckin' cryin'!" she yelled.

"Mommy!" I screamed. "Mommy, stop! Please."

My little brother cried and screamed until I heard his crying and screaming fading, and then I no longer heard Jamie crying. It just stopped. Everything stopped. It was a nightmare. My mother's boyfriend ran from out the bedroom and shouted, "Lorain, what the fuck! I'm not goin' to jail over this shit! Fuck, bitch!" He quickly left the apartment, fearing prison.

Moments later, my mother was arrested, and they dragged me off with some strange white lady. A few weeks after that, I went to live with my grandmother out in Jamaica housing, where I later ran into Shy and Jade. There were problems at first, but they worked themselves out.

My mother was sentenced to life in prison, and that's the last I heard or know about her. I think about my younger brother all the time and wonder if he was alive today, what would become of his life. Would he be in school, getting an education? Or would he be another one of these dope- or coke-pushing thugs that saturate these projects?

I know directly that every drug dealer in the projects didn't kill my brother. But indirectly, it was the poison they pushed into the addicts' hands constantly that was the cause of my brother's death and my mother's absence.

After my conversation with Jade, I placed the cordless on its cradle and retreated my ass back into my bedroom. Having my brother in thought and dealing with today's drama, I just wanted some solitude. My mood became a bit somber, and today's been a long fucking day for a sista. So I just laid in bed, closed my eyes, and went to sleep.

~ CHAPTER 4 ~

shy

"Shy, hurry up! Damn, what the fuck is takin' you so long?" Roscoe barked.

He was out in the living room, and I was still holed up in the bedroom, getting dressed. We were going out tonight. It was Saturday, and you know a bitch wasn't spending a beautiful October night cooped up in the crib.

He's been ready for about a half hour. But I had to throw the right outfit together. I had a bunch of shit in my closet, and when I go out, my gear gotta be right. I can't be going outside looking like some broke bum-bitch—especially to a club.

Roscoe and I were supposed to hook up with Jade and James at this club on Merrick Boulevard that was supposed to be popping off. Roscoe knew people at the party, so I was sure we'd get in for free with no fucking hassle from security. I was excited. Roscoe hasn't taken me out in weeks. He's been busy doing him and handling business out on the streets.

I put on what Roscoe brought me a week earlier: the red cropped leather jacket with the black collar and the skimpy matching red miniskirt. And I threw on my red and white Fendi shoes with my matching Fendi bag. I was looking too damn cute.

I walked into the living room, and Roscoe's jaw almost dropped. The he smiled as he gazed at me from head to toe, and from that response, I knew I was looking good. My legs were gleaming and looking right in Fendi.

"Damn, baby!" Roscoe said.

"You like?" I asked, doing a little twirl for him.

"You . . . you 'bout ready to make me wanna stay home tonight and do some things," Roscoe said.

He came up to me, but I put my hand out and said, "No, 'cause you're takin' me out. That can wait till later."

He sucked his teeth. I continued to gather the rest of my things. Roscoe grabbed his keys to the ride, and we were out. Roscoe was looking good himself. I just did his braids earlier, and he sported a black leather shirt, with the white T underneath, and black leather pants. He had the bling shining out of his shirt, and a diamond ring on his pinkie finger. I sported a cute thin diamond chain around my neck, which was a previous gift from Roscoe.

I walked out first, and I suddenly felt him grab my butt. I turned around and playfully said, "Stop." Roscoe smiled.

"Yo, you gonna get a nigga shot tonight, lookin' that good. I'm gonna have to fuck some nigga up, baby," he said. I knew he was kidding this time. But knowing Roscoe, sometimes he was dead serious. When it came to me, he don't like no man to disrespect me. He don't even like a nigga looking at me funny. When we go out, especially to a club, I try to stay real close to my man, 'cause I know how niggas be acting when they in a club, especially when a nigga is drunk. And I don't want no beef caused over me, and have my man fighting or, worse, killing a nigga, and he locked up over some dumb shit.

We got outside, and it was so nice that I didn't even need a jacket. We strolled over to Roscoe's pearl Escalade, and he opened the passenger door for me. When he got in, he put in a mixed R&B CD, and we drove off.

We got to the club in no time, and the line outside was ridiculous. It was like a half a block long. I think Roscoe said that Sean Paul was supposed to be performing, and that definitely drew in the crowd.

We got a lucky parking spot and strolled up to the hordes of people waiting to get in. I looked around for my girl. I called her cell phone, and she informed me that she and James were nearby.

As we stood outside, waiting for Jade and James to show up, I saw numerous eyes, especially the men's eyes, clocking me hard. Some tried to be subtle with it, being that I was with my man, and some men were with their female companions. But others, they didn't give a fuck that I was with my man or not. They stared hard, smiling—admiring and wishing they were with me.

"There they go right there," Roscoe pointed out.

I turned around an saw Jade and her man, James, coming toward us. I smiled. "Hey, girl." I gave Jade a hug and kiss and stared at James, knowing about him and Tasha.

James smiled and gave Roscoe dap, and they began chatting. Jade was looking cute. She had on this white leather mini miniskirt and matching halter top, with the bomb stilettos on, and her man came gangsta in the white tank top, showing off his muscles, some Sean John jeans, Timberlands, and of course, having the ice around his wrist and neck.

We didn't waste too much time standing outside socializing. We walked in, bypassing the crowds and lines outside, and security easily let our party in with no problems.

Inside was popping. I quickly got excited hearing my song "Tempted to Touch" blaring throughout the packed club. Ohmygod, I love this song. I started winding and gyrating my hips to the beat and started singing along.

"Before the end of the night . . . I wanna hold you so tight . . . You know I want you so much . . . and I'm so tempted to touch . . . tempted to touch, tempted to touch . . ." I opened my eyes and noticed the fellows watching me hard as I danced. Even Roscoe smiled at me.

But the DJ was killing me—he was definitely doing his thing tonight. He switched it up from "Tempted to Touch" to some Wayne Wonder, Sean Paul, Beenie Man, and Spragga Benz. I stood by the wall, grinding against my man, and had my hands feeling up my inner thighs, gyrating my hips against Roscoe's pelvis. I felt my man getting hard, but I didn't mind. Shit, if I had a dick, I'd get hard too, the way I was dancing up on him.

I was the center of attention. I even noticed the ladies watching me. Reggae and soca is my thing. My family is Jamaican, and you know I get down on the dance floor once I hear that beat and the smooth lyrics from my West Indian brothers.

I looked over at Jade and James, and Jade was dancing alone. James, I guess, wasn't much of a dancer, not to reggae anyway. He stood there next to Jade with a drink in his hand and observed the crowd. No one attempted to dance with Jade, especially when she had her thugged-out-looking man right next to her.

We all partied, drank, and got our groove on for hours. I ain't gonna front—a bitch was a little tipsy and shit. I had two Long Island iced teas, half of some Hennessey, and some Belvedere. Sean Paul got onstage and did his thing. He ripped the crowd and had everyone going berserk when he started to perform "Get Busy" and "I'm Still in Love with You."

By three, a bitch wanted to go home. The club was still jam-packed, and I observed that there were a lot more hustlers and thugs up in the place.

I was chilling by the bar, and Roscoe was off with some of his peoples. James came by the bar and ordered himself a drink. Then he turned and looked at me and said, "You look nice, Shy."

"Thanks," I said, being short.

I had no words for the man. He disrespected Jade, and I wondered what his excuse was for Jade to accept him back. He gazed at me for a moment, making me feel a bit uncomfortable. The man was sexy, I admit, but from Jade's mouth, he was fucked up and can be a jerk sometimes.

The roaring and thunderous sound of 50 Cent's hit song, "In da Club," boomed throughout the club and made it difficult to speak. Revelers jumped up and bopped around the dimly lit space, and it got so crazy that people started bumping into each other. This one fool who wasn't watching where he was going bumped into me and almost spilled his drink on me.

"Excuse me!" I shouted over the music.

This fool turned around and looked at me like I'd done something wrong. I glared at him. He smiled.

James sternly intervened. "Yo, apologize, nigga!" He glared at the man.

"My bad, ma," the man apologized, intimidated by James. And then he got lost in the crowd.

I turned to James and said, "Thank you."

"I got you, Shy," he said.

I took a sip from my drink and peered around the club while James stood next to me. I wondered what the fuck was he still around for?

Jade came up to us and gave her man a kiss. Jade got herself another drink, which James paid for, and she started chatting with me. But I couldn't really hear shit, so I told her to walk with me to the bathroom.

When we walked in the bathroom, I asked her, "Um . . . what happened wit' y'all two?"

"Nuthin'. He said what he had to say, and I listened . . . ," she explained.

"And that thing with Tasha?"

"Ill. I thought about it, I know James's taste in women, and Tasha ain't his type."

"So you just gonna let it be, and that's it?" I asked, somewhat bewildered by her nonchalant attitude.

"Shy, really . . . I ain't come here to discuss my relationship wit' James. He ain't perfect, and neither is your man, so let's drop it, okay," she said with a slight attitude in her voice.

I looked at her, like *What?* But before I could even utter another word, a bunch of ladies rushed into the bathroom, yelling, "They fightin'. They fightin'!"

Jade and I looked at each other, and I guess we both were thinking the same thing: James and Roscoe. We maneuvered through the thick sea of women that had taken safety in the bathroom and ran out into the club to see a brawl of men fighting in the middle of the dance floor. The lights were on, and it looked like chaos.

I looked around for Roscoe, and of course, he was in the middle of it, swinging a chair at someone's head. And James was pouncing on two guys.

I ran up to Roscoe, grabbed him by his arm, and shouted, "Baby, c'mon! Let's go!"

I looked down at the victim he was pouncing on, and it was that same fool that bumped into me earlier. His face was a bloody mess.

Roscoe looked at me, his face twisted with rage, and he grabbed me by my arm and ran with me out of the club. I turned around to look for Jade, but she was nowhere in sight.

We exited the club, and it was the same outside, niggas were wilding. I didn't even know what set this shit off, but I heard police sirens in the distance, and I damn sure didn't want me and my man getting caught up in the middle of this.

We both jumped into the Escalade and Roscoe peeled off around the corner. He drove fast down the backstreets; I know he wasn't trying to get pulled over by the police, because he had a loaded nine-millimeter under the driver's seat.

A few blocks on, and Roscoe finally slowed down. We came at a red light, and I looked at him. I took a deep breath and asked, "Baby, what happened?"

I noticed that he had blood on his hand as he gripped the steering wheel. "You hurt?"

"Nah, I'm good," he calmly replied. He still stared out the windshield.

I took his hand to inspect it, but he pulled it back from me. "I said I'm a'ight," he said, his voice raised a little.

I sighed. The light changed, and he quickly pulled off.

I wanted to know what went down back there. "Baby, you sure you're okay?" I asked, but he didn't answer me.

I thought about Jade, and I worried if her and her man made it out of there okay. I picked up my cell phone and started to dial up her number. But it rang and rang, until I got her voice mail. I dialed again, and I got the same thing, her voice mail.

"Roscoe, you think James and Jade made it out there okay?" I asked. But he didn't answer. I thought, *What the fuck is his problem now?*

We made it back to the hood in no time. Roscoe parked his truck, and we walked back to our apartment. I kept my mouth shut. I knew his attitude, and if he didn't wanna talk about it right now, I left it alone.

The minute we stepped into the apartment, Roscoe went straight in the bathroom, I guess to wash the blood off his hands. I went into the bedroom to get undressed.

After I slipped outta my clothing and put on something more comfortable, I picked up my phone and tried calling Jade again. I got her voice mail again. Fuck. Now I was more than a little worried. When Roscoe came into the bedroom, I asked him to call up James and see if they were all right. But he ignored me. I noticed that he wasn't getting ready for bed; this nigga was changing clothes to go back out.

Nah, I wasn't trying to hear that shit. I jumped up and barked, "Where you going?"

"Back out," he explained drily.

"Fuck you mean? You staying here," I said with attitude.

He smirked, looking like, *Whatever!*

"Roscoe, why you playin'? What if sumthin' happens to you out there? Stay here, baby. Don't worry 'bout out there tonight," I pleaded, gripping his shirt and looking him in the eyes.

But his stubborn fucking ass continued to get dressed, like my concern was unimportant to him.

"Baby, call James. Call him," I said.

"He a'ight," he said.

"How you know?"

"Because I know that nigga can handle himself."

"What about Jade?"

"Shy, go to bed. I'll be back," he said.

He strolled outta the bedroom and headed for the door. I followed him. I pulled him by his jacket, begging for him to stay. I wanted him to keep me company. I didn't want my man to leave. But he turned around and shouted, "Shy, go to bed! I'll be back! Damn!" And just like that, my fucking man bounced on me.

~ CHAPTER 5 ~

camille

It was damn near four in the morning, and my damn phone was ringing constantly. You know that pissed a sista off. I'm trying to get my sleep.

I reached over and picked the phone.

"Camille," I heard Shy cry out.

"Shy. What's goin' on?" I asked. I know Shy wouldn't call me this early in the morning if it wasn't important.

"It's Roscoe. Somethin' happened tonight, a fight broke out at a club, and we broke out. But I'm tryin' to call Jade, and she's not pickin' up her phone, and Roscoe left out here just now . . . ," she explained all in one breath.

"Shy, calm down," I said. "What happened again?"

"I don't know; everything happened so quickly. I need you to come get me."

"Come get you. Where you at?"

"Home. But I gotta find Roscoe. I'm worried about him."

"Call his phone," I said.

"I am, but he's not pickin' up. What if sumthin' happened to him?" she said. She sounded frantic.

"A'ight. I'll be over there in a half hour," I said.

"Thank you, Camille."

I hung up and reluctantly got dressed. Damn, I swear—these bitches and they drama. I'm like some kind of counseling center—they always come to me. I know I'm the oldest, but come on, give a sista a break.

I threw on some sweatpants, Nikes, and a light jacket and headed down the block to Shy's building. I knocked hard on her door, and she answered within seconds. I could tell she was crying: her eyes were puffy, and her face was stained with tears.

She let me in and closed the door.

"Shy, you a'ight?" I asked, concerned.

She sat on the couch and recapped the night's events. Now I'm thinking somebody got shot or killed, but she getting all worried and troubled about niggas brawling in a club. I mean, come on—niggas fight all the time, and I know this wasn't the first fight she's seen or been through. But I did understand her concern when it came to Roscoe. He could be a hothead, and there was no telling when he left out that door what his true intentions were.

So I calmed her down, and she called Jade up one more time. But Jade didn't pick up. Now I got a little worried myself. Shy wanted to drive back down to the club and see what popped off. But I told her it wouldn't be worth it. I had a better idea. I decided to call Jade's crib, instead of her cell phone. And guess what, this bitch picked up. Shy was so relieved. We all didn't waste time chatting on the phone. Shy and I went to her apartment.

We got to Jade's crib in minutes. She came to the door in her house robe and hugged Shy.

"Girl, you okay?" Shy asked.

"I was worried about you," Jade replied.

"I've been callin' your phone all night, and you ain't pick up," Shy said.

"I lost that shit," Jade explained. "I lost all of my shit—my purse, my cell, and my keys. It's a good thing James had an extra set."

"What happened to James?" I asked.

"He dropped me off and left," Jade explained.

"Roscoe too."

"I heard somebody got stabbed tonight," Jade told us.

"Who?" Shy and I asked in unison.

"I don't know, one of James's friends. I don't know how everything started, but James was really upset. His phone went off while we were driving home, and he dropped me off in front of the building and left."

See, that's why I don't fuck wit' none of these local shits, especially anything in Queens and Brooklyn. Manhattan, Long Island, I'll fuck with, probably, as long as it's upscale and niggas can't get in wit' jerseys, sneaker, Timbs, hoodies, and shit.

Well, of course I ended up staying the night at Jade's crib, gossiping and talking about what went down. We talked until my eyes became heavy. I tried to wait up with Jade and Shy, waiting for their boyfriends to come home, but I ended up falling asleep on her couch.

Morning came quick, and I woke up on Jade's sofa. I looked over, and Shy was asleep in a chair across from me. I looked at the time and it was 9 a.m. on Sunday morning.

Damn, I had been tired last night. The first thing I wanted to do was go home, jump in the shower, and brush my teeth. I had morning breath, for real. And sleeping on this couch didn't make waking up easier. I was still in my sweats and a tank top, and felt somewhat funky.

I peered around the room. I guess Jade was in her bedroom. I stood up, and that's when I heard someone at the door. I figured it was James, so I threw my jacket over me, trying to look somewhat decent.

James came into the room, looking furious. His jeans were dirty, and his wife-beater was torn and had a lil' bit of blood on it. He looked a mess.

Shy finally woke up. She immediately jumped up out of her chair and asked, "James, where's Roscoe?"

James looked over at Shy. I knew something had gone wrong last night. Before James could say something, Jade stepped into the room. She saw her man standing there, and she went up to him and hugged him strongly.

"Ohmygod, baby—what happened to you?" Jade asked, breaking away from him and observing his scruffy condition.

"Shit went bad last night," James said.

"Bad? I heard someone got stabbed," I said.

"What happened to Roscoe?" Shy asked.

James looked at Shy and said, "He got arrested."

"What?" Shy, Jade, and myself exclaimed.

"Arrested. Fo' what?" Shy asked, looking frantic.

"He down at Central Booking right now," James told her. "They chargin' him with murder and shit."

"Murder!" Shy shouted, looking baffled. "What the fuck happened?"

I saw the tears building in Shy's eyes. I thought she was bad last night; she damn near lost it right then.

"James, what happened? What did he do?" Shy asked, staring at James.

"Some cats wild out on us, and we did what we had to do."

I looked at this muthafucka and shook my head. Okay, Roscoe's locked up, and he's free to come home. That shit didn't sit right with me.

"So, why didn't they lock you up too, if y'all were together?" I asked.

"It's a long story, Camille. I need a fuckin' shower right now," he said offhandedly.

Shy was full of tears. Jade and I tried to console her while James went into the bathroom to take a shower.

"Why?" Shy sobbed. "What the fuck did he do? Why he couldn't stay his ass home?"

"We gonna find out what happened, Shy. Believe me," I assured her.

I knew James wasn't telling us the full story, and he was acting funny and shit. Shy's man was locked up, and he ain't stressing it like that. James can be a shysty individual. I never trusted him.

Thursday morning came, and I found myself down at the Queens criminal courthouse on Queens Boulevard with Shy and Jade. We got word of Roscoe's arraignment date, and I drove up there in my Beamer.

The line outside the courthouse was ridiculous. Everybody was waiting to go through the metal detectors and be searched. I hated this shit. The last time I came up here for a nigga was when I was seventeen, and Michael, my boyfriend at that time, got his dumb ass locked up for crack possession. He got city time and did a year in jail.

In front of us stood a young mother with three kids, one infant in a stroller, and she tried controlling the other young'uns. She had to be no older than nineteen, and was probably going to her baby's father court date. She was young, but you could tell that time and life has not been good to her. She looked worn out, with her long hair in a shabby ponytail, and her clothing looked like hand-me-downs from the Salvation Army.

Even though the line was long, it moved kinda fast. The courthouse had plenty of court officers doing their jobs up front. And they moved the line along at a good pace.

I got up to the metal detector, and one of the male court officers smiled and tried to kick it to me while he ran the wand across my body. He was a tall black and kinda cute. But fucking with niggas that work for the law ain't my style. I smiled and moved along.

We got to the courtroom, where they were supposed to bring Roscoe out. All three of us took a seat in the third row from the front and waited. Shy was quiet the whole time. Jade peered off into space, and I wished I was somewhere else. But I had to be there for my girl, Shy. I knew what it felt like to have your man locked up, and there ain't shit you can do about it. All she could do was wait and pray.

One thing I've learned about these arraignments is that they can be a very stressful time for friends and family. People don't tell you shit, and you can be waiting for hours until your people's docket number is called by the bridge or court officer.

The courtroom was semicrowded. I glanced at the time, and

it was 9:55. There was minor chitchat in the room, which caught the attention of the female court officer. She stood off to the side, rigid and observing her territory with a taut look on her olive skin.

"Quiet!" the court officer said in her loudest tone.

The chitchat eased up a little.

One by one, docket numbers were being called for the judge to review, and the judge, a silver-haired white man who looked to be in his early fifties, would say a few words to the attorneys and briefly acknowledge the accused.

Cases from robbery, crack possession, and even felonies were being called. It was a tedious process. About an hour passed until Roscoe's case was finally called.

"Docket number 448524745, Roscoe Richardson," the court officer announced.

Shy and Jade perked up, hearing Roscoe's name being called out. All eyes were up front.

Roscoe came into the courtroom, ushered out in handcuffs and looking mad at the world. He stood in front the judge and waited to hear his fate.

I noticed that his attorney, the one that came to represent him, looked different than the other cheap lawyers in the court. He had smooth white skin and sleek black hair, and he had on a gray pin-striped Italian suit, polished wing-tip shoes, and a Rolex around his wrist. I knew that Roscoe's lawyer wasn't one of these cheap CA (court-appointed) lawyers. He was the real thing.

He carried a real leather briefcase and had style to him, while these CA's wore cotton and polyester, sported bad scuffed shoes, and had busy head tops and five-o'clock shadows; they all looked like they've seen one too many cases.

The prosecutor spoke first. He opened up a manila envelope, peered up at the judge, and gave his deposition. "Your Honor, the people request that the defendant be held without bail, pending a grand jury investigation. He's the prime suspect in a murder five days ago. Also, he was found with a loaded nine-millimeter in his truck—" The male prosecutor went on putting Roscoe on blast, and his chances of freedom looked bleak.

Roscoe didn't flinch as he was being indicted on charges of murder, probably in the first degree, and criminal possession of a weapon.

A few more words were said by the prosecutor, including that Roscoe had a previous rap sheet which included drug arrests and other convictions.

Roscoe's attorney finally spoke. Standing next to his client, he stared up at the judge and stated, "Your Honor, my client claims that the shooting was done in self-defense. He feared for his life, and he also claims that the search of his truck was done illegally. . . ."

After all the bullshit was said and done from the defense and the prosecutor, the judge reviewed the case and said, "The defendant is remanded without bail. Next case." He sounded arrogant and shit.

I swear Shy was about to bust out crying. But she held strong, and only a few tears trickled down her face.

The court officers ushered Roscoe away back into lockup. He didn't even look in our direction. I knew he knew we were seated in the courtroom. But I guess he felt ashamed and shit.

After Roscoe was led away, the three of us quickly got up out of our seats and exited the courtroom. We followed Roscoe's attorney outside. Shy and the rest of us wanted to talk to the lawyer and get his insight and opinion on the case.

"Excuse me . . . excuse me," Shy said, trying to catch his attention.

He turned around and looked at us.

He spoke, looking like he was in a rush. "Can I help you?"

"I'm Shy, Roscoe's girlfriend. I wanna know what's goin' on."

"Well, your boyfriend is being charged with murder. He's looking at fifteen to twenty for murder in the first degree, which is an A-One felony; criminal possession of a weapon in the first degree; criminal use of a firearm in the first degree; and resisting arrest."

"Ohmygod!"

"What's going to happen?" I asked.

"The murder charge, I'll try and get it dropped to a justified homicide. But the problem is that they didn't find the gun on the victim. And there's a witness that the D.A. has who is willing to testify against Roscoe. I don't know how credible the witness is, but I'm on top of it. If your boyfriend cops a plea, the D.A. may give him ten years. But if he's willing to fight and take it to trial, it gets risky. He might end up doing twenty years."

Shy began to cry, and Jade consoled her in her arms, saying, "Shy, don't worry—we'll get through this."

"He's going to need all the help he can in this case," the lawyer said. He reached into his suit jacket and pulled out his card, which was off-white with raised lettering. "Here's my card. If you have any questions at all about the case, or his condition, don't hesitate to give me a call."

I took his card and peered at it.

"Sorry, but I'm in a rush," he said, and then turned and walked away.

Jade and I tried to ease Shy's stressful situation. We went to get something to eat at a nearby McDonald's, but Shy said she wasn't hungry. I knew she had Roscoe on her mind.

Shy was about to go through some bullshit. I know, because I've been there with two ex-boyfriends. The frequent trips to Rikers to go see your man and bring him a bunch of shit that he probably don't need, and the collect calls that total up and exceed your regular phone bill. When your man is home and he got all the free time to call a sista, he don't call. But the minute his ass gets incarcerated, he calling a sista everyday, talking about he need this and he need that. And most of the time he calls, it ain't about shit. He just want to hear your voice.

Shit, if Shy's dedicated and really loves Roscoe, she's gonna do time too if he's convicted and gets sentenced. And that shit ain't easy—going months, sometimes years without any dick—that shit gotta be love.

~ CHAPTER 6 ~

jade

I feel for Shy, damn, I do. She was a mess when I left her. The only thing I could tell her was to be strong, for herself and her man.

I mean, why the fuck did Roscoe do what he had to do? Why don't niggas listen? He was home, with his girl, but the minute some shit breaks out, they gotta go prove themselves in front of their boys and test who got the bigger dick, and end up getting killed or locked up. I was mad, I'll admit. But I was also thankful that I wasn't in the same predicament. Because it coulda been me too, and James's ass coulda been behind bars, and stressing me the fuck out. He came home.

I was lying on my bed, and James was in the shower. I was still curious about that night. James wasn't really saying shit about it. He left just like Roscoe did that night, and I knew that they both were furious about something. I just didn't know what. He asked about Roscoe and his predicament. I don't know why he didn't come down to the arraignment with us, but I guess he had his reason. Shit, thinking about Shy's situation made me forget about my own with James.

I was sprawled out on my bed in some panties and a large T-shirt, staring at the TV. I wanted to call up Shy, but thought against it—give her some alone time, and let her be.

I heard the shower stop running. I glanced at the bathroom. I sighed, because I wished I could be there more for her. But I was clueless about the judicial system just like the rest of my clique.

James walked into the bedroom with a blue towel wrapped around his waist, and his muscles gleaming from the water still on his skin. Damn, he looked so fucking sexy when wet.

James looked at me and smiled. "What you lookin' at?" he joked.

"Nuthin'," I sheepishly replied.

He walked up to the bed, still peering lustfully at me. "I know what you want, baby," he said.

"You do? And what's that?" I asked, trying to play along.

He slowly unwrapped his towel and dropped it to the floor, stood butt naked in front of me. "You lookin' for this?" he asked, smirking down at me.

I tried not to smile, but I couldn't help it. His big dick dangled in front of me like an anaconda swinging from a tree. My baby got the body of a god.

"You like this, right?"

I sighed.

"Don't front, Jade. . . . He takes care of you," James said, confidently.

"He a'ight," I said, resting my back against the headboard.

James slowly gripped his big dick and started stroking himself gently. I hadn't had sex in days. I was so busy looking after Shy and making sure that she was okay that I forgot to take care of my womanly needs. And right now, my thighs were tingling and my vagina felt really vibrant.

James came closer to me, and his dick got harder. He climbed onto the bed and approached me hungrily. The mattress sunk in a little as his thick frame rested against it. I just sat there and waited.

He grabbed me by my thighs and pulled me toward him.

"What you doing?" I asked, staring up at him.

"You know what I want, baby," he said.

He hovered over me, and I removed my panties and tossed them to the floor. James smiled. "That's my girl."

"I'm your girl, huh?" I stated.

"You know you are, baby," he said with passion in his voice.

I smiled.

"Just me and you, Jade . . . no one else. One day, we gonna get married and have kids. I promise you that shit. I'm gonna quit the game one day, and we gonna do us," he assured me. "I ain't tryin' to get locked up like Roscoe, and be away from my girl so long. It ain't happenin'. I'd go crazy if I don't see your face every day."

I swear, a huge smile spread across my face, and I felt like I was on cloud nine.

"You promise?" I asked.

"I promise," he returned.

It felt like a waterfall was rushing in between my legs. I wanted this man so fucking bad. I wanted to fuck until we couldn't fuck anymore. He leaned forward, and our lips connected and we started to kiss and tongue each other passionately. His warm fresh breath filled my mouth lovingly as our tongues entwined.

"Roll over on your back, baby," I said.

That smile James gave me . . . he knew what was up. He did so quickly, and his erection stood erect like a flagpole. I made my way down to his stomach, kissing him soothingly until my mouth came across his manhood. And I gulped him down like fine wine. I tried to take all of the dick in my mouth, deep-throating him, but the most I could take in was seven inches of his erection. But the way my man moaned, whined, and quivered, clutching the sheets, I knew my head game was on point. I was sucking my man's dick until his forehead caved in.

"Baby, stop," James pleaded. "You gonna make a nigga come up in your jaw, you keep suckin' me like that."

I smiled.

"Can't handle a lil' suction, baby?" I teased.

He blew a satisfied breath of air out his mouth. My job was done. James still laid on his back, and I wanted him to remain like that. I straddled my legs around him and let his erection enter me slowly.

I moaned the more dick he put into me. Shit, a bitch may be petite, but believe me, I can ride some dick, and James definitely knows it. He clutched my waist, as my hands rested against his thick smooth chest and my ass bounced up and down against him, and gyrated my hips against his broad pelvis.

Twenty minutes into our fucking, with me still riding him, James uttered, "Baby, I'm gonna come . . . shit . . . I'm coming!"

I didn't stop. I rode him faster and faster till James clutched my hips tightly, quivered, and grunted as he let one loose up in me. And by his body movement, I knew he came lovely. A sista did her job.

He was sprawled out on the bed, sweaty with me rested on top of him, panting lightly. The room smelled like sex.

After a few moments passed, I looked at James and asked, "Baby, what happened that night?"

"About what?" he countered, like he didn't know what I meant.

"Roscoe. Who did he murder?"

"Shit just got fucked up, Jade. You know we got enemies out there on them streets. You know how fucked up shit is," he said, like he was angry with someone.

"But that night at the club? Who were y'all fighting?"

"Some niggas that my man, Kay, had beef wit'. After y'all went into the bathroom, he came up to me and Roscoe and said niggas started beefin' wit' him by the door, and that one of 'em pulled out a knife and threatened to stab him. So you know, Kay, that's my nigga, and we wasn't tryin' to hear it, so we stepped to them. A few unkindly words were exchanged, and then shit popped off. And they stabbed my nigga Row in his chest."

"What?" I said. "So why did you drop me off and leave?"

"Like I said, Jade, shit went bad that night. It was drama, and you didn't need to be in the middle of it. We were gonna take care of it. Roscoe caught a bad one."

"His lawyer said he might plead for justified homicide. He said Roscoe shot in self-defense. But if not, maybe second-degree murder. But he said that they didn't find a gun on the victim, and that there might be a credible witness to testify against Roscoe. If his case goes to trial, they might serve him wit' twenty years if he gets convicted. But if he cops out, D.A. might give him ten."

James sighed. "Damn."

"Who did he shoot?" I asked.

"Jade, fo' real, it's a nigga that tried to come at us on some territory shit. Roscoe shot some nigga who felt big that night; some on-the-come-up nigga. That's all you need to know. I don't feel like discussin' this now. I'm fuckin' tired," he said, laying his head back.

I shoulda interrogated his ass first, and then give up the pussy. James had gotten what he wanted. He laid there with his head against the pillow with his eyes closed. I felt like playing Sherlock Holmes, but the dick wore me out a little, and I ended up falling asleep on his chest.

~ CHAPTER 7 ~

shy

I swear I'm tired of crying. I'm all cried out right now. Why muthafuckas gotta be dumb? I wish someone would answer me that. It's been a week since Roscoe's incarceration, and I'm a fucking mess. I haven't been to work, and I haven't left the house, none of that shit.

Camille and Jade, they're constantly calling or coming by, acting like a bitch is gonna kill herself. But I keep telling them that I'm good. It ain't like the nigga dead. Shit, he'll probably get off or something. We don't know that. He got a good lawyer who seems to know what the fuck he's doing. And I believe that Roscoe's lawyer is gonna take care of it. He gonna do my man right and have him acquitted of all charges. I believe that.

I wanna see my man, though, and I'm waiting for his call. A week had passed and not one collect call from him. So right now, I'm kinda pissed.

I know my man got clout up in them jails—he damn near ran shit in the hood. So I know he's not getting punked for his phone time in his housing. He's just probably too ignorant to call his girl and let me know what's going on with him.

I lay in bed, listening to the radio and thinking about my man. I started reminiscing about how we met, and the things we did. Two months into our relationship, I wanted to have his baby. But Roscoe wasn't ready to have kids. He said to me that he didn't want any of his children growing up in the projects and going through the same shit he went through when he was young. Roscoe's moms passed away a few years ago, and he never knew his pops. He grew up with his older sister. He told me that his moms, she wasn't the best mother, but she tried. She was an alcoholic who lost every job she had and stayed on welfare for as long as he could remember.

Roscoe wanted to give his children a good home, far from South Jamaica and the bullshit that comes along with it. He wanted to get a house and send his kids to the best schools out in Long Island, with a great education. Roscoe was a hustler and a thug, but the man had respect and morals for himself. He loved children. I remember on some weekends when he would pick up his sister's kids—she got three, two boys and a girl—and like a family, we'd go to the park, movies, Chuck E. Cheese, or just chill in the apartment and watch a Disney movie.

He told me once that he wanted twins, a boy and girl, so we could experience raising a daughter and a son at the same time. I like that. It made me feel special. Roscoe had so many dreams besides hustling that I knew that one day they were going to come true.

But tonight it seemed like everything collapsed. My dreams along with Roscoe seemed to be fading as I thought about him and not being able to touch and talk to him. I wanted to feel and make love to him. I was missing him so much that I threw on one of his Knicks jerseys and walked around the apartment in it all day.

He promised to move me outta the projects. He promised to take care of me. Tears trickled down my cheeks as I peered at a picture of us hugged up together and smiling. It was taken at Coney Island a few months back. And we looked so happy.

I remembered that night: Roscoe had on a black tank top that hugged his body so nicely and some denim shorts and white Nikes and, of course, being blinged out. He was so cute. I had on the white tennis skirt, with a short white T, sporting blue and white Nikes, and feeling so good.

Earlier, Roscoe took me out to dinner at City Island; afterwards, we took in the city and then headed for Coney Island. And after the park, he got us a stylish suite in the Sheraton.

"Baby, come back to me," I quietly whispered, staring at his image. "I'm missing you." I raised the picture to my lips and kissed it softly.

"Diary" by Alicia Keys played softly in the background. I looked at the time, and saw that it was 9:25. I plopped my head down against the pillows and peered up at the ceiling. I got lost in thought, listening to Alicia's lyrics.

A few minutes later, I heard the doorbell ring out. I sighed, not feeling for any company tonight, and got my ass up to go see who it was. But I figured who by the time I got to the door.

I glanced through the peephole and saw Camille and Jade standing outside my door. I sighed. But you know, they my girls, so I had to let them in.

I opened the door, and they both barged in like they own the place. I closed the door behind them and tried to look more upbeat.

"How you feelin', Shy?" Camille asked.

"I'm good," I replied, trying not to let my voice sound sad.

"You hear any word from Roscoe yet?" Jade asked.

"No. It's been a week and he ain't call a sista yet."

"Give it time, girl. You know it ain't like he can pick up a phone just like that and call you. Remember, he locked down. He gonna call," Camille assured me.

"I hope it's soon. I wanna hear what he gotta say, and make sure he's a'ight," I said, taking a seat.

"Well, James ran down some information on me the other night," Jade informed.

"About what?" I asked.

"He told me that it was his friend Row that got stabbed that night. He said Kay had beef wit' some dudes while we were in the bathroom, Shy . . . and that it went bad."

"Did he tell you who Roscoe shot, or if he did shoot someone?" I asked.

"He's bein' really sparse wit' information and shit, Shy. I don't know what's going on wit' him."

"Roscoe gonna let me know what went down," I told her confidently. "If he just calls me."

I looked over at Jade and Camille. "He's gonna be a'ight," I said, trying not to break out in tears. "He's comin' home."

Jade came over to me. "Shy, we goin' out tonight."

"No. I'm not goin' anywhere," I said.

"Yes, you are," Camille said. "You can't be cooped up in your crib stressin' dis shit. It's not good for you."

"Y'all two go wit'out me. I'm cool," I said.

"Shy, listen . . . I ain't takin' no for an answer. We gonna get dressed up and go out tonight and do us. Shit, when my man got locked up, you think my ass stayed in the crib all night and cried my eyes out? Yeah, it's fuckin' wit' you, but there ain't much you can do about it right now, Shy . . . sittin' here bitchin' about it ain't gonna change shit," Camille said sternly, being upfront with me.

Jade put her two cents in: "She's right, Shy."

I stared at the both of 'em, knowing that they weren't going to leave here without me. So I reluctantly told them yes and went into the bedroom to get dressed.

> Dear Roscoe,
>
> We came a long way, baby, and just to let you know, that our journey is still not at an end. The miles that we will travel, I know our road will never end. Our life together has just begun, so I'm holding on to you for an eternity. . . .

I began to write Roscoe a letter, wishing I could mail it to him, with a poem. It was a Thursday night, and I needed to free my mind, and writing always helped me to do that. I wrote my feelings down in this little notepad that I kept hidden. I showed it to only one person, and that was Roscoe. He read every one of my poems, and never criticized them—even the ones that I felt were corny. He said that they were all good, because they all came from the heart.

It's been a few days now, and still no word. I called up his lawyer, Don Shalley, and he assured me that he was still investigating his case. He didn't explain much to me. So that was really no help.

The room was so quiet and peaceful, and I had the lights dimmed over my writing material. I was in a trance, focusing on finishing my poem, when the phone startled me.

I quickly picked up the phone and heard the operator announce, "You have a collect call from Roscoe Richardson. To accept, press one, or just hang up."

Of course I accepted my baby's call.

"Shy?" I nearly melted into joy when Roscoe's voice transmitted through the phone receiver.

"Baby!" I hollered. I wanted to reach in the phone and give him a hug. "Why you ain't call sooner?"

"Long story, Shy. I'm getting processed and shit, and it's a bitch. So how you been?" he asked, like it's been years since we spoke.

"I'm worried about you. What's goin' on?"

"I know you heard that I got this murder charge lingerin' over my head. I'm sorry, baby," he apologized sincerely.

"You didn't do it, right, baby?" I asked.

He was quiet. "I can't talk about it right now, Shy . . . but I need you to come see a nigga. I miss you, baby."

"I miss you, too," I proclaimed, smiling from ear to ear. I didn't bring up the night he left out our door or any other shit, because I knew he was going through enough shit. I just wanted us to talk. I just wanted to hear his voice.

"So where they got you, baby?" I asked.

"Rikers Island, but get a pen and take down my information," he said.

"I got one already, baby. I was writin' you a poem when you called."

"Word? What you writin' me?" he asked.

"Sumthin'. But it ain't finished yet. I'm still workin' on it. It's nice, though."

"That's cool, that's cool. But yo, you need to write this down, especially when you come visit me."

"Okay."

"I'm in C76, 6M . . . and my number is 448524745. You can come check me next Friday around noon; I'm gonna have you registered down, and remember visitin' hours are over around two. And I need you to bring me a few things too. I need boxers and T-shirts, baby. These muthafuckas don't give you shit up in here, and deodorant. But listen, the T-shirts you get, they gotta be all white, and XXL, and the boxers, all white, baby. And also, drop me like fifty dollars into my commissary."

I quickly wrote all his information and the items that he needed down in my pad. "I got you, baby."

"Thanks, Shy."

"You know I'm here for you," I told him.

"So you chillin' for the night?" Roscoe asked.

"I ain't got nowhere to go. You ain't here, so what am I gonna do? Camilla and Jade been comin' over on a regular."

"Listen, you spoke to James?" he asked.

"No."

"Well, if you do, give him my information too. Tell him that I gotta holla at him."

"I got you, Roscoe. I'll let Jade know. So you good up in there? I mean, you ain't got any troubles, right, baby?"

He quickly sucked his teeth and replied, "Shy, you know I got this up in here. Niggas know who I be. I came into this dormitory and knew majority of the muthafuckas in here anyway. But you make sure you bring your fine ass and check me next Friday, a'ight, love?"

"I'm already there, baby. I miss you."

"That's fo' sure. I know they about to cut this phone convo short. But Shy—"

"Yeah, baby?"

"I love you, Shy."

I swear, when he said those three words, my heart almost stopped. I smiled. "I love you too, Roscoe."

After that, the phone went dead. I guess they cut us off, hating-ass jail. I hung up the phone and started to breathe easy. I felt good that night. I got to speak to my baby, and that's all I wanted. I wanted him to come home to me next.

But I wasn't going to cry. I knew Roscoe didn't want me shedding tears. He wanted me to remain strong and ride with him till the end. And I planned on doing that.

Next Friday couldn't come fast enough for me. But faithfully, I was on the E train on my way to Queens Plaza, where I transferred to the M101 bus to Rikers Island.

Camille gave me the instructions, because she's been through the routine far too many times. She volunteered to come, her and Jade, but I wanted to do this on my own. I was a big girl, and I wanted to spend time with Roscoe alone, even though we wouldn't be truly alone.

The E train was kind of crowded, and I was lucky to catch me a seat near the doors. I was dressed in my finest; I had on this cute Diesel peach top, with my thin diamond necklace showing, some black tight-fitted J.Lo jeans that accentuated my figure, and these cute pink Steve Maddens. I had silver hoop earrings in my ear and sported a butter-soft black leather jacket over my outfit. It was almost the end of October, and the weather was getting kinda cool. I was determined to see my man. I carried a bag filled with the things that Roscoe had asked me to bring.

There was this lady sitting at the end of the subway car who had a terrible cold. She was coughing and sneezing. I started smiling and tittering to myself, because for some funny reason, I started thinking about Camille and her crazy ass.

I remembered one time, the three of us was on the A train on our way to Manhattan. We were young, and we were seated across from this woman who had to be in her early forties or something. But anyway, she had this serious cold—the flu or something—and the bitch kept coughing and shit, and wouldn't bother to cover her mouth. She had her germs flying all over the place, and you know that made me feel uncomfortable.

But Camille, with her gangsta ass, glared over at the woman and shouted out, "Bitch, cover your fuckin' mouth! Ain't nobody tryin' to catch your nasty-ass cold and get sick from your dirty ass!"

I swear Jade and I started cracking up, laughing. That poor woman, she felt so embarrassed that she just stared at Camille, who gave her the screw face back, and everyone in the subway car took notice. But shorty, I guess she had no words and was too embarrassed to stick around, because after the train pulled into the next station, she grabbed her things, jumped up outta her seat, and left the train.

I'd looked over at Camille, laughing, and asked, "Why you do that?"

Camille sucked her teeth and replied, "Fuck that bitch. I know her parents taught her some manners. Coughin' in front of me like the shit is cute."

But that was Camille—in your face, don't give a fuck, and raw as can be type of girl.

Just then, I glanced over and saw this nigga watching me. He was with his girl, and he'd been clocking me for the longest now. He was tall and looked like he'd seen better days. His girl stared out into space, not even knowing that her man been gazing at me hard all this time. I tried to ignore it, but his eyes made me feel really uncomfortable. I wanted to get up and move.

But I'm glad I didn't, because then I heard, "Nigga, why don't you just go over and talk to her, you lookin' at her that fuckin' hard!"

"Yo, what you talkin' about?" he asked his girl.

"Willie, fuck you! I'm tired of your dumb ass!" she shouted, before mushing him in his head. Then she got up and caught a seat down at the other end of the train car. All he could do was sit there and look embarrassed. I chuckled to myself. He couldn't even look at me anymore. Now that was comedy.

Finally, the E train roared into the Queens Plaza station, and I quickly grabbed my things and exited the train, and ascended the concrete steps, coming outta the grungy subway station and making my way out onto the streets. I glanced around for the bus stop, but ended up asking a lady where to catch the Rikers Island bus. She pointed to a bus stop a block and a half away. I thanked her and went on my way.

When I got to the bus stop, I noticed about eight other females waiting for the bus, and they all stared at me like I didn't belong, even though I looked and dressed better than all of 'em.

One bitch stared at me all hard, then gave me a nasty smirk. But I paid them bitches no mind.

The bus came fifteen minutes later, and I was the last to get on, carrying this white shopping bag filled with packaged items for Roscoe. I had to catch a seat at the rear of the bus, because up front was all taken.

I figured that at least half of these women on this bus done made this trip before, and were either going to visit their boyfriends, baby daddies, brothers, or maybe fathers. They all looked like they needed a makeover, or was I the one who was overdressed?

Thirty-five minutes later, the bus pulled up to the visitors' entrance, and one by one, everyone exited the bus. We were greeted by three correction officers out front who made it clear that there were no cell phones, Walkmans, cameras, or any type of electronic equipment allowed inside the premises. And anyone found with any type of contraband would be subject to arrest and would be fully prosecuted.

I had nothing to worry about; all I had on me was underwear, clothes, and a few books for Roscoe to read.

We had to show ID and then proceeded into the building.

I was ushered through security, where we had to take off our shoes and belts, place loose items in a bin, and step through a machine and be scanned. The visitors' building was full of people and corrections officers. And this being my first time, I was totally baffled.

"Excuse me," I said to one of the officers, who was standing around, observing the ladies entering the place. "I'm lookin' fo' my boyfriend. He's in C76."

"You gotta go down to room seven"—he pointed down the corridor—"and give his name to the person behind the desk, and fill out a form."

"Thank you," I said, and walked off. I felt his eyes on me as I walked away. I turned around and caught him staring and smiling. The other male COs just watched me like I was doing something unlawful.

In room seven, there were two other ladies on line. I stood behind a hefty woman, who was black as night and needed a serious perm. She had buckshots in the back of her head, and dressed like she just woke up or some shit.

When it was my turn to approach the desk, I smiled down at the wiry light-skinned man with the horn-rimmed glasses and said, "I'm here to see Roscoe Richardson."

"ID," he said.

I went into my purse and passed him my state ID. I didn't have a driver's license, and this was the closest thing to it.

He glanced at it, then passed it back to me.

He went on his computer and searched for Roscoe's name, then looked up at me and uttered, "He's in C76 . . . dormitory 6M. Fill out this form, take a seat, and wait for the bus to arrive. It should be here soon." The instructions poured out of his mouth like liquid.

I took the forms from his hand and searched for the nearest seat. I sat next to this light-skinned mother who held her child in her arms. She smiled at me, and I smiled back.

"I like your shoes," she said, peering down at my Maddens.

"Thank you," I replied.

"What are they?"

"What?"

"Your shoes?"

"Oh, Steve Maddens," I replied, peering at my form.

She tended to her child for a moment, who looked tired, while I began filling out the information. It took me like five minutes. I was totally new to this, while everyone looked like they knew this place like the back of their hand.

"Who are you here to see?" she asked.

"Oh, my boyfriend," I answered halfheartedly.

"Well, I'm bringing him to see his father," she said.

I smiled lightly and said, "That's nice." Like I gave a fuck.

"He hasn't seen his father in a year, and I know Red is missing his son."

"Really . . . um." I smiled.

As soon as I was finished writing down what was needed on the form, I heard someone shout out, "Those of you for the bus to C76, we're loading now."

I quickly got up, grabbed my things, and followed the others toward the bus. We loaded in single file onto this white cheesy imitated school bus. The seats were stiff plastic and very uncomfortable, and the bus also reeked of a weird odor. But I roughed it just for Roscoe.

Minutes later, the bus stopped in front of C76, where the majority of the men and women started to file out of the bus one by one, anxious to see loved ones. I was next to last to get off the bus. We stood on another line, where a female CO came out and informed us about there being no electronic equipment allowed inside, and if you had any contraband, she pointed to an amnesty box and said now was our chance to remove it without any questions asked. Everyone was quiet, so she proceeded with the process. She collected our information, and we had to go through another metal detector and search. It was becoming a bitch.

It took me another thirty to forty minutes to see my man. I had to give 'em my ID, place everything that I had on me into a small locker, and wait to deposit shit into his commissary. And when I got the chance to, this bitch at the window told me that everything else was good, except for the boxers, because they weren't a solid white. They had blue and yellow stripes, and the inmates weren't allowed to have it. I'm like, *Bitch, drawers is drawers. Who cares about fuckin' color?* So I had to take those back home when I left.

Being ushered from one room to another and getting searched constantly, I felt like the fucking inmate. I mean, these muthafucking COs are thorough with they shit; it's a wonder how people be sneaking shit up in this bitch.

But finally, I was escorted into a large room, which was the gym mapped out to be a visitor's center. I looked around, gave the man my slip, and he instructed me where to take my seat.

I looked around, and there were over two dozen men and women seated around me. There was chatter throughout the room, but it was kept low. I saw a few cuties seated around me. They were incarcerated, but hey, I got attention too.

A few minutes passed. I sighed, turned my head, and a huge smile spread across my face when I saw them bringing out my man. He was in line with three other inmates, swathed in a gray prison jumper and wearing brown open-toe sandals with white tube socks.

I got up, and he came to me, all smiles.

"Hey, baby," I said ecstatically.

I gave him the deepest and most loving hug; it felt so good being held in his arms. It felt like it had been forever since I saw him. I kissed him, and didn't want to let him go.

"Shy . . . ," he said. "Umm, you feel so good, baby."

We finally took our seats, him across from me, with this miniature wooden table in between us. I was still able to touch and kiss my man. He held my hands across the table, massaging my fingers gently as he gazed into my eyes, smiling.

The chairs were red and plastic and looked like something out of a toy catalog.

"How you been?" he asked.

"I'm missin' you," I told him.

Roscoe looked good. He looked unscathed.

"I'm sorry, Shy. I know I fucked up. It's my fault. Shit went bad that night. I promised you that we were gonna do us, and I end up here."

I wanted to say it was okay, but in reality, I was scared. "What's gonna happen?"

"My lawyer, he's on top of things. He told me that the D.A. is willin' to plea wit' me. If I cop out and do ten. But I ain't doin' no dime. Fuck that. Fuck, I'll do a year or two, city time. I ain't tryin' to fuck wit' upstate. It wasn't even my fault, Shy. The nigga I shot had a gun. He was gonna shoot me first, so I had to react. But now I'm hearin' from my lawyer that they say the nigga didn't have a gun, or they can't find one, and they tryin' to hit me wit' first-degree murder and shit! He had a gun, Shy, I know it too. He had like .380 on him, and he came at me on some raw shit. Fuck, Shy!"

"Roscoe, I'm here for you, baby . . . no matter what happens. I'm gonna be right here, holdin' you down. We gonna beat this."

"It's bad," he said.

"No, it's not. You say he had a gun, right? And I know the truth is gonna come out."

"They tryin' to pin a witness on me. I don't even know who."

"They lyin', Roscoe," I said, holding his hand and wishing I could make this go away—make the situation for him better.

"But anyway, you look good, Shy . . . you damn sure do," he said, his expression turning from a frown to a smile.

"Thank you. You know I had to come up here and represent for you. Show these haters in here what you got at home waitin' for you."

He chuckled. "I like that. Any problems comin' up here?"

"No, but it's a bitch. Damn, they want you to do this, and take off this and that, remove this, go through this machine. No jewelry, rings, watches. Fuck, Roscoe."

"You think that's bad, try bein' on the other side of these walls, where these niggas don't give a fuck about you."

"Oh, I brought up everythin' you asked for. But they said they couldn't take the boxers because they weren't all white. I got you these cute boxers with stripes and shit. But they weren't allowed," I told him.

"Damn, niggas don't want you having any clean drawers up here. What the fuck! That's a'ight."

"And I put like fifty dollars in your account."

"A'ight."

Roscoe glanced around the room, looking at inmates and seeing who they were with. "I swear, majority of these niggas up in here are on some fake shit, Shy. Niggas come out here lookin' all hard, like they got it like that. But on the inside, it's a different story. Like that nigga right there." He discreetly pointed out a slim, tall man who was with his girl. "He on some down-low shit. He fuckin' pussy, Shy. He be fuckin' wit' this homo nigga on the regular. Now he up in here kissin' and huggin' up on his girl, like he don't take dick."

"Oh, that's fucked up!" I said.

"It's like that, though. I don't pay these fools no mind. I beat my dick first, before that shit pop off."

"You better," I said.

He smiled.

"You spoke to James?" he asked.

"Nah. I didn't get a chance to. Him and Jade been on some beefin' shit lately. They be wildin' out. The other day, they arguin' and about to fight each other in front of her buildin'," I told him.

"Yo, Shy, I'm gonna speak to James, and I'm gonna have him come by and drop some money off for you. I ain't got bail, and I don't know how long I'm gonna be up in this bitch. But James is holdin' down shop till whatever happens, happens. He gonna look out for you. I promised to look out for you—I don't care if I'm in here or out there. I'm gonna take care of you."

"Roscoe, I got a job, you forgot?"

"Yeah, I know that, but I know your lifestyle. You like rockin' that name-brand shit. And that little bullshit check you get from workin' at Mony's part-time ain't gonna do it for you."

"At least I get a ten percent discount off clothing."

"Yeah. A'ight."

I stared at his lips, and they looked so soft and enticing. I smiled, as he held my hands, and I motioned for him to come here. He smiled, leaned across the table, and we started to suck on each other lips, with people on all sides of us. Our action went on for a few minutes. I sighed, wishing I could take him home, or get a conjugal with him just for an hour. But I cleared the thought of sex from my head, closed my legs, and continued talking.

We talked more about his case and his lawyer, and Roscoe informed me that Don Shalley was the best. His lawyer's fees were already taken care of. Roscoe had cash stashed away just for situations like this one. He would give money to Don Shalley just off of GP. But I knew the more Roscoe tried to look unconcerned about his case and his freedom, deep inside he was hurting just like me. He had numerous charges lingering over his head, from felonies to misdemeanors. And his previous rap sheet wasn't peaches and roses. If worst came to worst, he would probably have to cop out to a dime and appeal his case later. But I didn't want it to go down like that. Ten years without having my man close to me, and no dick—nah, Don Shalley better be worth every penny he received.

It seemed like time went by quickly, because just like that, my visit with Roscoe was over. The CO came by and made it clear, our hour was up.

I stared at Roscoe with concern and love showing in my eyes. He looked back at me. We hugged and I passionately kissed him, sucking on his lips.

"You take care, Shy," he said in my ear. "I'm gonna be good."

"I'll be back next week, baby."

"You do that."

"I love you."

"I love you too."

He then reluctantly let go of me and walked back over to where he came in at. He was escorted through the thick brown shabby doors with two other inmates following right behind him. A few tears began to trickle down my cheeks as I watched him disappear from my sight. I quickly wiped them away with the palm of my hand and followed the male CO back to the exit.

Going home was painful for me. I cried on the train, thinking about my man.

~ CHAPTER 8 ~

camille

I was holding up a khaki jumpsuit by Jordache.

Cream stood in front of me, smiling, waiting for my approval. I was in his Brooklyn loft near Atlantic Avenue.

"You like it?" he asked.

"Yeah, this is tight. What else you got?" I asked.

Cream went into his luggage, which contained nothing but stolen garments and shoes from warehouses and department stores. He had everything from Gucci to Polo on sale for me at a reasonable price. He was my connect, and a very good one. I could depend on him to boost anything for me, from any store. He was good at what he did.

Cream was a few years older than me, in his early thirties, and he'd had a crush on me since the day we met. He was shorter than me, about five feet six, but cute and lean. He sported box braids and always wore throwback jerseys and stayed with a fitted cap on his head.

"I also got this for you," Cream said, pulling out of his suitcase a pink open-back dress by Donna Karan, with the pink Kangol to match. The outfit was tight. I wanted to keep it for myself.

I grabbed it and said, "Now this outfit, a bitch can definitely fuck wit', Cream. I might keep this shit fo' dolo."

"I knew you would like this one. That's why I saved it fo' you, Camille," Cream said, proud of his taste in women's clothing.

He had dozens of women's outfits spread out in front of me, but the good shit he kept concealed away in one of his many suitcases.

Cream had called me up yesterday and notified me of a new shipment that had just come into his possession, and since Cream has a serious crush on me and always wanted to fuck me, I'd be the first bitch he called up, so I could have first choice.

In my business, I needed top-quality shit to sell to these high-quality bitches that I call my clientele. Some live in the hood that I rest my head in, but most of my clientele stay out in Long Island, or Manhattan. And when I come through with items, these ladies know my merchandise is legit, authentic, and sometimes hard to come by. And they are willing to pay me whatever. I get everything for them—Gucci, Prada, Donna Karan, Versace, Fendi, Dolce & Gabbana, and even Louis Vuitton and Chanel. It's always COD, cash on delivery. And in one day, I'll make from fifteen hundred to two thousand dollars easy. And I give Cream thirty percent of my earnings. We make good business together.

I met Cream a few years back when I used to dance, strip, entertain—whatever muthafuckas call it today. He always came into the club looking so nice and dressed down in the latest costly fashion, from Sean John to Versace. He was always a fly nigga. He was still short, though. But he definitely had flavor. And from the day he first laid eyes on me, I had him.

He bought me a drink and tried hard to get into my pants, but I ain't easy, and I let him know that from jump. He respected me for that. Bitches were always turned on by his steady cash flow and his style. He'll fuck 'em, and forget about them the next day. Me, I saw a different angle than getting myself some quick dick and hopefully having him throw some cash at me.

We would talk, and Cream became a cool-ass nigga, mad down to earth. He'd be like, "Shorty, I like your style. You're different from these bitches up in here."

As the days passed, Cream started hooking me up with the flyest clothes to wear. He'd bring me gifts in the club like he was my man. It came to a point where I had to quit dancing, because bitches started hating on me hard. They'd try to steal my shit in the dressing room while I was onstage, or fight me when they had the chance.

Months later, I got to know what Cream was really about, and he was definitely about his paper. He had a tight crew, and on regulars, these niggas would go out to L.I. and do a string of B&Es, grabbing lucrative shit. I went along with Cream's crew a few nights, and Cream would be the one going up in the woman's closet and snatching all of her shit—minks, furs, clothing, jewelry—and he'd then sell shit off in the streets like it was candy. His cousin was a professional booster, stealing shit from shoes out of Macy's to grand theft auto and driving cars to chop shops. They had the right toys and equipment to commit such large and profitable schemes.

Cream was a hustler, and I loved that about him. He did him, and he did him lovely. He made his paper to the fullest. He pushed a Benz SL600, had a huge loft out in Brooklyn, and paraded his fortune like he was the Teflon don himself.

And I'll admit, we did hook up for a moment. Cream was a nigga who grew on me, and all of a sudden, I began to have a crush on him. One late night, we were drinking, cracking jokes, and chilling, and the next thing, I'm butt naked in his loft, sprawled out on his bed, and fucking him. He was all right in the bed. I had had bigger, and I had had smaller, but Cream made you feel like a woman—well, at least he made me feel like one. I don't know about these other hos out here. We continued to do us for weeks, and whatever I wanted or needed, Cream had it for me the next day. And he wasn't hung up on me. You know, always wanting to be up under a bitch, and being pussy-whipped. The nigga kept it real with his, and admitted to me one day, "Yeah, I still fuck other bitches once in a while. But yo . . . that's just me. We cool, Camille. Anythin' you need, I got you, boo. But I do me."

I couldn't get mad at the nigga. He was honest. We were together, but it wasn't like that—like some husband-and-wife type of shit. We had an understanding, and we took care of each other. And he was the first nigga that I had a threesome with, two women and a man. Cream was cool with it. He ain't flip out about me being bi.

Eventually, our relationship faded, but we remained cool. And now we've became partners in this clothing shit, among minor things too.

"So what you doin' tonight?" Cream asked.

"Don't know yet. Might hang out wit' my girls. Why?" I asked.

"Nah, just askin'. You lookin' good, Camille." He stared at me with lust in his eyes, but it didn't make me uncomfortable. "Why don't you try that pink dress on for me right now?" he suggested. "I wanna see how it fits you."

I smiled. "This one?" I flirted, holding up the pink Donna Karan dress.

"Yeah . . . that's da one."

"You gonna give it to me for free?" I asked.

He looked at me. "Yeah, I got you, Camille."

I shrugged my shoulders and began getting undressed in front of him. Cream smiled, licking his lips while he stared at me. "That's what's up."

I stripped down to my blue thong and nothing else. I didn't mind getting naked in front of Cream. It ain't like he never saw it before. I put on the dress and the matching Kangol, and started posing for him.

"Yeah, that dress looks real good on you," Cream said.

I looked around for the nearest mirror in his loft and found a floor mirror by the closet. He was right: the dress looked really good on me.

"Oh yes . . . I'm definitely goin' out tonight," I said, getting hyped off myself.

I posed a few more times, gazing at myself in the mirror, until Cream came up behind me and effortlessly wrapped his arms around my waist. We both stared at our reflection in the mirror.

"You want me to help take it off now?" he asked in a calm, masculine tone.

I smiled.

He squeezed me gently in his embrace, never averting his eyes from our reflection. I felt his hand start to explore my body as his warm breath brushed against my neck.

"What you want, Cream?" I asked.

"Honestly, I want you, Camille. It's been a long time," he admitted.

"Really?"

"You ain't got a man, right?" he asked. Like if I did, it would stop him now.

"Would it matter?"

"No."

"So why did you ask?"

"Thought it would be the polite thing to do."

I smiled.

He affectionately kissed me on the back of my neck, making my skin tickle. Then his hand grasped my breast, and I gasped, as his other hand slid up my dress, in between my thighs. I closed my eyes and licked my lips, feeling Cream's warm hands glide over my soft brown skin.

Within minutes, he slipped the dress off me and had me naked. I came here to do business with him, and now this man had me longing for him to enter me. Cream could be patient, especially when it came to me. We didn't see each other every day; sometimes weeks would go by, and then when we saw each other, it was always about business. The man never asked me any questions, especially about my personal life. But today, it was different. It was like something exploded within him, and he just had to have me. But I didn't mind, because it'd been weeks since I had any dick. Sierra could please a sista, but sometimes you just need the real thing, a flesh-and-blood hard-on thrusting into you instead of plastic and batteries.

Around midnight, Shy, Jade, and I decided to hit up a club. You know I had to show off my new dress. And I had hooked my girls up too. Shy opted for the Baby Phat leather skirt, and Jade went for the black Fendi shoes.

Shy was looking more spirited since she'd been hearing from Roscoe and seeing him on her regular visits to Rikers. And Jade's situation with James—that was her business. She can continue to be the fool if she wants. But I know what I saw, and if she don't believe me, then I ain't gonna stress it to her.

The club of choice was Club Vertigo in the city. The attire was upscale and classy, and I know we would have a good night out without worrying about any knuckleheads.

I sported my pink dress and received many compliments from my girls, as well as from complete strangers. I was the only bitch in our group with a car, so you know I had to drive. I pushed a sleek black Benz CLK500. I had had it for a minute now. Cream hooked me up. He helped with the down payment and everything. I make the payments every month, but whenever I'm short with money, Cream would buss me down with a lil' sumthin'.

I had to park in one of those high-priced city garages that charge you like twenty dollars an hour to park your shit. But I made Jade and Shy come out their pockets for parking. Shit, I ain't paying for gas *and* parking, and then buy drinks.

Vertigo was popping. The line outside was short; it took us no time to enter. They wanted twenty at the door. We paid, checked our jackets, and stepped into the dimly lit club, and the crowd was hyped, as the DJ popped off with some Fat Joe's "Lean Back." That's my joint right there.

We went straight to the bar, and I ordered myself a Long Island iced tea and started moving to my bitch Remy Martin's verse. I love her lyrics in this song. I noticed the fellows watching me, but I paid them no mind as I continued to dance by myself.

One nigga had the courage to try and dance with me. He moved a little close, swaying to the beat as he smiled at me, holding a Corona. I gave him a thin smile, but politely shook my head, denying his invitation to come closer. I wasn't feeling him like that. And I just got to the club. I wasn't trying to be all sweaty on a nigga already.

Shy, Jade, and myself took a seat at one of the nearest available tables and observed the scenery. It was a good mixture of revelers. You had the young and the old, black, white, Guyanese; even a few Asians were sprinkled around the place. And the DJ kept it diverse, from reggae, to pop, to rap, and even calypso.

I took a sip from my glass and peered at my girls as they sat close. We were catching so much attention that it felt like we were celebrities. We looked good, and our attire was on point.

"So Shy, what's up wit' Roscoe? He doin' a'ight?" I asked.

"He a'ight. I know he gonna get through this, and he's gonna be home soon. I'm visitin' him every week, makin' sure my man stay correct wit' clothing and shit."

"I heard he might take a plea," Jade said.

"Take a plea?" Shy quickly replied, looking at Jade with the *What the fuck you talking about?* look on her face. "My man ain't takin' no plea. He ain't guilty."

"Damn—my bad, Shy. You ain't gotta get all defensive about it," Jade said. "I just heard it from James. Roscoe called the house the other day, and they spoke."

"Well, you got it backwards, and why your man ain't locked up, too, Jade? He was there, too."

"Yo, y'all two, chill. We here to have fun, not talk about some bullshit," I said, trying to make peace.

"Nah, it's cool. You know, shit happens, Camille. I'm just

frustrated right now. I ain't had dick in weeks, and you know my pussy is throbbin' right about now," Shy said, looking like she was trying to make light of her situation.

Jade and I smiled.

"Well, you got plenty of men to choose from tonight," I told her.

"That bitch ain't gonna cheat on Roscoe. Roscoe would fuck her ass up. She's in love, Camille," Jade said.

"Who's gonna tell?" I asked.

"Oh, it's like that," Shy replied.

"Listen, you love him. I know you do," I said. "But y'all ain't married, that's how I see it. You can do you, and still be down for your man. He locked down right now, Shy, and I ain't tryin' to be negative about his situation, but ain't no tellin' when he's coming home. So don't keep stressin' yourself about bein' faithful, because a lot of brothas don't even know what commitment is. I mean, Roscoe a cool dude. I like him and all, and he respects you, but look, when that time comes, and you lyin' up in your crib, lonely, horny as hell, with a pillow clutched between your legs, listenin' to slow jams, and thinkin' about sex, havin' your man in prison ain't gonna help you none. And them collect calls are gonna get you even more frustrated. I've been there far too many times, Shy. Shit. So my advice is, get out there on that dance floor, and find you a quick booty call, because a bitch wit'out dick is gonna make you go crazy."

"I hear that!" Jade hollered, slapping me a high five.

Shy smiled.

"Shit, I got mines earlier today," I said.

"What? By who?" Jade wanted to know.

"Cream," I said.

"You still fuckin' wit' him, Camille?" Jade asked.

"Not like that anymore. We cool, peoples. But he came on strong to me today, and it's been a minute."

"I like him. He's mad cool," Shy said.

"Word. Tell that nigga to keep hookin' a sista up wit' the clothing. Yo, fo' real, any nigga that can hook a sista up wit' the nicest shit he be hookin' you up wit', Camille, I would have his name tattooed around my pussy," Jade joked.

We laughed.

"Yo, them shoes I got . . . you ain't gonna find them shits in no store like that," Jade said.

"He got connections, that's fo' sure," I said.

I took another sip from my drink and peered around the club with Cream on my mind.

"I say y'all should get back together, Camille," Jade advised.

"Yeah, y'all two did make a cute couple. I know he's shorter than you, but he's cute," Shy said.

"We're just friends," I informed them.

Jade smiled. "Yeah, whatever. . . . Y'all weren't friends a few hours ago."

"He's just some dick to call up when I need it, nuthin' else," I said, trying to look serious.

"Whatever, bitch!" Jade said. "I see it in your eyes; you still got a thang for him, don't you?"

I sucked my teeth. "Jade, please."

"Yeah . . . whatever."

Just then, our song came into play, Destiny's Child "Lose My Breath." Yo, I love this song. When it blared throughout the club, me and my girls went crazy, as so did every other bitch in the club. We jumped up outta our seats like they were on fire, and started dancing to the song like it was our last.

I swear, this song is so true, Destiny's Child be singing the truth. *Can you keep up? . . . Make me lose my breath.* I couldn't even said it better myself.

The night ended so good. I danced and drank till I couldn't hold water anymore. I had a good time, and so did Shy and Jade. We all needed a night out like tonight. Shy got a number, and he was a cutie. Jade did her thing and mingled with a few cuties too.

I was tipsy as fuck, but I still had to drive because both these bitches didn't have a legit license, and I keep asking them, what are they waiting for? You can't keep depending on some nigga to pick you up and drop you off all the time. Get your own shit, and go wherever the fuck you wanna go.

By the time we finally got home, it was like four in the morning and I was tired as fuck. Soon as I stepped into the apartment, I collapsed on my bed.

But before I could close my eyes and go to sleep, the phone rang. I reluctantly picked it up. I thought it was Jade or Shy on the phone ready to tell me about some more drama before I went to bed.

"You the bitch that's fuckin' my wife!" I heard a man's voice say.

"What?"

"Bitch, you heard me. Stay the fuck away from Sierra!"

"Nigga, who the fuck is you?"

"I'm warnin' you, you dyke bitch. You come near Sierra and endanger my family's well-being again, I'll fuckin' kill you," he threatened.

I lost it. "Nigga, who you threatenin'? Don't you ever disrespect me again!" I shouted. "Don't call here no more, you clown-ass nigga. I ain't fuckin' your wife!" I lied.

"You've been warned, bitch!" and then he hung up.

I swear that fucked up my night. I thought Sierra was careful with our relationship, but obviously I was wrong. She had her clown-ass husband calling my crib early in the morning, beefing with me, and that pissed me off. I wanted to call the nigga back and curse him the fuck out. But I put it off as nothing. He's probably just mad because I make his wife come better.

I thought about Cream before I went to sleep, and wished he was here tonight to hold me. Some nights, I do get lonely going to bed by myself, and Sierra rushing off to her husband every night after we have sex was kind of getting tiresome. But I'm a big girl. I moved my hand between my thighs, and started massaging myself gently while I thought about Cream. I end up getting one off before I fell asleep.

~ CHAPTER 9 ~

jade

I tried not to be, but I was jealous. Hearing Shy and Camille talk about they men last night—about how Roscoe loved and respected Shy, and how Cream stayed hooking Camille up with nice shit, and treating her like a woman, made me feel like shit. Both Shy and Camille had nothing good to say about James. And I thought about that, and his trifling ass. He never really did shit for me but fuck me long and hard, cause me to have a miscarriage when I was pregnant two years ago, and was probably fucking half the women in these projects. I wanted more than just a big dick and a cute face. I wanted this nigga to love me like I'm the only woman on this earth, and I wanted to be placed on a pedestal and have him worship the ground I walk on. But I guess I was asking for too much. Four years, and I started to wonder why we were still together.

I met James at Jones Beach during Greek Fest, one scorching June Saturday. I was walking in the parking lot with Camille and Shy, scantily clad in some enticing summer clothing and looking so cute. Niggas stayed trying to holla, but I flirted back and kept it moving. James shouted me out from a distance, while he was lounging and drinking with his boys. And when I saw him, he caught my eye immediately, and definitely had my attention. His biceps and chest ripped through his clean white tank top. He had smooth brown skin, and his thick lips were outlined with the trimmed goatee. He was tall, sporting a bald head and looking like he took pride and care in his appearance.

"Ma, you look nice. I like that fo' sure," he shouted out.

He waved me and my girls to come over, and Shy and I did. Camille stayed behind. I was young then, seventeen, and my boyfriend at the time wasn't doing for me anymore.

But James's presence was solid, and he was a thug, and I loved that. I'm so into thug niggas that that's all I know. He quickly invited me and my girls to chill with them, and later on in the evening, he wanted to take me out to a movie or something.

Well, of course we stayed around with James and his posse, and Camille did too, reluctantly. He was funny, and his demeanor let me know that he wasn't intimidated by us and our beauty.

We hooked up later that night, and sad to say, I fucked him. We got a room, and when I first saw his big dick, I was open, and when he thrust it into me, the nigga had me panting and calling his name, and a bitch was hooked. It was that easy for him. At first, it was hard to take the dick, because I never had it that big before, but with time, a bitch started to handle it like a porn star.

And like that, we started seeing each other, and in the beginning, like always, it was nice. He did little things for me, and when the nigga threw me over his shoulders and told me to touch the ceiling while he ate my pussy out, I swear, I wanted to marry this nigga.

The dick and the freaky sex kept me spending so many years with him. I never had anyone better, to be honest, and James knows it too. He's very fucking cocky.

But like I said, I met the nigga when I was seventeen, and back then, shit was different for me.

The phone rang, and I ain't rushed to answer the shit either. It was one of them days where I didn't feel like being bothered.

James was in the bedroom watching TV, smoking, and drinking. I picked up. "Hello." No one answered. "Hello," I repeated. But the other end was dead. I checked the caller ID, and I didn't recognize the number. And of course, whoever called immediately hung up after hearing my voice. But my instincts told me that it was another woman calling for James. I picked up the phone and dialed the number back, but blocked my number so it would come up unavailable.

Seconds later, a woman answered the phone. "Hello," I heard. And I knew the fucking voice.

"Tasha?" I said, shocked.

"Bitch, why you callin' my crib?" she answered in her stank voice.

"Ho, I know you ain't just call here lookin' for James. How the fuck did you get this number?" I said angrily, wanting to snatch her bald-headed ass through the phone.

"How you think, bitch? James passed it to me after he done finished fuckin' me the other day."

Mad was an understatement. But being in denial, I returned with, "Bitch, you fuckin' lyin'!"

"Keep bein' the stupid bitch, Jade. But you know what? You gonna get yours, bitch. I ain't forget about that day. Watch, ho. I'm still here, and I ain't goin' nowhere."

"Whatever! Come see me!" I shouted, and slammed the phone back down on the cradle. I then rushed into the bedroom, where James was sprawled out on the bed watching TV, and I smacked him across his head.

He jumped up and yelled, "Bitch, what the fuck is wrong wit' you?"

"You gave that ho my number?" I yelled, ready to hit him again.

"Fuck you talkin' about?"

"Tell me how that bitch, Tasha, just called here lookin' fo' your ass."

"Jade, you need to chill the fuck out. Word!"

"James, what the fuck is wrong wit' you?" I cried out.

"Ain't nuthin' wrong wit' me. You got the fuckin' problem, comin' up in here flippin' out. I told you about her already."

"Fuck you!" I cursed. I went up to him and tried to slap him again, but he grabbed me by the wrist and held on tightly, glaring at me.

"Get the fuck off me!" I yelled.

"Touch me again, bitch!" he said, squeezing my wrist and twisting my arm.

"Get the fuck off me!" I shouted, trying to free myself from his powerful grip. He was strong and never let loose. "I hate you!"

"You over-reacting, Jade. Calm the fuck down!"

I tried to swing my body around and swing on him, but I missed, and then James shockingly gave me a hard backhand smack across my face while he still clutched my wrist. I cried out, and he twisted my arm even harder.

"James, please. Stop, it hurts!"

"You gonna calm down?"

"Get off me!"

"Fuck you, stupid bitch!" he yelled, and then struck me hard against my face with his closed fist. It hurt like hell, and I collapsed down on the floor when he freed my wrist. He stood over me, glaring down at me, watching me sob. I cried, holding my face.

"Fuck this! I'm out," he muttered, and disappeared from my sight.

I didn't chase after him or do anything. For about an hour or so, I remained glued to the floor, in pain, and ashamed. The phone started to ring a few times, and I let the machine pick it up. Camille left a message, wanting to speak with me, and then my cousin called. I didn't want to speak to anyone. James fucked me up, and then left with no fucking remorse.

A few days later, we were at it again, arguing and fighting. I was in bed, chilling and trying to heal from our last fight. James came into the room and wanted some pussy. He had some fucking nerve. I told his dumb ass no, and he got upset. Then he tried to force himself on me. I fought him back, and he angrily tossed me across the room like it was nothing. I landed against the television, and it fell and smashed on the ground. I cried out, and again James had no remorse. He came up to me, snatched me up again, and threw me against the wall. He had his hand firmly wrapped around my neck, choking the shit out of me.

I grabbed his wrist, trying to loosen his grip. "James . . . let . . . go, please," I begged, gasping for air.

"Fuck you, bitch. Why you bein' like this fo'? I just wanna

fuck, that's all. Shit, you my girl. Now look, look what you made me do!" His eyes were filled with rage, and I was terrified to death. I actually thought that he was going to kill me.

But he let loose, and I slid down to the floor, crying. James continued to throw a fit, smashing things in our bedroom and in the living room.

He wasn't done with me. He dragged me into the living room, with me kicking and screaming and then threatened to throw me out of the window if I didn't start cooperating.

"Word, Jade, you think I'm fuckin' playin' wit' you?"

My body felt limp. I had no more strength in me to fight back. James stood a foot taller, and outweighed me by over a hundred pounds. It was like a chicken trying to fight off a pit bull.

For about an hour, my apartment felt like Baghdad—there was no peace until James finally grabbed his coat and left, leaving my home in shambles.

About fifteen minutes after James left, I heard a loud knock at the door. I assumed it was James again, forgetting something. But when I heard, "Police!" I dried my tears and wished they hadn't come.

I didn't want to see 'em, but I knew that they weren't going to go away unless someone answered the door. So I tried to collect myself. I picked up a few things and yelled, "I'm coming! Give me a minute."

I went into the bedroom to change shirts. James had badly ripped the one I had on, and it looked like I had been in a fight. After I changed, I went to the door, took a deep breath, and opened it.

"I didn't call the police," I said.

"Well, one of your neighbors did. Said it sounded like a fight in your apartment, and they thought that someone was being killed," the officer explained. He was as tall as James, black, and looked to be in his late forties.

"You okay?" the second officer asked. He was black too, younger in the face, and shorter than his partner. He looked at me with more care and concern than his partner had.

"I'm okay," I lied. I couldn't look them in the eye.

"What happened here?" the more concerned officer asked.

"Nuthin'. Me and my boyfriend had a little argument, that's all," I said.

"Little argument. Look at your apartment, miss. It looks like someone was in a fight."

"Well, I was cleanin', that's all."

"Listen, it ain't my business, but—"

"That's right it ain't none of your business. Please leave," I said with serious sarcasm.

"C'mon. She don't need us here," the taller officer said to his partner. He walked off down the hall while the shorter one lingered, looking like he wanted to stay and help. But I made things clear by slamming the door in his face.

I tried to straighten my place up, and get myself back in order. Suddenly, I heard another knock at my door. I sighed heavily and went to see who it was. When I peeped through the peephole, I saw that it was that same cop again. He had come back alone, without his partner. I opened the door for him.

"What is it this time?" I asked, attitude filling the air.

"Listen, miss . . . you can press charges, file a report, and I promise you that he won't touch you again," he said.

"Whatever! You don't even know what happened. Fuck you care for?"

"Because I do. Look at you. You're beautiful, and I would hate to see you end up dead. You deserve better than this."

I sucked my teeth. "You don't know me."

"I'm here to help, miss."

"Would you stop callin' me *miss*? I ain't that old, and I ain't your mother," I spat back.

"I'm sorry."

"Where's your partner?"

"He's down in the squad car. I told him to give me a minute. What happened here?" he kept on pressing. He was cute—I give him that. He stood about five-eight, had a pointy nose and brown eyes. His face was smooth, and his voice was gentle. He looked like Morris Chestnut in a way.

"Just a misunderstandin', nothin' else."

"Listen, I'm going to give you my card, and I'm going to write down my home number on the back," he said, reaching into his pocket. He jotted down his digits and handed me the card.

"Don't hesitate to give me a call if you need anything," he said, staring into my eyes.

I reluctantly took it. "Are you always this kind?" I asked, easing up a bit.

He smiled. "I just care a lot . . . and I'm just doing my job."

I felt a warm, gentle vibe from him. He wasn't no James, but he was still cute.

"Well, um . . . thank you, I suppose," I said.

"Yeah. Well, if you need anything, give me a call," he said again, backing away slowly.

"Okay."

"Oh . . . ," he said, halting in his steps.

I looked at him.

"Can I get your name?" he asked kindly.

I smiled. "Jade."

"Jade. I'm Officer Reese."

"I'll remember," I said.

He stared at me like he didn't want to leave, but realizing his partner was waiting in the car, he rushed away and let me be.

I closed the door and sighed. *What a day,* I thought. I looked around my apartment. I had some cleaning up to do. I wanted to tidy up this mess and spend the day alone, wishing James would stay wherever he was right now. I thought about changing the locks, but decided not to. I don't even know why. His temper was becoming out of control, and it always felt like I was walking on eggshells around him.

I placed Officer Reese's card in my jeans pocket and started straightening up the apartment. To lighten my mood, I put in a Mary J. Blige CD and listened to my girl break it down about love and the drama that comes along with it. She needed to write a song about my life. I swear it would go triple platinum.

~ CHAPTER 10 ~

shy

It was always good to see Roscoe. I'd been coming to see him almost every week now. He'd been incarcerated a little over a month. We hugged, kissed, and talked. It was November, and I knew that I was going to miss him even more around the holiday time. I remember last year we spent Thanksgiving at his sister's crib with her three kids. She had cooked up a big meal.

I became one of those women who made frequent trips to Rikers Island, knowing the routine like the back of my hand. I still came dressed cute, but I didn't overdo it like my first visit, wearing pink shoes and shit like that, because once you get through security, you looking worn out anyway. Shit is a bitch.

Roscoe held my hand softly and looked like something heavy was on his mind.

"What's wrong, baby?" I asked.

He looked up at me, and asked, "How you doin' at your job?"

"It could be better. My boss is becoming a dickhead, talkin' about I'm missin' too many days of work. But you come first, baby," I said.

He didn't respond.

"Roscoe, what you thinkin' about?" I asked again.

"Listen, James is gonna come by sometime this week, and drop you off some money. It should hold you down for a while."

"Okay. That's cool."

The visiting room was crowded, like almost every seat was full. The holidays were coming. This visit with Roscoe wasn't like the others, where he held down conversations with me, and told me to keep my head up and asked me questions. It looked like I was the one holding it down; trying to get him to say what was on his mind. I know my man. I knew when something was bothering him.

"Shy, I got somethin' to tell you," he began.

"What is it?"

"I might take a plea."

"What? A plea? Why, Roscoe, please . . . you can beat this, I know you can," I said, my voice frantic.

"Shit ain't lookin' too good for me. D.A. comin' hard at me with this one, and they about to present my case to a grand jury soon. My lawyer's doin' what he can, but wit'out a gun or some credible witness on my side, shit is bleak right now. If I cop out now, I might get ten, and do maybe six years straight. If we take it to court and I'm found guilty, I'm lookin' at fifteen, maybe twenty years, Shy."

Tears began to well up in my eyes. *What changed?* I thought to myself.

"Baby, six years. That's still a long time."

"Yeah, I know. But it's better than doin' twenty. I'll get out, and we can still have a life together," he said. "Look, Shy, I love you, and you know I'm always thinkin' about us, but I gotta do what I feel is best for me, and you. My lawyer, he ain't a miracle worker. I fucked up. This is a hard one for him. He's turnin' over every rock he can for me, but . . . I'm sorry, Shy. You deserve better, that's fo' sure. You don't need this."

"I need you, Roscoe. I need you home and wit' me. Why did you have to leave me that night? Why, Roscoe? If you woulda stayed your ass home, none of this shit wouldn't be happenin'," I barked.

"I know, baby. But you know my temper."

"And? What you had to prove, huh? Look at us. You had to go out and prove in front of your boys that you could pull a trigger on someone, and be the dickhead who ends up in jail."

"We gonna be a'ight, Shy," he tried to assure me.

"How you know that? I'm home alone every night, thinkin' about you and cryin' myself to sleep. You promised to take care of me. . . . Where's that promise?" I spat at him.

"Like I told you, James is gonna come through."

"Fuck James. I'm not talkin' about money. I'm talkin' about us, Roscoe, and our relationship. I'm talkin' about us havin' a family and movin' out of the projects. I'm talkin' about you not bein' up in here anymore. I need you. I need my man. But what I got is pain, sufferin', and fuckin' heartaches." I started to draw a little attention to myself as my voice got louder.

"Shy, lower your voice. I don't need these niggas bein' all up in our business," Roscoe whispered.

"I don't give a fuck about them! You feel embarrassed now. How do you think I feel out there on them streets? Everybody in our business. Everybody knows what went down wit' you, and I'm still fuckin' clueless to what happened. You don't tell me shit. James don't tell me shit. Your lawyer doesn't tell me shit. And I'm your woman, right?"

I was pissed off. He was taking a plea. And what made me mad was Jade knew about this before me. She's telling me about his business before I even knew. We up in the club, and she telling his business in front of everyone like the shit was cool. And I'm barking on her, because I'm thinking she don't know what the fuck she talking about, and she telling the fucking truth.

Roscoe tried to calm me down, but I was heated. Our time was up, and I just picked myself up and walked out. The CO told me that I had to wait—it was procedure for the inmates to be escorted back into lockup before any visitors could leave their seats.

Fuck that. I wanted out. I stood by the locked steel door and ignored their fucking procedures. Of course, corrections caught an attitude with me and threatened to deny my visits if I pulled a stunt like that again.

I was in full tears after I left the premises. I couldn't even take the bus home. I didn't want to be seen like this. So I caught a cab back home.

Two days had passed, and I was in the shower, thinking about my situation and Roscoe's. Twenty years, ten years—even six years, he was still gonna be gone from my life for a long time.

I sighed heavily, letting the water cascade over my body, and I started daydreaming. It'd been a minute since I had sex, and I started running my hand up my thighs until I was stimulating myself with wet fingers. I never went without sex for this long, almost a month and a half now. When Roscoe was home, we would fuck on a regular. Sometimes we used condoms, and sometimes we didn't. If he didn't use a condom, then Roscoe made sure he would pull out and bust off a nut on my stomach. He wasn't ready for kids.

I got caught up in the moment, having two fingers deeply in my wet vagina, and caught myself moaning out loud in the shower, thinking about sex.

It took a minute for me to hear the doorbell. So I rushed out of the shower, quickly wrapped a towel around myself, and yelled, "I'm comin'—don't leave yet."

I scurried into the living room, dripping wet, and leaving a trail of small puddles on the thick green carpet. I looked through the peephole and saw that it was James.

I secured the towel around me tightly and answered the door. "Hey, James."

James looked at me. "Oh, my bad. Is this a bad time? I can always come back." His eyes never left my body.

"No. I was just gettin' ready for work. Come in," I said. He walked into the living room and closed the door.

"I got some money for you. Roscoe said you needed it," James said, standing in the center of my living room. He reached into his brown Rocawear coat and pulled out a thick white envelope. He came over to me and put it in my hand.

"There's five grand in there, Shy. Enough to hold you down till the end of the month."

"Thank you," I said, clutching my towel, making sure it wouldn't fall off me.

"You okay?" James asked.

"Yeah, I'm good."

"I know it's hard, wit' Roscoe bein' locked up. He okay up in there? I ain't get the chance to see him. I'm holdin' shit down in the streets for him," he said, "but if you need anythin' else, holla at me."

"Thank you," I said again.

He looked hesitant to leave. He stared at me. I know it was fucked up for me to be standing in front of him with my body glistening, only wrapped in a bath towel but I wanted to get dressed and leave for work. I was already late.

"Okay, James, thanks. I'm late for work," I said, trying to give him the hint.

"You need me to take you to work? It's not a problem for me, Shy."

Shit, I was already fifteen minutes late if I left now, and my boss has been riding me hard lately—tripping and shit.

"I mean, if you want, I can wait out in the hallway until you get dressed," he said politely, like he was trying to be a gentleman and shit.

"Um . . ."

"I'm lookin' out for you, Shy. You're my nigga's girl, so I'm tryin' to make sure you a'ight. I'm willin' to hold you down until Roscoe gets home."

I hesitated for a minute. "Okay, give me like ten minutes." Then I dashed into the bedroom and closed the door behind me, while James waited in the living room.

I went into my closet and threw on the best possible outfit for me to go to work in. Roscoe had helped land me the job at Mony's, a women's clothing store on Jamaica Avenue. He knew the manager, who owed him a favor, and he told Mr. Beharry that I was looking for employment. Next thing I know, a week later, Mr. Beharry was calling me up and asking me when I can start. It was cool, even though Roscoe was taking care of me. It was good making a little extra something on the side for myself. I make like $155 a week.

But now, since Roscoe got locked up, Mr. Beharry been acting up, and thinking just because Roscoe wasn't around, he could start treating me like whatever, like he own me.

I threw on a pair of tight-fitted Guess jeans with a cashmere sweater and pulled my hair into a long ponytail, and walked out my bedroom to see James seated on my couch, looking at an old *Vibe* magazine I had left on the coffee table.

"I'm ready," I said. "Did I take long?"

He got up and looked at me. "Nah, I was just chillin'."

We headed out the door and proceeded to the elevator. He pressed the button and stood next to me. He was tall, and his expensive Rocawear coat fit his thick frame like it was made personally for him. His Timberlands were brand-new, straight out the box, not one mark or scuff on them. And his jewelry gleamed like it had fallen directly from the sun and landed on him. He had a remarkable presence.

When the elevator came to my floor, James allowed me to step in first. He pushed for the lobby, and we rode down in silence.

It felt awkward leaving my building with James and getting into his impressive gleaming black Hummer H2.

I thought about Jade, and wondered how she'd react, seeing me getting into James's ride without her. I mean, she lived in the building next to mine. The ride to work was innocent, but around here, people see shit like this and start taking on the wrong idea.

The only time I see James is when I'm with Jade or Roscoe. I don't really know shit about the man, except what Jade and Roscoe tell me about him. And the way Jade's been beefing lately about his cheating and his superficial ways, I already had my own preconceived notions about him. But the way he talked to me while I rode in his Hummer, I knew he was cocky and had game. I knew James was about him, and satisfying his own needs.

The traffic on Jamaica Avenue was thick with cars crawling to get to their destination. The holidays were coming, with Thanksgiving right around the corner.

James pulled his Hummer up to the curb on 164th Street and Jamaica Avenue and unlocked the doors to let me out. But before I stepped out, he asked, "You want me to pick you up after work?"

I looked at him and said, "No, I'm cool. Thanks for the ride."

"You sure? It's not a problem for me, love."

I didn't want to get too comfortable with him. He stared at me like he expected me to change my mind. But I held my ground and hopped out his ride.

I strutted across the street while James watched me from his Hummer.

"You're late, Shy," Mr. Beharry said, glaring at me like I had tried to rob his store.

"I'm sorry but—"

"But what? This is the fourth time in a week. I want you here on time tomorrow, or don't come to work at all."

"Mr. Beharry—," I started.

"Don't even start, Shy," Janise, my coworker, chimed in after our boss walked away. "You know he hatin' on you."

"Whatever," I spat.

It's funny, when my man, Roscoe, was out and running things, Mr. Beharry never flipped on me about coming in late or taking days off. Now, when my man ain't here, he acting like Roscoe never hooked him up with favors and helped him out when he had beef with these young hoodlums out here, who waited outside the store one evening just to fuck his ass up. But it's all good, 'cause I know when my man is out, he gonna see what's up.

For the rest of the day, Mr. Beharry had me doing inventory, and he criticized every fucking thing I did in the store. He was becoming a real fucking jerk.

"Shy, let me talk to you for a moment," Mr. Beharry said, walking up to me, smiling like we were best friends.

I was down in the basement, rearranging today's earlier shipment, and we were alone. I looked at him, wishing he was somewhere else at the moment.

"I'm sorry about being on your ass lately, but I'm just trying to look out for you, Shy." He came in close to me.

I took a step back and looked at him, annoyed. "Look, I know Roscoe is incarcerated right now, and it's hard out there for you. You need someone to take care of you, right, Shy?"

"Excuse me?" I said, catching a little attitude.

He came even closer, and had the nerve to place his hand on my hip. He was Guyanese, Indian or something, and had a bushy mustache and a receding hairline. His breath was tart, and he was very unattractive.

I moved away from him before it got ugly, but he followed me.

"Look, I want to be here for you, Shy. I want to take care of you," he said, licking his nasty lips. Then he grabbed me by my shirt.

"Look, I can take care of myself!" I barked back, jerking myself out of his grip.

He glared at me. "Not if you don't have this job."

"What?"

"I take care of you, don't I? I let you slide when you come in late, or don't come in at all. I treat you different than all the other employees. I hooked you up with this job. I deserve something in return." He was dead serious.

"Get the fuck out of my face!" I said.

"So, you're going to play me like that, Shy? After everything I did for you and your boyfriend? What can he do for you now, huh, bitch? That nigga locked up now! He can't do shit for you, Shy. But I can." He grabbed my arm and copped a feel on my breast. Then he tried pushing me down on the ground. But I fought back. I quickly pushed him off me. "Don't be like this, Shy. I wanted you so long now. Why can't we be together? I'm better than him, look," he said, and had the nerve to pull out his dick in front of me.

I swear, I caught a glimpse of his pathetic dick, and he was hung like a light switch. And he had the nerve to show it to me like he was packing. Somebody must have told him wrong.

That's when I thought, *Fuck this—I don't need this job,* and I bashed him in the head with a large crate. He stumbled and hit the floor.

I rushed by him, hearing him screaming in pain, and then heard him shout, "Bitch, you're fired! Get the fuck out my store, you fucking tramp!"

"Fuck you, nigga! Watch you get fucked up!" I shouted back.

Pussy muthafucka! He thought because Roscoe's in Rikers,

he can treat me like I'm some easy bitch off the street. He had another think coming.

Employees and customers took notice as I flew by them, cursing. Some of my coworkers wanted to know what had happened, but I ignored them and stormed out the store, fuming. I was coming back, and Mr. Beharry's ass was gonna get fucked up.

I was storming up 164th Street, when I heard my name being called out.

"Shy! Yo, Shy! Hold up for a sec."

I turned around and saw James. I thought he had left. But he was still here, probably conducting business. Sometimes him and Roscoe stayed for hours on the Ave. He saw the look on my face and asked, "What happened?"

"My fuckin' boss is what happened! He a fuckin' asshole!" I said, still heated.

"He touch you?" James asked. His face was all screwed up.

"He just fired me," I told him. "And he tried to fuckin' come on to me, showing me his dick and shit."

"What? Yo, I'm gonna handle this." James called over for his boy, and then he walked back to Mony's like a warrior on a mission.

I followed James, smirking. I couldn't wait to see the look on Mr. Beharry's face when he saw me coming back into the store with this tall thug and his man by his side.

When we entered Mony's, James told me to point him out. My coworkers knew that some drama was about to pop off; they stopped working and stood off to the side. I saw Beharry come out the back, and when he saw me, James, and his thuggish friend, he panicked, but he had nowhere to run.

James quickly stepped up to him, grabbing him up by his shirt, and knocking him down to the ground.

"What you want? What I do!" Mr. Beharry frantically shouted.

"You touch her?" James yelled.

"No, no! I leave her alone! Please don't hurt me!"

"Nigga, did you just not pull your little dick out in front of her?" James yelled. He smacked him across the face, turning it red and shit.

"Shy, I'm sorry! Shy, please! I know Roscoe!" he tried to plead.

I smirked down at him, mocking his pathetic attempt to bring Roscoe's name into this to save his ass.

"Nigga, listen here. You come near her again, you gonna have bigger problems next time I come around. You hear me, fool?" James screamed.

"Yes! I hear you! I hear you."

James then let go of him, and Beharry continued to whimper as he lay on the floor. His employees laughed at him.

"Fuckin' jerk," I insulted.

As we were about to leave out the store, two uniformed officers stepped in and asked, "Is there a problem in here?"

James and his boy kept their cool. James looked at the officers and replied, "Ain't no problem here, Officer . . . just a little misunderstanding."

"You sure about that?" the tall lanky cop asked, glaring at James. He looked like he was ready to lock someone up. He looked over at Beharry.

"We cool, right?" James said to Mr. Beharry.

Beharry got his ass up and walked up to the front, looking

sad and shit. "Everything's okay here, Officer. Like he said, it was just a little misunderstanding."

"See, Officer. We cool."

"You and your friend leave," the shorter cop said.

"I'm already out the door, yo," James said smoothly and ushered me out the door.

I ain't gonna front—I saw James in a whole new light after that. I saw why Jade loved him so much. He stood up for me like Roscoe would have done, and that was cool.

An hour later, I was up in James's H2, riding wherever. I just wanted to get the fuck off Jamaica Ave and be out somewhere.

"Thank you for that," I said.

"I got your back, Shy. You know me."

I smiled.

"Yo, fuck that job, Shy. You don't need to work there. I don't know why Roscoe had you workin' up in there, anyway. You too fly to have a job like that."

I smiled. "Nah, I opted to."

"Independent. I like that."

"I try."

"Word, though, if you need cash, Shy, come to me. I got you, okay?"

"I'm okay," I said.

We rode down the Southern State Parkway, coming into Hempstead, Long Island. James had the radio playing and the night was a little breezy. I had on my cream Baby Phat jacket, and just enjoyed the ride.

James pulled up to this neat bricked house with a small manicured lawn out front and a paved driveway. Parked in the driveway was a silver BMW. He put the Hummer in park, and asked, "You wanna come in?"

"I'll sit out here."

"A'ight, give me a minute. This is my cousin's crib. I came to pick up sumthin'," he said, and then stepped out and headed toward the house.

I sat waiting patiently in his ride, listening to the radio. I looked at the time. It was 9:20.

Another five minutes later, James came walking out of the house carrying a small black bag. He tossed the bag into the backseat and jumped back in the driver's seat.

To my surprise, he handed me another envelope.

"What's this?" I asked.

"It's a little extra sumthin' for you," he said.

I opened it, and saw that it contained about another five grand.

"Call it an early birthday gift," he said.

I didn't know what to say. I was stunned.

"Thank you," I finally said. Shit, a sista wasn't gonna turn down free money. And I just lost my job too.

James smiled and asked, "You hungry?"

"Yeah, a lil' sumthin'."

"Cool. I know this nice restaurant only a few miles from here. We can go and check it out. You'll like it, believe me."

Fuck it, I thought. It was only an innocent meal, right? He started up his truck and made a quick U-turn.

God, I hated myself right now. I had crossed that line. The line that no friend should ever cross with her friend's man. But there was no turning back. I moaned and sank my teeth into the pillow as James ate me out. It'd been a minute since I had sex, and there were other men willing to give it to me, but I had to go around and fuck my best friend's man.

We had had dinner, and it had been cool. James kept complimenting me on my looks, saying that Roscoe was a lucky man to have me in his life. We had a good vibe going, and next thing I know, he pulled up in front of a motel, we were getting a room, my clothes came off, I sucked his dick, and now he was doing me right below.

His tongue licked around my thighs as he fingered me softly and a few tears began to trickle down the sides of my face. I thought about Roscoe; I thought about Jade. I wanted to yell stop, but the pleasure kept me mute. *Why am I doing this?* my mind was saying, but my body was saying, *You need this, Shy—it's only one night.*

I felt James climbing on top of me. His big dick looked like it was coming at me. That shit was big, about ten inches or so. And Jade was taking that in every night? No wonder she had four years with him.

"Ahhh," I gasped, clawing at his back and feeling him push inch by inch into me. I swear my eyes rolled in the back of my head as he penetrated me.

He began to thrust, humping in between my widely spread thighs.

"God . . . I wanted you for so long, Shy," James whispered in my ear as he fucked me. "Damn, you feel so good. . . . Damn, I've waited for this."

He had my legs rocking back and forth in the air. He then gripped both my ankles and spread my legs apart even wider, as he leaned up, pressed against his knees, and pushed his dick deeper into me, causing me to lose control and scream. Shit felt like it was nesting in my stomach. Next thing, he fucking me like Speedy Gonzales—rapid and shit. It felt good, a little, but his dick was too big for him to be trying to push all of that in me so fast. He started sweating and shit.

An hour later, we were done. I was sprawled out on the bed while James went to use the bathroom. I was out of it. I couldn't even get up. But my conscience was tearing me apart. I stood up and looked at myself in the mirror over the dresser.

"Shy, you a foul bitch," I said softly to my reflection. "How could you do that? Jade's your girl and you know how grimy James is. Him and Roscoe are best friends."

"You said somethin', Shy?" James shouted through the closed bathroom door.

"No."

I started to tear up, feeling like shit. I had never cheated on Roscoe. I love that man with all my heart. I was mad at him. I was envious of Jade. She still had her man around, getting the dick every night, while I was left with toys and my fingers night after night. I'm not used to spending time alone. I always had a man around, even my bitch-ass father when he was alive. I always had someone to love me and keep me company. Since I was fourteen, I had a boyfriend. And in one night, that changed for me. My man was on Rikers, while Jade's man came home to her every night.

I quickly jumped off the bed, collected my things, and shouted to James, "James, I'm ready to go."

"But we got the room for another five hours!"

"I'm ready to go now," I said, getting dressed.

I heard the toilet flush, and James stepped out of the bathroom, still butt naked.

"Shy, why you trippin'? Don't nobody know we here. We way out on L.I. Chill, baby," he said calmly, coming over to me.

"No, I need to go now," I repeated, pushing him away from me.

He sighed. "Whatever."

Within the next hour, we had checked out and were headed back to Queens. During the whole ride, I tried not to cry, but Roscoe was on my mind.

I had James drop me off a few blocks from my building. I didn't want anyone seeing me exit his Hummer this late at night. I didn't even say good-bye to him. I just hopped out his truck and walked briskly to my building.

When I walked into my apartment, the first thing I saw when I turned on the lights was a picture of Roscoe and me that had been taken at Coney Island one night. It was sitting on the wide-screen TV. I broke down crying and collapsed on my bed.

"Baby, I fucked up," I whispered to myself.

~ CHAPTER 11 ~

jade

For it to be November, it was so nice outside, the weather man said it would feel like a spring day, with temperatures reaching up to sixty degrees. I decided to spend today outside, enjoying the day, not cooped up in the crib, worrying about my man or waiting for him to bring his ass home whenever he felt like it.

I wanted to look nice today, and threw on a short cute white skirt, my Fendi shoes, sporting a cream Baby Phat jacket that Shy and I bought together one afternoon, and to top it off, I rocked a blue and white Yankees fitted. I had to admire myself.

I strutted out my building, thinking a bitch needed a job or something. Shy worked. Camille had her hustle. I waited around for James all the fucking time. And I was so tired of that. I needed to be independent like my girls. I moved outta my mother's crib when I was eighteen and landed right in James's apartment, where he promised to take care of me forever and shit. And a bitch believed those promises. I was young and so fucking naïve. When the truth came out, it was too late for me. My mother moved to South Carolina, and I was stuck living with James. I got cousins and aunts, but they have their own damn problems, and you know a bunch of women living under one roof is going to cause problems. I didn't need the extra headaches in my life.

Soon as I stepped out of my building, I saw the eyes watching me, loving me. The fellows said, What's up, and kept conversation friendly and respectful toward me. They all knew James, and they all knew his reputation. So they let me be. But you had a few that were bold enough to come at me on some different shit, sometimes even all disrespectful and shit.

Like Charlie. Now this nigga has had a crush on me since we were both in grade school. And he definitely didn't like the fact that me and James had hooked up. He would always let his feelings for me be known, and he even started talking disrespectful about James. We had been together for a year then. Charlie would buy me flowers and candy, give me cards on my birthday, and if I needed a favor, he was there.

I tried to warn Charlie, letting him know to chill on the gifts and his feelings for me. James was becoming furious and had threatened him a few times. But Charlie, being who he was and never scaring easily, kept up his pursuit toward me, dissing James. "I don't give a fuck about him. Jade, we knew each other for too long! Fuck him! He ain't stoppin' me from doin' shit!" Charlie would say.

Then one night, I was coming out of the bodega, and Charlie was standing out front. He saw me and approached me, smiling. He volunteered to help me carry my groceries to my apartment.

We didn't even get to cross the street when a black SUV suddenly screeched to a stop in front of us and about five niggas, including James, rushed out and attacked Charlie in front of me. They beat him with bats, fists, and whatever else they had so badly that he was in a coma for weeks. James yanked me by my arm and dragged me into the truck. I was yelling and terrified. I looked at Charlie's bloody, abused, and battered body slumped against the curb as they pulled off. His face looked like hamburger meat.

When we got into the apartment, James let me have it. That was the first time he ever put his hands on me. He said he hit me because he loved me and because he was so jealous. After the black eye and swollen cheeks, he promised never to touch me again, which was a fucking lie. I had been so embarrassed that I stayed indoors for weeks, ducking Camille and Shy for days.

After that incident with James, I never saw Charlie around the way again. Some claimed that he died in the hospital, but I didn't believe 'em. Charlie was an example to other men who even dared tried stepping to me. James put the message out clearly that I was his woman, and not to be messed with.

I strutted across the street to the nearest bodega. I needed a cigarette. I had tried to quit smoking when I was pregnant, but after I lost the baby, the craving quickly came back.

I saw a police car drive down the street, and I thought about Officer Reese. He was cute. But dealing with a cop in my neighborhood was the wrong thing for a sista to do. Muthafuckas are quick to criticize you and shit—thinking you snitching or something. That's okay.

"Let me get two looseys," I said to the Hindu store clerk. I passed him a dollar, and he gave me two loose cigarettes.

"Let me get a pack of gum too. Winter fresh."

I walked out the bodega, thinking about taking a cab over

to my cousin's place. She had a basement apartment over on Merrick. She lived there in peace with her son.

Then I heard someone shout out, "Hey, Jade!"

I turned around and saw Officer Reese coming my way. His partner was in the car, seated behind the driver's seat. Officer Reese smiled, being clad in his dark blue uniform, his belt clustered with cop shit, gun holstered on his right hip, and his shoes looked Payless.

"Officer Reese," I said, surprised.

"How you doing? Everything okay with you?" he asked. His right hand rested lightly, almost casually, on his gun.

"I'm okay. I was just on my way to see my cousin," I said.

His smooth brown skin shone in the sun, and he looked taller than the last time I saw him.

"It's good to see you out. You're looking good," he said, staring at me.

"You too," I said.

Our conversation was sparse. Maybe he was nervous, but I knew for sure that I didn't want the attention talking to a cop.

"Um . . . well, you still have my card, right?" he asked.

"Yeah, I still have it."

"Give me a call sometime," he said, but his eyes said that he wanted to say more to me than just give him a call.

"I might. Been busy."

"Oh, that's good. Well, it's nice seeing you. I got to run in here and get a few things for my partner and myself, but I want to hear from you whenever you're free, Jade."

"Maybe," I said, flirting a little.

He smiled.

His partner honked the horn, shouting, "Reese, come on! We ain't got all day!"

"See you," I said.

He walked into the store, never taking his eyes off me. I knew he liked me, and it was cool. It was funny to see him act kinda nervous around me. Here he was, a cop, here to protect and serve and probably acting like a hard-ass on the streets to have a reputation, but when he came around me, he became sheepish and humble. It made me feel good, like a woman, having NYPD blush.

I got to my cousin's crib around two that afternoon. My cousin Shana, we tight like that. She got one son, J.J., short for Jakim Jr. Now her story, it belongs in a book and should become a bestseller. Because Shana, she's been through some shit.

Shana is two years older than me, being twenty-three, and her son is three. I always heard stories about my cousin and her promiscuous ways back in the days. Her baby father, Jakim, was killed a few years ago by his best friend, and till this day, my cousin feels guilty about his death. She talks about it with me once in a while, but I can still see it be fucking wit' her. Jakim was so cool, and he was cute. I met him a handful of times. I had a little crush on him when I was fourteen, fifteen.

I remember my cousin talking to me about her relationship with Tyrone, and how they got down. Then admitting how wrong it was for her to mess with friends like that. But like myself, my cousin was into thugs back then. That's all she dealt with, and the dick had her open. But I respect my cousin Shana, because despite all the trouble she's done been through in her life with men, her friends, and the law, she still landed on her feet and is doing her right now.

She got the nice two-bedroom apartment on Merrick for her and her son. It's comfortable, and she ain't got no man paying her bills for her. She goes to school at York College, and she's holding down a cushy job at some insurance company on Hillside Avenue. Word, I love her for doing her. We don't see each other as often we would like to, but when we do, it always love between us.

"Hey, Jade," Shana greeted, giving me a hug as I stood in her doorway.

"What's up, Shana?" I said, all cheery and shit.

"What brings you by here?" Shana asked. "I haven't seen you in a while."

"I was around and decided to stop by and see what's good wit' you," I said.

"You in trouble?" Shana asked.

"No, nuthin' like that. I'm cool."

"You sure?"

"Yeah, everything cool wit' me, Shana."

"A'ight now . . .'cause you know if anything pop off, I got your back."

"I got yours too."

She smiled and gave me another hug. I walked into her nicely arranged apartment. I loved her place. It wasn't the biggest apartment on the block, but it was comfortable.

Shana cut her hair short, sporting a bob. I don't know why, and she gained a little weight, but she still looked good.

"Where's J.J.?" I asked.

"He's over at my mother's," she said.

"Damn, I wanted to chill wit' lil' man. I haven't seen him in weeks."

"He fine, wit' his lil' bad ass. When you gonna babysit for me, Jade?" Shana asked, smiling.

"When I start havin' kids on my own," I joked.

"Oh, I see . . . it's like that, huh?"

"Yeah, it's like that," I said teasingly.

"Yeah, look at you, you're too cute to be babysitting little badass kids, coming outside in a skirt and those shoes."

"Shana, you know how we get down. Everyday is important for me, and it's nice outside. I had to show off a little sumthin' to tease these niggas wit'."

She chuckled. "You want sumthin' to eat or drink? I just went shopping yesterday and got a fridge full of shit. I don't know why; J.J. and I can't eat everything."

"So why you buy it?"

" 'Cause my ass got greedy."

I laughed. "Yeah, give me a soda or sumthin'."

I took a seat on her couch and took off my shoes. Shana doesn't like people wearing shoes in her apartment. Her carpet was new and rich, and she kept her place tidy.

Shana came out of her kitchen with two sodas in her hands; she passed one to me and then took a seat in a cushioned chair near the kitchen.

"So what's up, Jade? How is Shy and Camille?" she asked.

"They a'ight. You know Shy's man got locked up a few weeks ago. He caught a murder charge," I told her.

She sighed. "Roscoe? You know it's funny—he kind of reminds me of Jakim somewhat."

"Roscoe?"

"Yeah, but Jakim wasn't hotheaded like Roscoe."

"But Shy's holdin' on. She be going to see him every week in Rikers . . . bringin' him clothing, money, and other shit."

"Damn, tell her to keep her head up," Shana said. "And Camille." Shana laughed. "That's my girl. She still flippin' on bitches in the projects?"

"You know Camille's gonna stay gully wit' her hood ass. We all went out to the club the other night. I wanted you to come; it woulda been so nice for all of us to hang out like that."

"Yeah, but you know with school, work, and taking care of J.J., I ain't got time like that anymore. That's y'all thing, it's not my life anymore."

"Please, girl, you ain't that old, actin' like you sixty years old up in here. You can still hang out—you just don't want to," I said.

"Anyway—," Shana said, getting up out of her seat and walking back into the kitchen. "So, Jade, you still fuckin' wit', um . . . James?" she asked from the kitchen.

"We gettin' along a'ight," I lied, wishing she didn't bring him up.

"What you mean, y'all a'ight?" Shana asked, walking out of the kitchen with a snack in her hand.

"It could be better, and it could be worse," I said.

"Fuck you talkin' about, Jade? Y'all cool or not?" she asked, prying more into my relationship.

"Look, we goin' through our little drama right now, but I know he still loves me. That's what you wanna hear?"

"Don't catch an attitude with me, Jade. I was just askin'. You know you my cousin, and if that nigga's actin' up, then let me know."

"Look, I can handle myself, Shana; you know what I'm sayin'? We got our problems, I'll admit, but we workin' it out right now."

"Okay. I was just makin' sure everything was okay with you. I heard about you and your girls fightin' up on Guy Brewer a few weeks back."

I sighed. "And who told you this?"

"Jade, please, I ain't that out of tune wit' the neighborhood. I still know about some things that goes on. Just be careful around there, and be careful around James," she said worryingly.

"James? Why you worryin' about him for?"

"Jade, I'm gonna keep it real with you. Since the first day I met him, I didn't like him. He's triflin'. He reminds me of Tyrone. He's selfish, arrogant, and he's shady. And I know you can do better than him."

"I've been wit' this nigga fo' four years now, Shana. I ain't just gonna leave the nigga like that. He's my man."

"Listen to me, Jade. I've been through this shit before, and don't let a big dick and a thuggish attitude get you in some shit that you're gonna regret later on. It ain't worth it. If you gotta fight a bitch on the corner for this nigga, leave his ass alone."

"How you know that I was fightin' a bitch over a nigga?"

Shana looked at me like I was full of it. "C'mon, Jade, this me you talkin' to. I fought bitches in clubs and almost got my face sliced open one night."

"Camille's been runnin' her mouth to you again, right? She tellin' you my business?"

"I ain't talk to her in months."

"Listen, Shana. I know you my cousin and we family and all, but the shit I go through wit' James, that's my business. He's my man, and I can handle my goddamn self, a'ight! I got this under control," I lied. I didn't want to look weak in front of my cousin. I didn't want her to know that this nigga been beating my ass on the regular and he had me in tears almost every night. My cousin was strong and always had a very strong attitude. And I wanted to be like her, and I tried to fabricate in her eyes that I was just like her, handling my business and letting no nigga put me under.

"Listen, if anything jumps off, you better give me a call," Shana said.

"I got you."

She looked at me.

"What?" I smiled.

"You think you're cute, huh?"

"I don't think. I know," I said.

"If we weren't cousins, I'd be hatin'," Shana said jokingly.

"I know."

"Whatever, bitch," she said, laughing.

She took my soda can and placed it in the recycling bin in the kitchen. "What you doin' for the day?" she asked.

"Nuthin'. Why?"

"Because I was about to head up to Jamaica Avenue and look for some shoes to wear tonight."

"Tonight?"

"I'm goin' out tonight."

"Oh, word, wit' who?" I asked.

"A guy," she said, being sparse with details.

"I *know* a guy—you ain't gay. But what's he like? Is he cute?"

"What you think?"

"Okay, he's cute. Where did you meet him?" I asked.

"Damn, Jade, what are you, my mother?"

"No, your cousin, and I deserve to know."

She laughed.

Shana promised to explain to me later about her date. She wanted to get dressed and go shopping on Jamaica Avenue before it got crowded with schoolkids.

We continued to chill and talk. Shana browsed through some shirts on a rack in Mony's on Jamaica Avenue. As she looked around, I thought about Shy and wondered if she was working today. I didn't see her in the store.

"I met him at my college," Shana said as she held up a cute Rocawear shirt.

"Who, your date?"

"Yes. His name is Henry."

"Henry. He a white boy?" I asked. I don't know too many brothas named Henry.

"No, he's black, and he's from the South. He's a senior and trying to get his bachelor's in political science," she said.

We went looking from one rack to another, looking through different shirts. Shana pulled out another shirt and continued to talk. "He's twenty-eight, tall, and nice."

"Nice?"

"Yeah, nice," she said, smiling.

"What you know about nice and nerdy guys? I know you're still into the bad boys," I said.

"For me, that's so played out. I want a man who can take care of me and my son. I want someone with a future and a regular job. I ain't tryin' to deal wit' no nigga hustlin', and worrying about the feds kickin' in my door eight in the mornin'. Jade, that happened to me once, with Tyrone, and I ain't tryin' to go through that ordeal again."

"Oh. Well."

"Oooh, this is nice," Shana said, picking up a denim skirt.

"Yeah. It's cool."

"Now, this would look so great on me, but it's gettin' cold, and I ain't tryin' to freeze my legs off. Henry just gonna have to wait till the summer to see me in a skirt."

"So, you really like him?" I asked.

"Yeah. We've been seein' each other for about two months now."

"Two months, damn. You fucked him yet?"

"Damn, Jade, can you ask in here any louder? I don't think the people outside heard my business that clearly."

"I'm sorry," I said, lowering my voice.

"And no, I didn't fuck him."

"Why not?"

"Because I've been busy, and we don't see each other like that. He works a lot, and I'm busy with everything else," Shana said.

"But you're goin' to, right?"

"What is this, Twenty Questions?"

"No. I'm just curious."

Shana smiled. "I might. He's been patient. I'm fond of him."

"You gonna fuck him tonight, right? That's why you out here shoppin', tryin' to look nice for him? You already got plans for the dick."

Shana smiled, confirming my suspicions. "Listen, you mind your business."

"Yeah, yeah, yeah. We family. We supposed to share every-thin'," I said.

"Not everythin'."

"Okay, not everythin'," I said, smiling at her subtle remark.

I glanced around for Shy, but didn't see her.

"Okay, I'm gettin' this," Shana said, holding up a cute pink and white J.Lo blouse. "And I'm gettin' these jeans."

"Shana, I wanna ask you sumthin'."

"Like what?"

"I met someone—," I started to say, but Shana cut me off.

"Word. He's cute?"

I sucked my teeth.

"Okay, he's cute. And what else?"

"But it's his job," I said.

"Oh, oh, Jade found herself a working man too; look out now. Let me find out, we got sumthin' in common now with the men. What is it, Jade? He's not making enough money to support your rich and fabulous lifestyle? He can't afford Gucci and Fendi?"

"No, it's not like that. I know he makes pretty decent money. But it's just . . . I met a cop. There, I said it."

Shana looked at me in shock. "A cop," she muttered. "You talkin' to a cop?"

"We met the other day. But I've been thinkin' about him more than often. He's cool. And I'm attracted to him."

"You want it to get serious?" she asked.

"I don't know him like that."

"What about James—he knows?"

"C'mon, Shana, what you think? He don't know shit. You know he a thug, and you know how he feels about five-o like that."

"Listen, Jade, I'm gonna tell it to you like this. If you're feelin' him, then go for it. Just be careful. And don't have everybody knowin' your business. If he's a cop, fuck it—he a man, right? He seems nice, and he got a job. I'm tellin' you, leave these hustlin'-ass niggas alone, because in the long run, it's goin' to be more trouble than it's worth. But don't rush into shit. Feel homeboy out, see what he's about," she said.

"I know. I'm just bein' careful. People see you hangin' around five-o like that, and they gonna start thinkin' the wrong things. I ain't snitchin' on no one."

"Jade datin' a cop," Shana said teasingly.

"We didn't date yet," I said.

"Listen, get rid of James and move on. You'll feel better about yourself."

I sighed. James had been in my life for four years, and just getting rid of him so easy wasn't gonna be easy. It's sad to say, but I was still in love with him.

"I'm definitely gettin' this outfit here," Shana said, holding up a blouse and some tight jeans.

"That's nice. Yo, let me see if Shy's workin' today, because she can get you the ten percent discount."

"Do that."

I went up to one of Shy's coworkers and asked if Shy was working today. She looked at me and said, "Shy don't work here anymore. Some shit popped off with her the other day, and she quit."

I was shocked. "What?"

Her coworker went on. "She had a beef wit' the manager, and then she brought some thug-lookin' nigga up in the store, and he just wild out on my boss."

Oh, shit, I thought. I had to give my girl a call and see what popped off with her recently. I haven't spoken to her in a few days, and I wanted to see if she was okay.

Shana paid for her things, and we left the store.

I thought about Officer Reese and decided to give him a call in the future. Shana was right. I needed to try new things in my life.

~ CHAPTER 12 ~

camille

"Girl, you got that dress in a size six?" Shannon asked me. She peered at the red corset minidress I held up for her, while she sat under the hair-dryer.

"Of course I got your size, girl," I said.

"I want it. How much, Camille?" she asked, reaching for her purse.

"For you, Shannon, I'll take a hundred."

"Cool." She rummaged through her purse and passed me two fifties.

I've been taking orders all day. Cream came through and hooked me up with the nice stuff. I was at Tomeka's beauty and hair salon in Hempstead, and the orders wouldn't stop. Everybody in here knows me, and they trust me. They know my product is legit. So far, I already made about five hundred dollars for the day, and it wasn't even noon yet.

"Camille, I want those shoes you showed me the other day," another client in the shop said to me.

"What, those pink and white Fendi shoes?"

"Yes. I just bought this dress the other day that would go perfect with them shoes," she said.

"I got you, girl. They're still in my trunk."

"God bless you, Camille."

"Girl, you know I got you."

Business was booming. After I left here, I had to run out to Brentwood and drop off a few orders in that town too. Tomeka's a cool friend of mine. She started up her own business with her boyfriend's drug money a few years ago. And to show her how I appreciated her for letting me run business out of her shop, I would give her stuff for free on the regular.

Tomeka's a thick and healthy-lookin' woman in her late twenties. She sported thick locks in her head, and her black skin wrapped around her like night. But she was beautiful. Men swarmed around her like she was Beyoncé.

"Camille, I'll take that dress in the chair."

"Camille, I need some shoes for next week Saturday."

"Camille, how much for that black dress?"

"Camille, when you comin' back to the shop?"

They all asked and hounded me like I wasn't coming back. But I wasn't complaining. That's my clientele, and without them, I would be out of business.

"Girl, why you always causin' uproar in my store with your overpriced clothing?" Tomeka joked, coming out of a back room. "Shit, business keep goin' this good for you, and I'm gonna have you start payin' rent up in here, like my other employees."

"And I'm gonna have to start chargin' you for all the free stuff I be blessin' you wit'," I said teasingly.

Tomeka smiled. "Nah. We can't have that."

"A'ight now."

"So, what you got new for me?" Tomeka asked.

"What you lookin' for?"

"Michael is takin' me out to some fancy restaurant tonight."

"Really?"

"Yeah. But he lookin' for some booty later on. He ain't been gettin' no ass from me recently."

"Why not?"

"'Cause he be actin' up, and I cut him off for about two weeks. Now he wanna take me out to dinner and a hotel afterwards," Tomeka said.

"Work it, Tomeka."

"So I need somethin' that's gonna scream out . . . *damn* . . . and get this nigga's dick so hard that it hurts," she said.

"I got you, Tomeka. Come with me to the car."

She followed me to my car. I popped the trunk and displayed some more exotic garments for her to choose from.

"Oooh, you definitely got choices," she said, and began looking through some of the plastic-covered garments.

"Don't I always?"

I decided to pick for Tomeka and pulled out this beaded silk dress that stopped just above the knees and would hug her figure like skin itself.

"Oooh, now that's nice, Camille. I love it."

"I know. We got similar taste."

"Michael is gonna love it."

"He's gonna love takin' it off you," I replied.

Tomeka smiled. "Ain't that the truth. Thank you, Camille."

"No problem."

My phone went off in my purse. I reached for it, looked at the number calling, and saw that it was Sierra. "Hold on,

Tomeka. Let me take this," I said, taking a few steps away so she wouldn't hear.

"What?" I answered bitterly.

"Hey, Camille," Sierra said.

"What's up?" I asked. I haven't heard from her in weeks, so I assumed that her husband put her on lockdown.

"I miss you, Camille."

I sucked my teeth. "You need to control your damn husband, Sierra. He's very disrespectful."

"I know. I'm sorry about that, but my husband has been trippin' lately. But he's out tonight with the kids, and I got time to spend with you. You want to go out to dinner, and then maybe get a room afterwards?" she suggested.

"I don't know. I gotta think about it. I thought you had him under control. I thought you were good at keepin' secrets from him," I said.

"I am. But he suspected somethin' with me and went through my phone when I was asleep. He saw your number and some of the text messages I had sent you and got pissed. It won't happen again, Camille. I promise," she assured me.

I sighed. "I'll call you back in two hours."

"You better do that. I definitely wanna see you tonight," Sierra said, sounding a bit desperate.

I looked over at Tomeka, and she was still admiring the dress I gave her.

"Where are you now?" she asked.

I lied and said, "Manhattan."

"Oh. What you doin' out there?" she asked. Now she was getting in my business too much.

"Sierra, I'm out here on business. Don't worry about what I'm doing. I'll call you back and let you know what's up, okay?"

"Okay, boo . . . call me."

I hung up on her and sighed. Here she is married with a lunatic for a husband and sweatin' me. *Why did I get involved with this woman in the first place?*

I walked back over to Tomeka. "Who was that, your man?"

"Somethin' like that," I replied quickly.

"Camille, I'm definitely wearin' this tonight," she said. She had the dress draped over her forearm.

"I'm glad you like it. Oh, give these shoes to Jennie. She already paid me for them," I said.

"A'ight."

"I gotta run, Tomeka, but tell the girls I'll be back around next week wit' some more stuff."

"You do that, girl."

I jumped into my car and headed for the Southern State. My phone sounded again, and it was Cream. I quickly picked up and said, "Hey, I've been thinkin' about you."

"Oh, word? What you thinkin' about?" he asked soothingly.

"Just you."

"I like that. So what you doin' tonight?" he asked.

"Why, you got sumthin' planned for us?"

"Yeah, a lil' sumthin', sumthin'," he said.

"Like what?"

"You'll find out later."

"Why you teasin' me?" I said.

"Because, it's my job to. Just come to my place around eight."

"I'll be there."

"Eight, Camille . . . and don't be on that CP time."

"I won't." I smiled. He hung up, and I was in a good mood. It was still early in the day, and I had some free time on my hands. So I decided to stop by a nearby Friday's and have lunch alone.

By three, I had totally forgotten about Sierra. I quickly picked up my cell phone and speed-dialed her number.

"Hello," she answered.

"Sierra, it's me. About tonight, I'm sorry, but I'm not going to be able to make it."

"Why not?" she asked. She sounded disappointed.

"Sumthin' really important came up," I told her.

"Like what, Camille? I was lookin' forward to spendin' some time alone with you. Can we see each other for a moment?" she asked, sounding desperate.

"Sierra, I'm sorry, but I'll make it up to you. Promise."

I heard her sigh, knowing she was upset. "But I don't know when I'll be able to get away. My husband been tryin' to keep me around him more often. You know he's been trippin'."

I didn't want to spend too damn long on the phone with her. She had dick in the house which she had access to 24-7. I lived alone, and Cream was a busy man, so for him to call up a sista and bring up that he had something special planned for me, I couldn't let the brotha down. I had to show him some love.

I told Sierra, "Next time." She became upset, and said she didn't want to hear from me again if I couldn't stop by for a quick minute. But I remember plenty of times when I wanted to see Sierra but that wasn't possible because of her husband and sometimes because of her work schedule. Sierra had a problem, thinking everything and everyone had to work around her life, and if she wanted to spend time with me, and I wasn't available, then it became a problem. But I never took her being self-centered personal. It was pussy, and like men, I never tried to get too attached, because like dick, pussy too can come and go.

I had Cream on my mind all day. I fucked him a week ago, and just like that, he had me open again. Cream and I, we always had an understanding: he does him, and I do me. But when it came to me, Cream would put me first before any fucking woman, and I'll do the same for him.

Jade would always joke around, sayin', "Y'all two need to stop frontin' and get married." And I be like, "It ain't that serious with him." But I started to think, maybe I was fooling myself. Maybe it was becoming that serious with him. I began to think, what if Cream got seriously involved with another woman, and she took away my time and my love. Would I become jealous? I thought about it, and fuck yeah, I'd hate on the next bitch. I can't even lie about that. And that's why I tried to avoid these type of predicaments, seeing Jade and Shy and other bitches that were caught up in good dick and a nigga. I didn't want to become that stupid. I'm my own woman, and I tried so hard not being tied down by no one. I wanted to do me and have no strings tagging along a guilty conscience as I fucked him or her.

It was seven thirty, and I drove hastily down Atlantic Avenue, racing against traffic that kept me from doing sixty on the busy streets. I cursed cars and pedestrians for becoming obstacles and making me mash on my brakes repeatedly. I was fifteen minutes from his place, and I know Cream likes his woman to be punctual.

But I know once he saw me, he would forget about me being late. I wore a ivory wrap top with bell sleeves, tight clean-front leather pants that accentuated my figure, leather boots with stiletto heels, and my long hair falling off my shoulders. I looked too good, and I was his tonight.

Finally, I reached in front of Cream's place. The outside of his building didn't look much; it looked industrial and desolate, and neighbors were sparse. He lived a few block from Atlantic. But Cream felt at home here.

I jumped out my ride, glanced at the time, and muttered, "Shit." It was five minutes after eight. I strutted up to Cream's building and pressed the buzzer. Soon afterwards, the door buzzed, indicating that it had been unlocked, and I quickly stepped into the building. I took the large lift with the iron gates up to the second floor. The building was old and huge; it used to be a factory or something. Cream bought the building and made it into his home. He told me that he loved it, the open space; it made him feel so free. To me, the place could be a little creepy, especially at night. I hated coming to visit him when night descended. I always felt that I was being watched, or someone was going to loom out from the dark and attack me. But Cream said he had security cameras set up all around the building and that I was safer here than anywhere else in Brooklyn.

I stepped into Cream's open domain, and the first thing I noticed were the fragrant candles and rose petals nicely spread out on the sleek wooden floor. He had the stereo playing a Kenny Lattimore CD, with the lights dimmed. I became touched. I smiled but didn't see Cream.

I proceeded into the room.

"You're late," I heard Cream say. I looked around, but didn't see him.

"I'm sorry, baby. I ran into traffic on the way here," I said.

Then I saw him coming down the stairs, and he was looking good. He had on a Giorgio Armani pantsuit, Armani button-down shirt, tie, and a pair black expensive wing-tip shoes.

"Oh, my God," I muttered. I was in shock. I never saw him in a suit before. But what really caught my eye, and had me in complete awe with my hand over my mouth, was when I saw he had cut off his braids. He was showing off a baldy. I was used to seeing Cream in jeans, Timberlands, Nikes, throwbacks, and a fitted.

But tonight, he looked like a whole new man. He looked good—damn, he looked good. I was silent, as Cream continued to approach me.

"I said eight, and it's ten after eight," he said.

"I'm sorry," I apologized flirtatiously. I began batting my eyes at him.

"You know you gonna have to make it up to me," he said.

"I know."

He smiled.

"I love this. Ohmygod, Cream, when did this change take place?" I asked. I was still in awe.

"I assume you like the new me," he said, running his hand across his bald head.

"Baby, you look good."

He smiled harder. "I knew you would like it."

"Is this the surprise?" I asked.

"Some of it. I got more for you."

"And the suit, Armani. Cream, you definitely went all out."

"Well, this suit cost me a little over two grand. But it looks nice on me, huh?"

I looked at him. I was definitely impressed by his newfound image. I wanted to fuck him right there and now. But I contained my hormones and took in a deep breath.

"Damn, Camille, you look gorgeous, ma. I like the outfit. Damn, leather pants, and the shirt . . . ummm, you got a brotha lovin' you right now."

"That's how it supposed to be. You know I always come correct," I said.

Cream smiled. He then took me by my hand and led me to the kitchen. I loved every minute of it. I thought he cooked up a meal, but to my surprise, he had a gift or gifts waiting for me in the kitchen. What I saw draped over the back of a kitchen chair was a pumpkin-colored leather jacket, and a shoe box placed next to the jacket on the table.

My eyes got big. The jacket was Escada ostrich. "It costs twenty-six hundred," Cream proclaimed.

"Are you serious?" I shouted.

"Yup."

I rushed over to the jacket and picked it up. The leather jacket I had on now was nice, but an original Escada . . . The shit was priceless.

"Open the box too," Cream said.

I picked up the box, knowing it was shoes. But when I saw that they were Manolo Blahnik pumps to match the jacket, I damn near passed out.

"Baby, why?" I asked. I mean, I got gifts before, and Cream came across expensive clothing like it was nothing, but tonight, he outdid himself.

"I'm celebratin'," he said.

"For what?" I asked.

"I'll tell you over dinner. I got reservations at the Park Avenue Cafe."

"Oh, really? I thought you made dinner here."

"Nah, I want to dine out."

"At the Park Avenue Cafe?"

"Yeah. And I don't want to be late."

The Park Avenue Cafe was located at 100 East Sixty-third Street between Lexington and Park. It was elegant and comfortable, with an upscale Americana look.

Cream and I arrived a little after nine thirty; we were quickly seated and began ordering our meals. Cream immediately ordered a bottle of wine, and a few hors d'oeuvres before our meal came.

"What's up wit' you tonight?" I asked. I took a quick sip of the wine.

Cream bit into an hors d'oeuvre and sat back in his chair. We looked like a Hollywood couple that night.

"So," I uttered, dying for him to tell me what the celebration was about.

Cream smiled. "Camille, I'm on my way."

"On your way to what?"

"Remember my record label that I started up wit' a friend of mine two years ago?"

"Yeah."

"I got a distribution deal, Camille. With Sony. Mike hooked it up."

"Are you serious?" I said, excited.

"Yeah, baby. Our attorneys worked everythin' out. The

contracts were in order, and I signed last week. We about to blow up. You know we already got three rap groups under our company, and they're nice."

"Ohmygod, Cream, I'm so happy for you! You always loved music, now you're about to become a hip-hop mogul," I said, smiling.

"Yeah. But I'm movin' out to California for a few months, Camille," he said.

Hearing that made my bubble bust. "What? Cali? When are you coming back?"

"I'm gonna be out there for a minute, Camille, gettin' things in order and workin' on these groups."

I sighed, because as always with good news, the bad news is right around the corner.

"But check it, I want you to come with me," he said.

"What? Me move out to Cali—?" I said with shock.

"Yeah. I want you out there, by my side. I want you with me, Camille."

I didn't know what to say. California is a long way from home, and I never left the state of New York, except for traveling to New Jersey.

"We can get a place out there, get the fuck out of New York for a minute, and do us, baby. It's gonna work out. I know it. I'm settin' everythin' up now."

"When are you leavin'?"

"Sometime before the New Year."

"It's so soon," I said, surprised.

"Yeah, I know. But we gotta make moves. I don't want to leave you here. . . . Say yes."

I sighed. "I need to think about it."

"I understand, with everythin' being so sudden, but—"

"This is my life here, Cream. Everythin' I know is here, in New York. I don't know nuthin' outside of this town."

"But that's the beauty of it, experiencin' new and better things. You don't need this, Camille. You lived in the projects all your life. You're better than the ghetto. You deserve better things in life, and movin' to California, it's going to be a start for you. I can get you into modelin' and videos. We can build so much, Camille."

Oh, God. I thought about Shy and Jade. They were my girls, and what would they do without me around to hold shit down when it got rough in the projects. Then, Cream was my connect to my lil' clothing business, and when he leaves, I'm gonna be fucked. It's hard to find a good, reliable help like Cream. I had to think long and hard about this one. What was good for me? I know a lot of bitches would jump to the opportunity with no questions asked, but I always thought things out before I leap. I wanted to make sure that this was the right thing for me to do.

The food came, and Cream went on talkin' about California and his music label. Cream is a nigga about business. He got that street savvy and that business savvy. How many niggas you know own a fucking small building in Brooklyn and arranged it to make it a comfortable living situation? He makes money, and he makes it big.

The night ended with me staying the night at his place, and we made love. I wanted it to be soft, romantic, and passionate. I just didn't want to fuck his brains out. The night was so perfect, that I didn't want it to ever end. But I thought about California while I lay up in Cream's arms. It was about two or three thousand miles away. I thought about Dr. Dre, Snoop Dog, and

Death Row Records. I thought about palm trees, Hollywood, Sunset Boulevard, and the weather being nice year-round—no snowstorms and cold arctic winds nipping at your ass during the winter. But Cali did have earthquakes and mudslides, and having the ground shake under your feet scared me.

~ CHAPTER 13 ~

shy

Everything good wit' you, baby? You've been kinda quiet," Roscoe said. I had accepted another collect call from him, and we'd been talking for about ten minutes. I heard the phone ring while I was naked in the bathroom. It was a little past nine, and I knew it was Roscoe calling, so I threw a bathrobe around me, rushed into the bedroom, and snatched the cordless off the cradle.

"I'm okay," I replied drily. I sat in a chair and stared at the wall. I was still feeling guilty about fucking James a few days back.

"James came by and gave you the money, right?" he asked.

"Yeah. He came by a few days ago."

"Cool."

The conversation went dead for a few seconds. But then Roscoe sparked it back up by asking, "Shy, you still mad at me for takin' a plea?"

"You did what you had to do, right?" I replied with a little attitude.

"Shy . . . c'mon, don't be mad. Yo, I can't be up in here,

thinkin' you pissed off at a brotha. I need you, baby. I'm in court, and you ain't there—"

"I come see you, right?"

"Yeah, but—"

"Roscoe, this is hard for me. I love you—you know I do. But I'm scared," I said.

"We gonna be a'ight," he told me.

"Baby, how?" I asked. I didn't tell him that I lost my job. I figured he had enough to worry about already. And I didn't want to tell him about Beharry.

"James is gonna look after you while I'm locked down. And you got Jade and Camille by your side. . . . They cool peoples. You still got your job, so you're good."

I sighed. I wished it was that easy.

"Roscoe—," I began, but then the call cut off. I guess his time was up. Shit, I hated how our phone calls would sometimes end so abruptly with no indication at all. I didn't even get the chance to tell him a proper good-bye.

I sighed heavily and placed the cordless back on its cradle. I stood up and stared out my bedroom window. It was raining hard, and it looked chilly outside. I could hear the wind smacking against my window as the cold rain cascaded down the glass. My bedroom was quiet. I was lonely. Some nights, I'd become afraid to stay in the apartment by myself. I yearned for some male company. I wanted to be held during nights like tonight.

I went back into the bathroom and started to wrap my hair. The situation was new to me—alone, frightened, and just a little stressed. I wanted to pick up the phone and call Camille or Jade, but thought they probably were busy right now. Besides them, I don't fuck with no other bitches around here.

After I was done wrapping my hair, I tied a scarf around my head and quickly brushed my teeth. I walked back into my bedroom, and that's when I heard the doorbell.

The doorbell caught me off guard and kinda startled me. It echoed throughout my quiet apartment, breaking the stillness and making me wonder who was coming by this time of the night.

I tied my robe tightly and looked through the peephole. I let out a quick sigh when I saw James standing outside my door.

I thought about not opening the door, but maybe he was dropping sumthin' off or had some news to tell me. So I unlocked the door, and there was James, his tall thuggish figure in some designer clothing and clad in a thick brown leather jacket.

"Did I come at a bad time?" he asked.

I wanted to say yes, but when I opened my mouth, I heard myself saying, "No. I was just gettin' ready to go to bed."

"Oh—"

"What do you want?" I asked. I tried to be stern with him, but my voice was soft.

"I wanted to come by and see how you were doin'. I haven't heard from you in a few days. I'm just checkin' up on you. You know, nights like tonight, no woman should be spendin' alone," he said. His eyes looked past me and stared into my apartment.

"You lookin' for sumthin'?"

"You got company?"

"What, no!" I replied quickly. I was a bit annoyed. "Why would you ask that?"

"You look busy."

"I just got off the phone wit' Roscoe," I told him.

"He a'ight?"

"I would hope so."

He stood there, waiting for an invitation into my apartment. I knew if I invited him in, it would start something. So I had him standing out in the hallway. But the demons in between my legs wanted me to open my mouth and say the opposite. I was alone, and he was company.

"Can I come in?" he asked.

I was silent. I didn't tell him yes, and I didn't utter no. I should have *shouted* no, but stillness became my answer. My eyes looked down at the floor as I gripped the door with my body leaning slightly against it.

"James, you can't be in this buildin', especially in my apartment. What if someone sees you?" I questioned.

"Shy, I got peoples in this buildin' that I come by to see on the regular. People see me walk in your buildin', they don't know that I'm comin' to your apartment; none of 'em live on your floor anyway. As far as they know, I'm here on business."

It became quiet. I contemplated the idea. It was getting late. James continued with, "Only for a few, Shy. I just wanna make sure you okay. You know."

He didn't wait for a response; he kinda nudged me to the side and made his way in slowly. I sighed, glanced up at the ceiling, shaking my head, and closed the door behind him.

James took a seat on the couch and quickly made himself at home. He took off his shoes and looked up at me.

"What about Jade?" I asked.

"She cool. Why you ask?"

"Because we're best friends, and how it looks havin' you up in my apartment this time of the night?"

"Shy, relax. Jade don't know I'm here, and she don't need to know. This is between you and me. I know you care about your girl. Shit! I do too. But we lookin' out for each other. You feel me?"

"Fuck you mean by that?" I asked.

He got up and came to me. He stood close and placed his hands against my hips and said, "I know you're lonely, and I know you miss Roscoe. I miss the nigga too. But what's done is done, Shy. Yo, don't stress it. You're young, and I want you to come out right. I wanna be here for you anyway possible. You feel me?" His words were soft and somewhat assuring. He gazed into my eyes, and then he pulled me into him closer, embracing my petite figure.

Our lips touched, and I felt his large, strong hands gripping my butt.

"This is what you came here for?" I asked softly. I felt his hands fondle and grope my seminude body. "For some pussy?"

"I came here for you, Shy. Honestly, that night at the hotel, I truly enjoyed that wit' you. I've been thinkin' about you a lot lately," he said.

James then untied my robe, opening it up, letting it fall off my shoulders, dropping it down around my ankles. I stood naked in front of him. My nipples became rigid, and in between my legs started becoming wet.

I wanted company, and I feared being alone, so I allowed him to stay. We made our way into the bedroom, where James began to strip. He then pushed me onto the bed and climbed in between my thighs and thrust his erection into me.

He didn't even take the time to strap on a condom. He pushed his dick into me raw. I weakly said, "James . . . get a condom."

"Hold on, Shy, let me feel you raw for a quick moment," he grunted. I felt him thrust into me.

A moment turned into a half hour of unprotected sex with him, and then I felt him come in me. I felt so fucked up. It was stupid of me. And I knew I couldn't reverse what just happened.

James passed out beside me, snoring and shit. I went into the bathroom to be alone and shed a few tears as I sat on the toilet. I was weak. How could I allow this man to come into my home and take what belonged to Roscoe for a second time? The first time, shit happens, right? But fucking him a second time, on the bed that Roscoe and I shared every night, *How could I?*

I woke up early the next morning, seeing James getting dressed. I glanced at the time and saw that it was 9:20.

"Shit!" I mumbled.

"You okay?" James asked, zipping up his jeans.

I didn't say a word. I just looked at him, having my conscience eating me up inside. He was wrong for that, I thought.

"Why didn't you get a condom?" I asked.

"Yo, you a'ight, Shy. I don't get bitches pregnant on the first go-around."

"Excuse me!" I replied angrily.

"Listen—," he started. He approached me in his wife-beater. "I'm sorry. I just got caught up in the moment wit' you—that's all." He sat next to me while I rested my back against the headboard. He touched my leg and stared at me. "Yo, next time I'll strap up. Promise!"

"Next time?" I said. I looked at him like he must be crazy.

"C'mon, Shy, last night was nice. I enjoyed that, and I'm sure you did too." He said it with a smug look.

"I think it's time for you to leave," I said.

"It's cool. I'm gonna let you be," he said. He got up off my bed and continued getting dressed while I remained in bed, clutching my covers.

"You gonna let me out?" He threw on his leather jacket.

I got up out of bed, feeling a little bashful in just my underwear—which was crazy, because I already fucked him twice. I threw around me my feather-embroidered robe and walked him to the door.

Before James left, he turned around, went into his pocket, and pulled out a wad of cash. He peeled off four hundreds and pushed it into my hand.

"Take it, Shy," he insisted.

I sighed and reluctantly took the cash.

"If you need anything else, call me," he said. He then leaned forward and tried to press a kiss against my lips, but I pulled back and told him, "I can't right now."

James looked at me, and he didn't say another word. He just shrugged his shoulders and left my apartment. I closed the door and slid down the door with my back against it. I started to tear up. I clasped my hands around the back of my head and asked myself, "What the fuck is wrong wit' me?"

~ CHAPTER 14 ~

jade

It was ten something in the morning, and my man hadn't come home last night. He had been out all fucking night, and I started to become worried. I knew about the life he lived—the hustling, countless money coming in, the thugs and criminals he dealt with from day to day, and I thought he could be in jail, or hurt, probably dead somewhere. I called his cell phone a few times, but I kept getting his voice mail.

During these past few days, James and I had reconciled our differences and made up in a good way. We'd planned to spend Thanksgiving alone at the Sheraton on Long Island, have dinner at a nice restaurant, and then afterwards, dine on each other. And I was looking forward to it.

I thought about Officer Reese a few times, having his card hidden away so James wouldn't come across it. And I was tempted to call him a few times, but I changed my mind. I was willing to work things out with James. I didn't want to end it with him so easy, especially since we had four years together.

I went into the kitchen and started cooking up breakfast for myself. I scrambled some eggs, began boiling some water for some grits, and placed a few pieces of bread in the toaster.

I heard James come in. I looked up at the clock and saw that it was a quarter to eleven. James didn't say a word to me. He rushed past the kitchen and headed straight for the bathroom.

"James!" I called out. I followed him to the bathroom, and the door was closed. I knocked on it and asked, "James, you a'ight?"

"I'm good. I'm about to jump in the shower," he shouted through the door.

"You want some breakfast? I'm cookin' grits and eggs."

"Nah. I'm good."

I didn't say anything else. I went back into the kitchen to continue with breakfast. After breakfast was done, James was still taking a long shower. And I ain't gonna lie, a bitch was horny. Last night, hearing that rain and wind outside my bedroom window made me think of James, and how he would throw down in the bedroom during nights like last night. We would have the radio playing in the background, and he'd be grinding between my legs, fucking the shit out of me.

I took a few bites from my plate, and then got up and walked to the bathroom, stripping off my clothing on the way, leaving a trail of bedtime garments from the kitchen to the bathroom.

I knocked on the door gently. "James, hey, baby."

He didn't answer, so I took it upon myself to make the first move, and luckily for me, he left the bathroom door unlocked.

I casually walked in and went straight for the shower. The mist from the running hot water saturated the mirrors and lingered in the bathroom, making me unable to see my reflection in the glass. I pulled the glass shower door back, seeing James's thick, strapping young body drenched with the steaming warm water flowing from the shower head above.

James turned and looked at me, as I stood naked in front of him. My nipples were stiff, and I was in need for some dick. No words were spoken. I hopped into the shower with him and gripped his dripping, rock-hard body and started kissing him all over. I heard him moan, as my tongue danced across his chest. I gripped his dick in my fist, stroking him gracefully.

"Fuck me, baby!" I cried out passionately, with the water cascading off our skins like a human waterfall. James said nothing, he turned me around, bent me the fuck over, and shoved his big black dick into me. My hands clasped the shower walls, as I tried to hold on and screamed out his name with so much obsession. He gripped my ass and continued to fuck the shit out of me. I came within minutes, and he did next, pulling me closer and grabbing my titties as he exploded into me.

Our actions continued on from the bathroom to the bedroom. James tossed me on the bed and began devouring my pussy. He gripped my legs strongly, with his lips and tongue doing a sista so fucking right. Of course, after an episode like that, I had to go down on my man, and tried deep-throating the huge erection that he had up again. After that, I straddled him and rode his dick till a bitch came again. Afterwards, I collapsed against his chest, breathing kinda hard—dick done did me justice.

I didn't even question him about last night and his whereabouts. I got so caught up in our crazy sexual escapade and having three fucking orgasms in one morning that I let it be.

James took a quick nap, with me still rested by his side. I was worn out too. So I closed my eyes and napped right along next to him.

My quick nap ended an hour and a half later, and I didn't realize that I was still so damn tired. I looked over, and James wasn't by my side. But I heard him in the bathroom. I was sprawled out across my bed, feeling the sun's radiant rays casting down on my nude body from my opened bedroom window. Outside seemed nice, but NY1 said that temperatures would reach a high of forty-five degrees and being a bit chilly, which meant my thickest leather and my boots.

James finally came out the bathroom, and he had on his jeans and his beige Timberlands. I looked at him, surprised that he was getting dressed.

"Nigga, I know you ain't goin' out again," I barked. I wanted him to spend some time home with me, and do us for a while.

"I'll be back," he said. He buckled his belt.

"What? James, you come in here after ten in the goddamn morning, and now you're leaving here again! Why can't you stay your ass home?" I shouted, jumping out of bed and reaching for my robe.

"Jade—," he started, but his cell phone went off, catching his attention. He opened the phone and said, "Yeah . . . what up?"

I glared at him. He had the phone pressed against his right ear and his shoulder, and he threw on his button-down navy blue Rocawear shirt. Nah, I wasn't having this. He wasn't gonna come home, get himself some quick pussy, having me throw it at him while he was in the shower, and then leave me in this apartment out to dry. Fuck that! I scurried around the room and started getting dressed too.

He paused his conversation on the phone and finally paid attention to me, saying, "Jade, what the fuck you doin'?"

"I'm comin' wit' you."

"No, you're not. You stayin' the fuck here," he said, and then returned back to his conversation over the phone.

I wasn't having that. I didn't care what the fuck he said. I continued getting dressed, ignoring his statement. But by the time I was almost done, James was damn near out the door already.

I rushed up to him, pulling him by his leather and trying to pull his ass back into the apartment. James jerked his arm free from my pathetic grip, saying, "Jade, get the fuck off me! I don't need you babysittin' me today."

"What? Are you serious, James?" I asked. I was about to tear up. I felt he was dissing me right now.

"I'll be back," he said. He gave me a cold-face look and proceeded to the elevator.

"James!" I exclaimed from the apartment door, watching him wait for the elevator. "James! James! James!" But the nigga ignored me, like I wasn't even standing there. I continued to call his name out. The elevator came to the floor, and he walked in like I was nothing.

What the fuck! I thought. This nigga done flipped the script on me. *Fuck that!* I threw on my leather jacket, grabbed my purse and a few personal things, and rushed out the door a few seconds after he left. I rushed down the pissy, foul-smelling staircase because I didn't want to wait too long for the elevator.

When I made it out of the building, I saw James walking down the block. His truck was parked across the street, and he didn't even bother to get in. That meant his journey was nearby. I tried to be inconspicuous, and followed him the best I could. He walked down about three blocks, not even looking back to see if he was being followed. But knowing James, he probably was so fucking stupid and arrogant, that he thought he had this game of his down pat. He probably thought that I stayed my ass in the apartment like I was told.

James pulled out his cell phone, called up a number, and then he began talking. I was about a block away from him. I kept my eyes glued to him like he was magnetized. James finally stopped trekking it down the street and stopped in front of one of the project buildings.

I stood hidden from James's view, watching this ignorant muthafucka and waiting to see what he had going on. I couldn't help it, but my heart began to beat faster and faster. I began to feel envious about seeing him with some new pretty bitch he hooked up with recently and dissing me for her. I tried to hold my own, thinking about Camille and hearing her mouth, talking some shit like, "Jade, you followed that nigga? Why? He ain't worth the trip. You need to leave that nigga alone. Fuck him!"

At first, I wanted my girlfriends to love him like I did. I wanted Camille and Shy to be jealous of me—it was fucked up, but I was young. James was so fine that I wanted to be the envy of all Jamaica housing and all of Queens. I wanted to praise James, and have bitches wishing they could be me for snagging up my boyfriend. I felt and thought I was the lucky one. But truth be told, I was really the unlucky one. The trials and tribulations, along with the heartaches and pain I've been through with this man for so long, was definitely having its toll on me.

I watched and waited for about five minutes. I gawked at James standing in front of the building lobby with his hands placed in the pockets of his leather jacket. After watching and waiting, I caught the surprise of my life. My mouth dropped, and my attitude flared up, when I saw Tasha walking out of the building and going up to James giving him a strong hug and then kissing him on his fucking lips. The shit was a joke. No, this nigga didn't. Nah, he ain't just leave out the crib with me, after he just fucked me, and then caught an attitude with me about him leaving to run outside in the cold to see this dumb dirty-bird bitch. He must be smoking or using that crack he was pushing— Nah, Lord, this ain't happening. He swore that Tasha wasn't his type and he wasn't fucking her. But now I'm seeing him hugged up on her outside in the cold, out in the open, where people could see and then later on talk. And then when I beef about it to him, his excuse always was, everybody spreading rumors about him and trying to break us apart. Fucking bullshit!

I was hurt and, at the same time, fucking furious. I caught this weird funny feeling in the pit of my stomach. My face tightened up; I clenched my fist and muttered, "A'ight!" He think he had it made? *Fuck that!*

I briskly walked up to the two of 'em. They had their backs turned from me and not paying attention. I glared at Tasha. She had on a black leather coat, a miniskirt, black stockings, and some shin-high leather boots, and her weave looked decent for once. The bitch looked proper like what, one day out of the fucking year. I became even more furious, thinkin' James probably paid for all of her shit.

James finally turned around, catching me coming up to the both of 'em like a bat out of hell.

"Fuck!" I heard him mutter when he saw me coming.

That bitch Tasha turned around and twisted her ugly face at me. James released his arm from around her, knowing he was busted.

"Nigga, what the fuck is this!" I shouted.

"Jade, fuck you doin' here? I told you to be easy and stay up in the crib."

"Nah, nigga, I thought you said you wasn't fuckin' wit' her. Why is this bitch here, huh, James?" I shouted, with my arms flaring all over the place.

"Bitch! Who the fuckin' you talkin' to, ho?" Tasha countered back.

"She fuckin' busted, James, and you dissin' me for her! Fuck is wrong wit' you! Bitch probably got AIDS or some shit."

"What?" Tasha shouted.

"Jade—"

"James, you don't need that bitch. Who the fuck is she! I know you ain't talkin', dumb bitch!" Tasha cursed, stepping forward.

"What bitch?" I barked. I got up in her face.

I was causing a scene and did not give a fuck. I became reckless, and wanted to hurt both of 'em bad. I was two seconds away from whipping this bitch's ass.

"Yo, Jade, chill," James said.

"Nah, fuck you and fuck this nasty ho! She needs to find her own fuckin' man!" I screamed. I became so furious that she was with him that I spitted phlegm dead in Tasha's face.

Tasha didn't even attempt to wipe the spit that rested in between her nose and left eye as she came at me, swinging. I grabbed her jacket and punched her in her neck, and then caught her again, punching her on the side of her head. We struggled, falling against the black-ironed three-foot gate that was fenced around the building.

We tore into each other like hungry lions. I tried to grab her hair and pull her shit out, but she pushed me off her and then charged at me again. She lunged at me like a fast discharge from a loaded gun and knocked my ass down on the concrete.

"Get the fuck off me!" I yelled. I tried to protect myself from the quick blows that she rained down on me.

A crowd gathered around, and James, this fucking asshole, just stood there and watched the whole thing, I swear, while this bitch was pressed down on top of me, striking me with punches. I sworn I saw him sneered down at me, like the situation was cute to him.

I wish my girls were here by my side, because Tasha had the advantage over me for a few seconds, scratching my face and digging her dirty nails into my skull. I was little, but I was going hard.

I don't know who separated us from each other, but I was grateful when I felt her being pulled up off me. I got back on my feet still acting a fool.

"Yeah, what bitch? What you got now!" Tasha shouted, being contained by a stout dark-skinned man with glasses.

"Fuck you, ho! You nasty! Fuck you . . . fuck you! You can have him. I'm done wit' him!" I shouted. This older bearded man held me tightly by my arm, keeping me from thrusting after her and wanting my revenge.

"Don't hate, bitch! Don't fuckin' hate! You got your ass whipped, bitch. . . . Watch, Jade . . . you think I'm playin'!" Tasha exclaimed, with her hair in disarray.

"Let that bitch go . . . let her go . . . let her the fuck go!" I screamed. I tried to jerk my arm free from this man's grip. I twisted and belligerently yanked and tried to release myself from his grip, but he wasn't having it.

"Calm down," the man holding me said.

"Nah, fuck that!" I yelled. I was crying. I was hurt. I felt disrespected.

"Yo, what kind of man are you, having these two women fighting out here like this?" the man holding me said to James.

"Nigga, what? Mind your fuckin' business!" James said.

The guy James cursed out didn't return with a remark. He just looked at James in disgust, pretty much the way I looked at him now too.

"Get the fuck off me!" I yelled.

He did, without me having to ask twice. I stormed off down the block, cursing and fuming. I didn't even turn and look back. The bitch ripped my sweater and scratched up my face. I swear, if I had a gun, both of 'em would have been dead.

I walked away, not even bothering to turn around. I was in full tears and not knowing what to do with myself. A part of me, though, did want to turn around, and I wanted James to run after me, apologize, and say something. But he stood behind. He never came up to me. He never said a fucking word to me. Fuck him! He can have that bitch.

An hour later, somebody was at my door, but I didn't want to be bothered with. I cried on the couch, listening to Beyoncé's CD. The words to her song "Dangerously in Love" lingered in my head as I clutched a pillow to my chest with crazy thoughts spinning around in my head.

I heard the doorbell, which was followed by hard knocking afterwards.

"Jade, open up! It's Camille," she shouted. "Open the damn door, Jade!"

I unwillingly got up from my position on the couch, and

walked sluggishly to answer the door. I took my time unbolting the three locks, and cracked open the door. Camille ran into my place like there was a fire out in the hallway. She looked at me and said, "Jade, you a'ight? I heard what happened. Where that bitch at!"

I just looked at her, still clutching my pillow to my chest with my back pressed against the wall. Word travels quickly. She examined my face, like a mother to a hurt child, and became furious. "We gonna fuck that dirty bitch up. Where the fuck is James?" she asked angrily.

"I don't give a fuck!"

"What happened, anyway?"

"I fought the bitch," I said, saying no more.

"I see that."

"Listen, she done and over wit'," I told her, trying to hold back the tears that began welling up in my eyes. I thought about James, and he was making me hysterical.

Camille looked at me, and I knew she saw the hurt in my face. "You okay?"

I tried to be strong, but my hard image collapsed when I heard a certain song airing over the radio that made me instantly think old times. It was Brian McKnight's "One Last Cry."

I lost it and broke down in front of my best friend. "Why don't he love me anymore?" I exclaimed. I had a river of tears streaming down my face. "I mean . . . I do so much for him, Camille, and he keeps dissin' me. Why? For that dirty bitch, Tasha. What the fuck she got over me? I'm supposed to be his woman."

"Fuck that bitch-ass nigga, Jade. You don't need him. He don't do shit for you, anyway. Right now he fuckin' up your life."

"Niggas are fucked up!" I cried out. "You do so much, and they still go out and cheat . . . fuck him . . . watch . . . watch. Camille, I'm gonna leave him, and he gonna miss me. He gonna miss me," I proclaimed. I broke into tears again and fell against the couch.

Camille came up to me, consoling me and saying that it was time for me to move on.

"You know what you need to do? Change the locks and keep his ass locked outside your crib. This is your place, Jade. I don't care if he helps you pay your rent. You do you, and kick his triflin' ass out. Stand up on your own two feet, Jade. If you need help with money, you know I got you."

"Thanks, Camille."

"You know what else is gonna make you feel a whole lot better," Camille said, smiling a devilish grin.

I looked at her with tears in my eyes and asked, "What?"

She got up, went into the bedroom, and soon came back out with arms full of James's clothing—Rocawear, Sean John, Phat Farm, Versace, and other shit like that.

I let out a slight smile and asked, "What you gonna do wit' his shit?"

She walked up to the window, opened it, and tossed all of his designer clothing out the window. "That's what!" Camille said.

She encouraged me to do the same. I walked into the bedroom, grabbed a bunch of James's shit, and repeated Camille's action, tossing a bunch of his shit out the window, and seeing it spread out across the grass under my window. Camille and I repeated this for fifteen minutes. We threw everything—his Timberlands, Nikes, shoes, clothing, and even his jewelry—out the window, and I'm talking about platinum rings and chains, watches that were worth an easy five thousand dollars, and his PlayStation 2, including the fifty or so games he collected.

"You feel a little better?" Camille asked.

I took in a deep breath, and said, "Yeah. I'm okay now."

"Now you need to change the locks and put that bolt across your door," she suggested.

"Believe me, I will." I had to. I knew that when James came home and saw his shit out the window like that, he was gonna flip. But I wasn't scared. He touch me, I'll get his ass fucked up.

Camille hung around until evening came. I felt safe around her, but when she left, my fear surfaced again. I knew James was gonna be furious. So for protection, I retrieved a kitchen knife and kept it gripped in my hand all evening.

I sat listening to the radio and thought about my options. Yeah. James paid my bills, and he took care of me, but was it worth getting dissed and having him constantly beat on me, and pretending to be happy? Can this really be my life? Was I blinded by a big dick and a fine-looking face? I went into the bathroom and peered at my reflection. "Jade, you're too beautiful to be puttin' up wit' this shit." I needed to find a real man who would appreciate me. James, he didn't appreciate me. He said he loves me, but if what he gave out to me was love, then what was hate?

I glanced at the wall clock and saw that it was a little after eight. I sealed the door with the bolt going across it, thinking, *Will that do any good keeping James's ass out when he comes home?*

I went into the bedroom and searched for Officer Reese's card. I thought it was time for that call. I picked up the cordless and slowly dialed his cell phone number. The phone rung about three times until I heard, "Hello, Officer Reese?"

I didn't answer right away.

"Hello?" he repeated.

"Officer Reese . . . Hello, it's Jade," I said. I was now the nervous one.

"Hey, it's about time you called. How's everything going?" he asked. He was excited hearing my voice.

"It could be better," I said.

"Oh. You're not in any trouble?" he asked with concern.

"Everyday is a problem for me," I replied. "Are you at work right now?"

"Yeah, but I'm on lunch. We can talk."

"I don't wanna get you in any trouble."

"No, not at all. I definitely have time to talk to you."

I smiled. It was nice hearing someone say that they had time for me. I became quiet over the phone, not knowing what to say.

"Jade, you still there?" Officer Reese asked.

"I'm still here, Officer Reese."

"Hey, do me one favor, don't keep referring to me as Officer Reese. If we're gonna be friends, then you need to start calling me Casey.

"That's a nice name."

"It's cute . . . thank you."

I became quiet again. James crawled into my thoughts. I wanted to feel safe. I guess that's why I called up Officer Reese. I wanted to hear his voice, and to be honest, I wanted to feel protected.

"Jade, you're quieting up on me again. Are you sure you're okay?"

"Yeah. Everything's okay," I lied.

"Do you need me to come by there and check up on you?"

"There's no need for that. I'm a big girl."

He tittered, "Well—"

"Oh, you starting to have jokes about my size already," I joked.

"Nah, it wasn't even like that."

I smiled and chuckled just a little, getting my mind off of James somewhat.

"So, Jade, when are we gonna go out? I wanna have a decent date with you. I want to see you."

"When are you off?"

"I'm off next week—Thanksgiving, and that Friday too."

"I'm good then too. But I know you'll probably want to spend Thanksgiving with your family."

"I do, but you know what, I want you to come along too," he suggested. I was shocked.

"What? . . . Uh. I can't, Officer Reese."

"Hey, hey, what I tell you about calling me Officer Reese?"

"Okay, I'm sorry, Casey. But I can't meet your family. You don't know me like that."

"Jade, how can we be friends if I can't bring you around my family? Hey, as long as you're black, a female, and completely beautiful, my peoples won't mind. They are gonna love you."

I sighed. He didn't know me from a hole in the wall, and here he was willing to introduce me to his people that easily. I felt somewhat flattered, but I was nervous.

"I'll do it . . . but under one condition," I stated.

"And what's that?"

"That we see each other before Thanksgiving," I told him.

"Okay, not a problem. I'm definitely looking forward to it," he cheerfully said.

"Okay."

"When? I work the three-to-eleven shifts in the day. So we can meet before my shift or after my shift. You decide."

"How about after your shift? I'll meet you somewhere."

"That's cool with me. You pick the place."

"I was hopin' you would," I said.

"Um . . . do you know where Chantell's is at on Merrick?"

"Yeah, of course."

"Okay, meet me there Monday night around midnight. It gives me time to run home and freshen up for you."

"Monday night around midnight it is," I repeated.

"So, I'm definitely looking forward to seeing you," Casey said.

"Same here," I told him.

I hung up with a smile on my face. But that smile and warm feeling were short-lived, when I suddenly heard banging and James shouting at my door.

"Jade! Bitch, you fuckin' crazy! Bitch, open up this fuckin' door! You threw all of my shit out of the goddamn window. Bitch, I'll fuckin' kill you!" he shouted from behind the bolted door like a fucking madman. The only thing that kept him from entering the apartment and coming at me was the bolt I put across the door from the inside. He had the door unlocked, but he couldn't push it in any further; the dead bolt prevented him from pushing his way into the crib.

I screamed and reached for my knife.

"James, go away. I don't want you here!" I yelled. I was terrified.

"Jade, open the fuckin' door!" he yelled, kicking and banging against the door, trying to force entry. "Bitch, you must be stupid! Open the fuckin' door now, Jade. Open the fuckin' door, you stupid bitch!"

Every time I heard his threats and screams, I cringed and scurried into a corner, crying and fearing for my life.

"James, go away before I call the cops!" I yelled. "I'm not fuckin' playin' wit' you anymore! I'm callin' the cops on you. I don't want you here anymore!"

"Why you had to throw my shit out the window like that? You fuckin' over-reactin', Jade. It ain't that damn serious!"

"Yes, it is," I countered.

"Bitch, I ain't goin' no-fuckin'-where. I live here too. Who put you up to this? That bitch, Camille, huh . . . she did this? She told you to toss my shit out the fuckin' window like that? She can get it too. . . . *Now open up this fuckin' door now, bitch!*" He screamed so loud and kicked the door so hard that I thought he actually succeeded and made his way into the room.

"James, go away . . . please . . . go the fuck away!" I had the phone gripped in my hand and was tempted to press 911.

"Hey, I'm callin' the cops!" I heard a neighbor shout. "It ain't no need for all this goddamn racket up in this building."

"Bitch, I'm comin' back!" James said.

I was balled up in the corner, crying, with a kitchen knife gripped in one hand and the cordless in the other. I was shaking, and actually fearing for my life. James was crazy. And I didn't know what to do.

I stayed scrunched up in the corner for several moments, trying to get myself together. My tears stopped, and I got up, went to the door, and saw that James almost succeeded in kicking in the door. It was almost pushed back and looking soon to come off the hinges. I sighed. I had to get out. I had to do sumthin'. I knew for sure that I didn't want to end up on the ten-o'clock news one night.

~ CHAPTER 15 ~

camille

You and her did that . . . fo' real?" Cream asked in disbelief. I told him about Jade's situation and how fucked up James was, so we had to toss all of his shit out the window. He laughed about it.

"Yeah, we did. . . . Fuck that nigga. He ain't gonna keep disrespectin' my girl like that, and keep thinkin' he gonna keep gettin' away wit' it. She had to make a stand. So I helped her," I said, my voice sounding a bit irate.

Cream smiled as he drove, clutching the steering wheel and peering out the windshield. We were on Long Island, on a Sunday evening, and it was a beautiful day out, despite the cold. I was happy being with Cream.

"Camille, you a gully ass, bitch. . . . No disrespect," he proclaimed.

"None taken."

"Yo, I feel you, though any man that puts a hand on his woman, or any woman at all, should be put in the fuckin' ground . . . fo' real. I don't play that. He ain't beefin' wit' you, right?" Cream asked.

"Nah. He don't fuck wit' me. But he fuckin' wit' my homegirl, and if you fuck wit' her, then that's like messin' wit' me. Jade and I, we sistas. We tight. We like family. . . . Nah, fuck that, we *is* family," I stated proudly.

"I hear that. Sometimes your peoples close to you can be all you got in this world . . . and that's why you stick by them through thick and thin," Cream said, glancing at me.

"I feel you," I replied, smiling. "And that bitch, Tasha—mark my words, Cream . . . she gonna get hers. I'm gonna get at that bitch personally. I can't stand that fuckin' ho! The bitch is triflin'."

"Camille, just don't get your ass locked up, okay?"

"You know me, Cream—I'm gonna do it right."

We drove for a few more minutes, without saying a word to each other. I peered out the window and thought about my girl Jade and praying she was okay. I knew if some shit popped off, my cell phone woulda been ringing like crazy.

"So, Camille, you thought about goin' with me to California?" Cream asked, breaking the silence.

Damn Cali, I thought. "I'm still thinkin' about it," I said.

"Camille, don't let this opportunity pass you by. I want you out there, baby. I need you out there."

"I know, Cream. But I'm worryin' about my friends, and I want them to be okay if I decide to go out there with you."

"Jade and Shy can handle themselves. You ain't their mother. You can't be there forever, lookin' out after them. They chose their way, and you gotta go yours. I'm not sayin' to dis 'em, but later on, you gotta let them be."

I sighed.

"Think about it, Camille. Don't let anyone hold you back from doin' what you gotta do and movin' on with your life.

Jamaica housin', it ain't forever. Some people move on, and some don't. Don't get stuck in that realm where you feel the projects is gonna be your home forever and there ain't anythin' better fo' you. There's always sumthin' better."

"I know, Cream . . . but . . ."

"No buts, Camille. Stop second-guessin' yourself, do you, don't let anyone else do it fo' you. Stop thinkin' about others, and start thinkin' about yourself, and your life. You gotta make yourself happy."

Cream was right. I needed to make myself happy. I needed to start doing me. I couldn't be around Shy and Jade forever. The drama in New York was really stressing a bitch out. I sighed, wishing everything could be so easy.

We turned into a twenty-four-hour diner on a busy street. It was early evening, and I haven't eaten all day. I was ready to order everything on the menu as soon as we stepped in.

Cream parked the car, and I stepped out, zipping up my coat, because the wind picked up very heavy in the past hour.

"Shit, it's gettin' cold out here," I muttered.

"Man, this ain't nuthin' but some refrigerator weather," Cream said, having on a not-too-heavy jacket. He wore a black Sean John jacket, which was unzipped, and he was looking unaffected by the cold wind.

"Baby, you ain't cold?" I asked.

"Nah, I was born in this. You know my birthday is in January."

"Yeah. I know. But I don't want you catchin' a cold and gettin' sick on me," I said to him in a concerned way.

"I'm built like a rock, baby. Let's go eat."

He proceeded toward the diner, and I was a few steps behind him. As I walked, somethin' caught my attention. Right across the street was a motel, and I saw a Hummer, one just like James has, pull into the parking lot. I observed the H2 for a moment and noticed a woman who looked just like Shy from a distance stepping out from the passenger's side.

Nah, it ain't—it couldn't be, I thought. But when I saw James come from behind the driver's side and put his arm around a woman who looked like Shy, that confirmed my suspicion.

"That bitch!" I muttered. I stared at them, shocked. Nah, she ain't go there. Had she? She wouldn't. If Shy disrespected Jade like that, yo, I swear—

"Camille, you comin' in or what?" Cream asked. I caught myself standing in the middle of the parking lot with my full attention focusing on the motel across the street.

"Yeah, I thought I saw something, that's all," I explained. I walked forward, and when I glanced over across the street, I saw James staring over my way. I wondered if he saw me. Shit, I hope so—let that muthafucka know he busted. And Shy, I was going to have a serious talk with her when I get home.

Cream asked no questions. We strolled into the diner and were quickly seated. We ordered our meals minutes after our arrival. I sat, being quiet and thinking how trifling and fucked up that was to see James and Shy getting a room together out here on Long Island where they thought no one was around and that no one was watching. It was a small world, and I've learned, what you do in the dark will later come out in the light.

Cream dropped me off in front of my building around midnight. He had to run out to Manhattan and take care of business. He asked me to come along, but I declined. I was tired, had a full stomach, and my mind was occupied with what I saw out on Long Island. Shy and James, they had to be fucking; there ain't no other reason for the two of 'em to be together and alone, getting a motel room early in the evening.

"So, I'm gonna call you," Cream said, reclined on his leather seat, with the volume on the stereo turned down. He stared at me with his beautiful brown eyes.

"You better."

"And think about it, Camille. I want you out in Cali with me. It's gonna be good fun," he stated.

"Give me time. I'll have an answer for you in a few days."

He sighed. "A'ight. Take care of what you gotta take care of, and get back at me," he said, with his enthusiasm trailing off toward me.

I kissed him good night and stepped out of his ride, smiling. He drove off slowly. I stood in front of my building, watching him leave, until he disappeared turning the corner.

I blew out air, kinda missing him already. The cold air suddenly picked up, and I rushed into the lobby, clutching tightly my coat and my purse. It was quiet and still around, and kinda eerie. I've walked into my building dozens and dozens of times alone during nights like tonight, and I never felt afraid or awkward. People, especially all the thugs and stick-kids knew me, and they left me alone, never fucking with me. But tonight, I felt uncomfortable, having a feeling that someone was watching me, like someone was close by. But being me, I tried to shrug it off and went for the elevator, pressing for it, and instantly, the thick black elevator door slid back into the wall and allowed entrance. I quickly stepped in. I went to press for my floor, having my side turned against the door, but suddenly noticed movement from my peripheral vision. Before I could react, the shadowy figure quickly swooped in with me, and viciously pushed me against the wall of the elevator. He gripped my right arm and twisted it around my back, and brandished a huge sharp knife next to my face.

"Don't you fuckin' move, bitch!" he threatened. I could smell his breath, with his face an inch or two from mines. He had my face and chest pressed tightly against the wall, with his large body compressed against me. I tried to cry out, but the force he used, made me whimper. I couldn't reach for the blade I had hidden in my pocket for protection, for moments just like this one.

"Bitch . . . you like to be in other people business, huh? You ain't so fuckin' tough now, bitch. Go ahead, try sumthin', and I'll slice you the fuck open," he warned with his voice low but fearsome and raspy. He tightened his grip on me, causing me to cry out.

"This is a warnin', you dumb bitch: Stay the fuck out of James's business! You think you slick, havin' his shit thrown out the window?"

My eyes began to tear up, and I wanted him off me. I was alone with this lunatic, and there was not a soul around.

"Mind your fuckin' business!" he continued. "If you don't, then I'm comin' back, bitch!" He pressed the knife against the side of my face. It was cold. Then he cupped my breast with the knife in his hand and licked the side of my face. Then he took off, and I never got a good look at him.

I cried out, dropping to the floor. I was in shock. I lived in these projects all my life, and I never had an incident like that ever happened to me.

I didn't get up right away. I just rested down on the dirty

stained elevator floor and tried to get my composure together. To say that I was mad or upset was an understatement.

After I got myself together, I pressed for my floor, and the door closed. I reached into my purse and thought about calling Cream, but thought against it and placed my cell back into my purse. Cream was probably halfway out to Manhattan by now, and beside, I knew how to handle my business. I wasn't gonna let James and his punk crew intimidate me. Fuck that! Jade was my business. So whatever happens to her happens to me.

I wasn't hurt, but I was a bit shaken. It took me a while to get to my apartment door, but I made it there and walked into my dark apartment. Soon as I got in, I went straight for the bathroom and turned on the shower. I stripped and quickly jumped in the tub. I wanted this nigga's smell off me right away.

As I stood under the running shower, I got angry at myself. How could I allow myself to be so vulnerable? I should have known better than that. I should have been more alert with my surroundings. I had gotten careless. But I wished I was able to see that nigga's face clearly. I was only able to hear his voice and get a quick profile; the rest of him was a mystery to me.

But I wasn't gonna sit in my apartment and cry all night. I knew who sent him, and it was payback. James had fucked with the wrong bitch.

~ CHAPTER 16 ~

shy

For James, one night turned into two, and two turned into three. I knew he had had a serious falling out with Jade, but he didn't get into details with me. I tried calling Jade a few times to see what went down, but I kept getting her voice mail and her answering machine at the apartment. I called Camille, too, and it was the same with her. *What's going on?* I thought to myself.

It felt funny having James spend continuous nights with me. He came knocking on my door a few days ago and asked if he could stay, and my dumb ass told him yes, and now he up in my place like he's Roscoe.

But the sad thing was that I allowed James to set up shop in my apartment, so he could produce and package that crack/cocaine he sold on the streets. He promised to break me off some money from the profits. He came into my place with a stranger, and quickly set up a small area in the kitchen where he and his friend began cooking up the drugs. I never saw it done before, and even though Roscoe was in the drug business, he kept me away from it. Roscoe said he never wanted me involved. Roscoe never disrespected our home by bringing in any drugs or anything related to drugs. The most he kept in our apartment was one or two guns, and about ten thousand dollars in cash. He knew that if our place ever got raided because of a snitch, his home would be clean, and the feds couldn't touch me.

But James was the opposite. He had, in my kitchen, about one kilo of pure raw coke, baking soda, pots and pans, boiling water, razors and knives, and about five dozen small vials to put the crack into after it was cooked.

The man James brought into my apartment was gaunt, with a long thin face and dirty fingernails. He looked like he smoked the same shit he was cooking up. I gave James a disapproving look about bringing this man into my home, but James just shrugged it off.

After a week of them cooking up and bottling the crack, I noticed the stranger getting high in the corner of my kitchen. I flipped out and was about to knock him upside his head with a frying pan. But James stopped me, told me to let Rico do his thang; he worked hard and needed a quick break. I cried out to James, told him I was stressed. I was scared. He gave me a hug, and then said the unthinkable to me: "Shy, you wanna take a hit? It will do you some good." I couldn't believe that he just asked me to smoke crack. "Yo, Shy, this shit will get your mind off of a lot of shit. I know you stressed right now, baby. Let me take care of you."

He pulled me into the bedroom. I forgot about Rico getting high in the kitchen, and allowed James to slowly undress me. He pulled off my sweats, then my panties, and began eating me out. I moaned loudly as James fucked me with his tongue and fingered me at the same time. Then he got undressed and thrust his big dick into me—once again, no condom. But I didn't care. I was so enthralled with the dick that I let him cum in me repeatedly. Afterward, James lay beside me and said, "Yo, take a hit of this." He had a crack pipe in his hand. I was skeptical. I had forgotten about Rico getting high in my kitchen.

"Shy, you know I ain't gonna let nothing happen to you. I got so much love for you," James said. "Trust me, this is just a lil' sumthin' to help you get your mind off of shit. I'm letting you smoke this for free, because I care about you."

I looked at him.

He continued, "If you don't like it, you ain't gotta try it again. But it ain't gonna hurt to try it once. I do it sometimes too."

He passed me the pipe and I reluctantly took it into my hands. James smiled.

"It's gonna make me feel better?" I asked.

"Trust me, you'll forget about your problems quick."

I looked at the pipe, and James lit it with a lighter, heating it up. The crack sounded like Rice Krispies crackling. I slowly put my lips to the glass dick, and inhaled. I suddenly felt this exhilarating rush. James smiled. "That's my gurl." He then disappeared under the covers, spread my legs, and buried his face in my pussy. I moaned. My legs began to quiver.

"Hit that shit again," James said. And I did. I put the pipe to my lips and inhaled, this time even stronger. I panted, feeling James's soft lips devouring me from below. I felt my heart racing, I felt a sudden rush, and then it happened. I cried out loudly and had a strong orgasm. I knew my neighbor heard me. I clutched the sheets tightly and panted again and again.

"Take one more hit, baby," James said. He emerged from underneath the sheets and looked at me. "Feels good, right?"

I didn't respond. I was in a trance. I didn't know if it was the crack, or if it was James's skills down below.

"I'm gonna make you feel good tonight," James said. He climbed in between my legs and penetrated my walls again, causing me to gasp. I picked up the pipe one last time, and took another big hit. James smiled and said, "Didn't I tell you that shit was gonna make you feel really fuckin' good?"

I was high. "Fuck me, baby!" I cried out. I wrapped my legs around James and clawed at his back. He pushed his dick into me hard and fast. I swear, this nigga made it feel like the earth was shaking. We fucked for an hour straight, and after that, a bitch couldn't move. I was done. I no longer cared about Rico getting high in my kitchen. I was high and numb.

I was beginning to worry about people talking, because in the projects, ain't nothing a secret, especially when you're screwing around with your best friend's man. I didn't want any beef, especially with my girls, Jade and Camille. But the dick—ohmygod, the dick. James was pushing that shit deep into me night after night, and had a bitch hooked, or addicted like I was a dope fiend with the needle stuck deep in my arm. And the way he ate pussy, he had me clawing at walls, especially last night when he threw me over his shoulder and told me to touch the ceiling as he hoisted me up in the air and had a bitch howling as he dined between my legs. I ain't gonna lie; James had the biggest dick I ever saw. I mean, Roscoe was good—he's my man and all—but shit, I know it's fucked-up to say, but he ain't home right now, and a sista like myself needed her itch scratch once in a while.

I missed my visit with Roscoe last week. I got caught up in some things. But he still calls me every other night around eight, and I still accept all of his collect calls. He beefed with me about not coming to visit him last week, but I lied and told him some bullshit excuse and promised I'd visit him around Thanksgiving. I never told him that I lost my job. I was scared to.

I was trying to be careful, because I knew I was playing with fire. But I was lonely at nights, and it felt good waking up to a warm hard body next to me and rolling myself over on some dick and getting me some. I had toys, but they could only take me but so far.

Thanksgiving was right around the corner, and I had nothing planned and nowhere to go. I wanted as much company as I can have.

I glanced at the time and saw that it was fifteen minutes past eight. I knew Roscoe would be calling soon, but that didn't mean I told James to stop, as he had my legs spread and went back and forth from eating out my pussy to my asshole, sticking his tongue in both and causing me to grunt, pant, clutch the sheets, and feeling heaven out this bitch.

"Oooh, don't stop . . . don't stop . . . do that shit . . . yes, yes . . . oh, shit . . . eat that pussy, eat that ass . . . right there, yes . . . RIGHT THERE."

James had me animated. I gripped his shoulders. I squeezed my breasts. I clutched the sheets and pillows. The nigga had me on cloud nine right now—oh, God.

Suddenly the phone rang, and I knew it was Roscoe. James stopped and lifted his head up from between my dripping thighs.

"It's Roscoe," I said, breathing heavy. "Ssshhhh. He can't hear anybody in the room with me," I told him.

"I'll be in the living room," James said, leaving my bedroom with his bare ass showing.

I picked up after the fifth or sixth ring.

"You have a collect call from . . . Roscoe Richardson . . . if you accept, please—"

"I accept!" I hollered into the receiver, not giving the operator time to finish her speech.

"Hello."

"Hey, baby," I said with joy. I propped myself against the headboard, my pussy still throbbing for some more action.

"Shy, what's good? You comin' to see me soon, I hope?" he asked.

"Yeah. I missed you. How you holdin' up?"

"I'm good. My next day in court is December seventh. You gonna be there?"

"I'll try."

"What you mean, you'll try? I want you there."

"Why you still in court? I thought you took a plea?"

"Yeah, well, my attorney came up wit' some good news. Remember when I told you that there was a gun? Well, forensic unfolded vital evidence that the nigga I shot had fired off a gun that night. They did some test, and some shit came up positive in his right hand."

"Are you serious?"

"Yeah, but it's too early to celebrate now. I'm still goin' through motions and shit. And guess what, some nigga picked up the shell casin' from a .380. My lawyer tryin' to investigate deep into this shit. Yo, I think somebody tried to set me up, Shy."

"What? Why?"

"I don't know. You know how niggas hate on me out there. I make money, and some hardheaded niggas want me out, so they can move in. But when all the bullshit is done, Shy, I'm gonna find out who . . . That's my word; we gonna see what's up."

Hearing this brought hope and a smile on my face. Ohmygod, if everything goes good, my baby might be coming home earlier than expected.

"So what is your lawyer sayin'?" I asked.

"He sayin' don't go celebratin' yet. I still might have to do some time for the gun charge and other shit. He sayin' everythin' is a hunch right now about me being set up, but he got NYPD lookin' hard into it. Word, Shy—my lawyer is worth every fuckin' penny I'm payin' him."

I smiled.

"So what you doin' right now?" he asked, changing the topic.

"Me?"

"No, I'm talkin' to the fuckin' Easter Bunny," he replied sarcastically.

"Why you gotta get smart?"

"Because, why you asking, 'Me?' when you're the only one on the phone?"

"Please. Well if you wanna know, I'm naked and I'm lyin' in bed."

"Naked? What you doin' naked?" Roscoe said, sounding a bit upset.

"Because I knew you were going to call, and I wanted to be naked and maybe have sex with you over the phone," I lied.

"Oh, word? That's what's up," he said, sounding so happy.

"I got my legs spread for you, baby," I said enticingly, reaching my hand down my stomach and in between my thighs.

"Damn, Shy. Yo, I'm missin' you like crazy, love. . . . You don't know."

"Word, you missin' me, baby . . . you missin' the punanny? You wanna smell the punanny?" I asked seductively.

"Yeah, put your pussy to the phone," he said, sounding a bit desperate.

I took the cordless and placed it between my thighs, and said out loud, "You hear the punanny callin' you, baby?"

"Yeah, I hear it," I heard him shout.

I started playing with my pussy, with the phone near my goods. I placed two fingers inside of me and moaned out loud. "Oooh, it's wet for you, baby. It's wet. I got my fingers in my pussy, and it wants you. I want you, baby. . . . Oooh, yes . . . Roscoe . . . yes."

"Damn, Shy . . . you gonna have a nigga plan an escape, you keep fuckin' around like that!" he said.

I laughed. I placed the phone near my ear and said, "You like that?"

"Oh, shit. Hells, yeah. Damn, you got my hand in my pants jerkin' off to you, Shy."

"You by yourself?" I asked.

"Nah, not really . . . but niggas don't give a fuck up in here. Shit, it's either this or get at one of these homo-thugs up in here."

"Oh."

"And you know I ain't tryin' to swing that way, no matter how many years I get."

"That's right, baby. Pussy for life."

"Yeah," he chuckled.

"I missin' you so fuckin' much, Roscoe," I proclaimed. I suddenly found myself getting a little emotional.

"Don't worry, Shy. We gonna be good again. I promise. But,

yo, let me get off this jack, I know they about to cut my shit short. But I love you, baby."

"I love you too, Roscoe."

Our conversation was soon over. And right after, James stepped into the room. It brought me back to reality.

"Roscoe's cool?" he asked.

I didn't say a word. I looked up at him with a few tears trickling from my eyes. My guilt surfaced again. Here I was fucking his boy while he was locked away and expressing his love for me. Oh, God, I was trippin'.

James came swinging his dick back into the bedroom, and sat down next to me. He placed his hand on my thigh and rubbed it gently.

"So where did we leave off?" he said, amused and shit.

I gave him an unpleasant look. Was he serious?

"Please. Not now." I got up off the bed and reached for my robe.

"What you mean not now? I'm fuckin' hard, and you were ready to go at it a moment ago. But all of a sudden, Roscoe calls and you frontin' on me, Shy. C'mon."

"James, I got a lot of shit on my mind right now. And besides, ain't you curious to hear about what he had to say?"

"Yeah. What did he tell you, anyway? Y'all were up in here chattin' it up kind of lively."

"He told me some good news. He said that if shit goes right, they might drop the murder charges. His attorney says that he believes Roscoe was set up, and that the man he murdered, they found out he did actually fire a gun at Roscoe. His attorney is doin' a heavy investigation."

"Oh, word . . . that's what's up," James said, nonchalantly.

"I know."

"That's cool," James said, getting up from the bed and walking up to me. My eyes never left his. He came up to me and placed his hands against my waist, slowly moving me toward him.

"James," I said.

"What?" he answered devilishly as he smiled.

"I just talked to Roscoe."

"And?"

"And I don't feel right about this right now," I straight up told him.

"You fuckin' serious? You're startin' to feel fuckin' guilty after we done fucked countless of times—you ain't give a fuck about your man then."

"Neither did you," I countered smartly.

"C'mon Shy, be fo' real."

"I am. Please . . . can you leave for the night? I want to be alone," I proclaimed. I was stunned. I actually told him—and myself—that I wanted to be alone for the night.

He stared at me. And the look on his face frightened me.

"Why the fuck you actin' like a bitch for, Shy? This nigga calls and—"

"James, just one night, please. . . . That's all I'm asking. I just wanna get my head straight. I just wanna be alone for one night."

"You know what? Fuck it!" He stormed past me, picked up his clothing, and started to get dress. I sighed in relief, thinking that there was going to be trouble. But I was wrong.

James got dressed quickly. He threw on his Timberlands and coat and went for the door. He left without a good-bye. After he left, I felt a tad better. I just couldn't fuck him tonight, after the conversation I had with Roscoe. It didn't feel right. I wanted this night to belong to Roscoe; it was his night, even though he wasn't here with me physically. I felt him. I wanted to celebrate the small accomplishment that his attorney made over his case. It was a start, and a very good start. Maybe all the charges against Roscoe will be drop, I thought. Shit, you never know. It can happen.

I called up Jade first; I wanted to share with her the news. I called her crib and she picked up, finally.

"Hey, girl," I hollered, sounding joyous.

"Hey, Shy," she answered, not seeming to be in the same mood that I was in. Then the thought of her man just now leaving my crib crept into my thoughts, and I felt fucked up. "What's goin' on?" she asked.

"I just talked to Roscoe." I lowered my enthusiasm a bit, with my conscience eating away at me.

"Oh, yeah. He okay?"

"Yeah. He informed me that they might drop the murder charges against him."

"You serious? What happened?"

"A bunch of bullshit, that's what happened. He might be coming home sooner, Jade," I stated.

"I'm so happy for you. But don't get all bent up about this just yet, Shy. . . . You know I'm not tryin' to rain on your parade, but be there for him. It's a start, like you said, but anythin' can go wrong."

"I know Jade. I know."

Jade became quiet. I heard her breathing over the phone, and I got curious. So I opened up my big mouth and asked, "What happened between you and James?"

She sighed heavily. "You ain't talk to Camille?" she inquired.

"No. Not recently," I said.

"Same ol' bullshit, Shy. He a fuckin' asshole, that's what. I'm so done wit' him."

"Damn."

"Listen, Shy, I gotta go. I don't mean to cut you short, but I got a lot of shit to do tomorrow morning, and I need some rest."

"I understand, girl. I'm gonna call you later."

"Call Camille, Jade. She'll put you on about what went down," Jade said.

"A'ight."

After I hung up with her, I called Camille's cell, but there was no answer. I called her apartment next, and I got the same results.

I decided to call it a night. I stared at a framed picture of Roscoe and me while I rested on the bed, and I started writing him a poem.

So many things I wish that I could say.
So many things I wished that we could play.
So many words that's stuck deep in my head.
I keep asking myself, how I can express myself
to my man in the most sensitive way.
Say to him, my man is irreplaceable and insatiable,
the two ingredients that make you sensational.

~ CHAPTER 17 ~

jade

It was Monday night, and I was nervous about meeting Casey in a few hours. He'd called earlier to confirm our date, and I told him I'd be there.

I haven't seen or spoken to James since he tried to kick in my door, and that was a few days ago. I tried not to become wary and frightened of my boyfriend, but I couldn't help it. James could become a lunatic when he's upset. He has a really dark and ugly side to him. And it was dangerous. He had a history of violence, and many people in the neighborhood feared him. I've seen the worst in him, and I've seen the best in him.

Saturday, I had the locks changed. I was fortunate that Earl, the locksmith, made time out of his busy schedule to come do me a favor. Earl's shop on Guy Brewer always closed around two in the afternoon. But he came by my way a little after three to change all of my locks. I was grateful. He really saved my life. I knew Earl through my mother, and he watched me grow up, and as long as I could remember, Earl had that shop located on Guy Brewer forever. He was a really nice guy. He was from Barbados and been in the neighborhood for over thirty years now.

He was in his mid-fifties, had a thick gray beard, and was a stout man with a receding hairline. I remember him always having a crush on my mother.

But Earl, he would always warn me about James, saying, "Jade, that boy no good for you . . . ya hear? You're young woman. . . . You need to go out and find you a Bajan, and stop dealin' wit' deese Yankee boys, ya hear?" You could still hear a bit of his Bajan accent as he talked.

I smiled. And thanked him. Earl was one of the few folks that never feared James. If he saw James, Earl would tell James about himself, straight up, not caring about James's street reputation.

I glanced at the time and saw that it was 11 p.m. I'd just gotten out the shower and was in the bedroom preparing for my date. I'd barely leave my apartment anymore, fearing I might run into James. So I tried my best to stay indoors. And it was fucked up that I had to live my life like this. I was scared to go out for food or anything else. But it was November and cold outside, so I knew I wasn't missing much on a daily basis. But still, the predicament that I was in was un-fuckin'-believable. But tonight, I was willing to risk running into James to see Casey. He was a cop, but I no longer cared. He was cool, generous, and nice.

I didn't know what to wear for the occasion. I had a closet full of clothes, and I was wedged, not knowing what to put on. I searched from drawer to drawer, and examined my closet fully—something casual, or street, maybe a little formal? I thought, *Fuck it, something nice, lay back, but still classy.* I threw on my white turtleneck sweater, a pair of tight jeans, and my knee-high black-with-cream-trim leather spectator boots with the stiletto heels. Now all I had to do was throw on my black leather jacket, and I was good to go. My twists were done, and I had just the right makeup on. I peered at myself in the mirror and loved my image.

I called a cab earlier, and they said twenty minutes. Some cabs don't come around here no more, fearing they might get robbed or beat up, sometimes even murdered—but my cabbie, he was cool, and he grew up around here, so he never feared his neighborhood. We dated when we were fifteen. But other than that, whenever I needed a ride somewhere, all I had to do was call Johnny up, and he'd come by just like that.

It was fifteen minutes to midnight. And I was waiting for that call. I poured myself a quick drink and waited around in the living room.

The phone rang. I quickly picked up, and it was my cabbie, telling me that he was outside. I told him I'd be out shortly. I grabbed my things, even a small razor for protection in case James or any other asshole came strolling around.

I exit out my apartment with caution, observing my area and locking my door. I quickly strutted to the elevator. I didn't want to take the stairs, because sometimes there be too many crack-heads and hustlers lingering around, especially when it's cold outside, and plus I didn't like the smell of urine and I just didn't want to risk it.

The door opened on my floor, and I quickly stepped in. When the doors closed, I went into my purse and pulled out my small weapon just in case a bombshell was waiting for me down in the lobby. I was nervous as the elevator descended two floors.

I got to the lobby, and it was empty. I exhaled lightly, being relieved. I saw Johnny, my cabdriver, waiting for me out front. I walked hurriedly to my cab, and when I made it inside the car, I sighed with relief.

"Hey, Johnny," I said, getting comfortable in the backseat and closing the door.

"Hey, Jade. Where you goin' to?"

"Chantell's, up on Merrick Boulevard."

"Got you. Everythin' okay wit' you?"

"Yeah, I'm tryin' to be good . . . but you know, livin' here, drama is always around."

"I hear you, Jade."

He put the car in drive and moved forward. I rested against the old cracking leather seats and closed my eyes.

Johnny pulled up in front of Chantell's ten minutes later. The ride was quick. I gave him a ten and thanked him for the ride. Before I got out the car, he told me to be careful. He heard about my situation with James. I told him that I was all right and headed for the entrance.

Chantell's was a lounge and bar, and it was a cool place to chill, mingle, and stray away from home when you didn't feel like going. There were no lines, no bouncers out front, and no fleet of cars parked outside with drug dealers, thugs, and ballers profiling. If it was a Friday or a Saturday night, the place would have been swamped with people and business. But being that it was a Monday, Chantell's seemed more laid-back and tranquil.

I walked in, and it was damn near empty. There were a handful of folks scattered throughout the place, talking, eating, and drinking at the bar as a Destiny's Child song played throughout the place. No one paid me any attention when I walked in; it was like the wind just blew in.

Casey and I agreed to wait for each other at the bar, and there were two men already seated at the bar, and none of 'em was Casey. So I made my way over and ordered myself a quick drink while I waited. I glanced at the clock behind the bar, and it was 12:10. I knew he would be coming off work, so he needed time to change. I was reasonable.

By 12:25, I was becoming a little bit impatient. The female bartender tried to make conversation with me, saying she knew me from somewhere, but I couldn't place her face. I shrugged her off, and she went about her business.

I sighed, downing my second drink, and was about ready to pick myself up and leave. This nigga's wasting my time, I thought. I peered at myself in the hazily lit mirror behind the bar, gazing at my reflection between the Johnnie Walker bottle and the clear Armadale bottle.

Chantell's felt invisible—it wasn't even lively. It was like I wasted my time, and it was my idea to meet before Thanksgiving, and now I was having second thoughts about that too.

I rested my chin in the palm of my hand, with my elbow pressed against the bar counter, looking at myself—looking like a bored bitch.

"Honey, you okay?" the bartender asked.

"Yeah."

"You need another drink?"

"I'm still good wit' this one."

"Okay," she said, and then attended the other two men. She was a bit taller than me, with locks down to her back and dressed like she lived out in the Village.

I closed my eyes and pictured a better place, a better place for me and my soul mate, if he ever came. I heard George Michael singing "Father Figure" from the speakers that were situated over the bar. Father figure. I chuckled. I never knew my father. He abandon me and my moms when I was three, and his sorry ass never came back. My mother, she was my father. She raised me the best she knew how to. Shit, I remember my moms struggling trying to make ends meet day after day, working two, sometimes three jobs at a time. She always tried to be strong, but sometimes life would kick her in the ass and tell her to stay there.

When I was eight, that's when the men started coming around. The first one I remember meeting was Angus. He was nice, but not the best-looking man in the world. He was a bit stout, had short black hair, and was light-skinned. I always saw him in suits, never in streetwear. I guess he was a businessman or something. But every evening, Angus would come by, drop a twenty in my hand, and hang out with my mother. Every time I saw Angus, he had money to give, either to me or my mother. At nights, I would hear the both of 'em moaning and panting. I knew about sex at an early age, so it wasn't a shock to me, knowing what they were doing. I later found out that Angus, he was about business, but his business didn't take place in the corporate world; he handled business out in the streets, moving heroin like it was sugar. And I caught on to why my mother was dating him. He helped her with the bills, rent, and even spoiled her with jewelry, dinner, and money. Life was bringing her down, so she found a way to get around it, and that was through dating hustlers and having them take care of her. After a while, Angus stopped coming around, and I never asked my mother about him.

After Angus came Chaz. Now he was a pretty boy—light-skinned, with S-curls, tall with a medium build to him, and stayed looking nice in expensive clothing. He was the opposite from Angus; Chaz never wore suits. He always wore jeans,

Adidas, sweatsuits, and sported a lot of jewelry. When I first met him, I was ten, and I thought my mother hit the jackpot with him. He was cute. But he was a straight thug, and he wasn't nice like Angus. Some nights he could become an asshole and beat on my mother. But after the fights, he'd apologize to her and me and then shower our apartment with gifts like it was Christmas. But a week later, it would be the same old bullshit. It was like a recycling trend in our apartment: first there were the fights and, later on, an apology, and expensive gifts followed. But Chaz was shot in his head outside our building when I was eleven. I heard it was over a beef with a girl he was cheating with while he was dating my mother. Apparently, his mistress had an overzealous boyfriend with a hot temper.

After Chaz came Tommy, and after Tommy came Morris, Edwin, Justin, Alishma, and Angel—it was one hustler or thug after the other.

But my favorite and the most remembered man my mother dated was Kahlil. I was fifteen when my moms met Kahlil. He was a smooth-ass pretty-boy nigga. He was dark-skinned, sported a fade, drove two cars—a Porsche and a Benz—and dressed really nice in suits and street clothing. He carried nothing less than two grand or more on him at a time.

Kahlil was a few years younger than my mother, and a few years older than me, but the respect he received in the hood was unbelievable. Everybody, and I do mean everybody, gave him his props, from the young to the old. He was the hustler of hustlers. When my moms got with him, bitches started hating hard, because they were jealous of my mother being with him, and it trickled down to me.

Kahlil was only twenty-six, and already he owned grocery

stores, laundromats, restaurants, and a clothing store on Jamaica Avenue. He had so much money that he would buss me off with a G sometimes—why, because he could, and he did. My mother benefited lovely when she was fucking Kahlil. She was thirty-five at the time, and Kahlil bought my moms her first car, a '93 cherry red Benz, and all my moms had was her permit. The nigga even took us to fucking Disney World one summer. I was in shock.

With Kahlil around, I went to school every day fly, and having bitches wishing that they could be me. Niggas gave me respect, knowing that my mom was fucking with Kahlil. If I had a problem, Kahlil took care of it. He ran these niggas in South Jamaica like they were puppets on strings. When he told them to do something for him, they did it with a sense of urgency.

I developed the biggest crush on him. I think I loved him more than I loved my mother. But he always saw me as a fifteen-year-old girl, no matter how many years passed and how endowed my body became. To him, I was like his little sista. Because of Kahlil, I fell in love with that thug, that hustler, and that get-street money lifestyle. Kahlil was my image of the perfect man—smart, thuggish, cute, rich, and don't take shit from no one. He always treated my mother fair, even though he was still going around fucking other bitches. I saw him, and knew my man or my husband had to be just like him, or somewhat close to his image. Because Kahlil was an icon.

Kahlil fucked with my mother for three years. A few months before my high school graduation, the feds came down hard on Kahlil and his crew. They ransacked through his homes and took away all of his business. That drug lifestyle of his finally caught up to him, only because of two snitches who didn't want to go to jail for a very long time. So they gave up Kahlil and a few of his associates, and they charged him with A1 felonies, conspiracy, and the drug kingpin act, and Kahlil got twenty-five years in a federal prison.

I cried when he was found guilty and was sentenced. I think I took his incarceration harder than my mother did. But we kept in touch over the years, writing each other letters and sometimes talking over the phone. I tried supporting him during his time in lockup, and it was hard. Kahlil knew about James and me, and he had no beef with it. James wasn't no Kahlil, but he was definitely close.

I've dated and been around a lot of hustlers, players, killers, and even pimps in my short lifetime, and I found it to be ironic that I was waiting for a cop, my date, to show up. Not in a million years would I see myself going out with a cop. Growing up in my hood, police, 5.0, po-po, they were always the enemy; you don't fuck with police unless they were throwing you in the back of a squad car.

"Waiting for me?" Casey said, coming up behind me.

"It's about time—it's almost goin' on one." I said.

"I'm sorry, Jade, but I ran in late at the station. I promise I won't keep you waiting again."

"I was about to leave."

He smiled. "Thank you for waiting this long. I'll make it up to you. You had a drink already?"

"Two."

"Well, the rest are on me tonight. You want to get a table?"

"Yeah. I'm tired of sittin' at this bar."

I got up off my barstool and followed Casey toward the back. He looked nice tonight. This was my first time seeing him out of uniform. He had on loose-fitted blue jeans, brown and white Timberlands, a button-down, and a nice-looking brown leather jacket. He had a small thin chain with a small cross around his neck.

We took a seat at a nearby booth, with him sitting across from me.

I chuckled.

"What's so funny?" he asked.

"You look like one of the brothas from the hood dressed like that," I mentioned.

"Oh, really?"

"You don't look like a cop right now. You look good. I definitely like it." I smiled.

"Well, thank you. I'm flattered. You know the uniform does come off when I leave work," he joked.

"Ha, ha," I replied. "You got jokes."

"Nah, but this is me off duty. Relaxed and not tryin' to think about the job," he said, picking up the menu. "I'm human just like everybody else, Jade."

"So how long have you been a cop?" I asked.

"About five years now."

"You like bein' a cop?"

"It's cool. I feel the benefits are great. And the job's not boring, and I get to carry a gun."

"So, you're one of these action-adventurous types of men, who like to chase down bad guys, get into car chases, and duck bullets, thinkin' they Superman?" I said.

"Never been in a high-speed chase yet," he said, smiling, mocking me.

"You makin' fun of me?"

"Nah . . ."

"Yes, you are—stop it," I said, tittering.

He was cool, and his vibe was great.

"Might I add, Jade, that you're lookin' fine yourself. I love it. You're definitely beautiful," he said, causing me to blush.

"Stop messin' wit' me, Casey." I smiled more, trying to avoid eye contact with him.

"I'm glad we came on this first date," he said.

"Same here."

"So what you orderin'?" he asked, peering at me.

"You got nice eyes. I never really noticed them. What color . . . hazel?"

"I get 'em from my mother. . . . She's part Italian."

"You serious? You got Italian in your blood?"

"My father's black, and my mother's Italian. And please, no mob jokes."

"It wasn't even on my mind." I told him, laughing a little.

"So what about you—you askin' me about my life, I want to know about yours, Jade," Casey said, putting down the menu and focusing his attention completely on me.

"Ain't much to tell," I started. "I never knew my father; he bounced when I was three. And I grew up in the projects all my life. My mother, she's still around, livin' in South Carolina now, and doin' fine for herself."

"Any kids?"

"No," I quickly replied. I didn't want to bring up me losing my baby a few years ago. "What about you? Do you have any kids?"

"I have one. A son. His name is Randy. He's eight."

"That's nice. And what about the mother—is she still around?"

"Straightforward are we, huh? That's cool. Well, Candy, she's a lost cause. I tried being there for her, but she's a chickenhead."

"So, y'all not together?"

"We haven't been together in four years. My son stays with me or his grandmother. I'm raisin' him."

We ordered drinks and a few appetizers, and our conversation never stopped. Casey, he was very interesting. And he was fun to talk to. I was on my fourth drink.

"Casey, how old are you?" I asked.

He smiled. "How old do you think I am?"

I examined his face, his eyes. He was mature, responsible, and I knew he had to be in his twenties, I say late twenties. "Twenty-eight," I blurted.

He smiled. "I'm twenty-five."

"What . . . fo' real? And you became a cop when you were twenty, I guess."

"Hey, you're listenin'. That's cool."

"So, if you're twenty-five now, and your son is eight, damn . . . you must have had him when you were—"

"Seventeen," he chimed in.

"Damn, you were young," I said.

"Yeah. I was young, foolish, and a wild boy back then."

"Where you from, anyway?"

"I grew up in Brooklyn . . . Brownsville."

"What made you become a cop?" I asked, taking a sip from my drink.

"I don't really know. I just saw that they were hirin', and took the test one day. I never took it serious. Shit, I never though I'd pass and make it this far. But I did, became a rookie cop, and now it's been five years and I'm workin' at the Hundred third."

"You grew up in Brownsville. I knew a nigga out there."

"Really. Y'all dated?"

"Nah. He was friends with my cousins. But he was into drugs real heavy," I said.

"You like them thug niggas, right?" he questioned.

"What makes you say that?"

"I see it in you. That's your preferences."

"I'm sayin' . . . thugs and hustlers are the only men I know. I grew up around them. My mother dated them. My friends, my cousins . . ."

"So have you ever dated someone like me?"

"No. But then again, I don't really know you like that; you may turn out to be a knucklehead just like the rest of 'em. You dress like one. But so far, you gain some positive points around me."

He smiled. "Jade, not to be in your personal business, but what's up wit' you and your situation?"

"What situation?" I replied, naïve about the question.

"Jade, I hate to ask . . . but are you in an abusive relationship?"

"Please, nigga, why you bringin' the shit up on our first date? I was havin' a good time wit' you."

"I'm not trying to cause you to be upset—"

"Then don't!" I barked, leaning back against the padded chair and catching an attitude.

"Listen. I just met you, but I care about you, and I'm tellin' you the truth. The only reason why I'm bringin' it up is because I don't want to see you get hurt or worse—"

"Listen, Casey . . . I know how to take care of myself. Nigga, it ain't your business anyway," I spat, getting ghetto on his ass. "Is this the reason you brought me here, to fuckin' investigate my ass, huh?"

"No, no . . . please, I didn't mean to offend you," he apologized. "I just wanted to talk."

I was sighing, crossing my arms, and was about ready to get up and leave, and have him sitting here by himself. I didn't want to think about James tonight, but here Casey was, bringing my drama up and reminding me of the bullshit that I was going through at home. Sitting with Casey was the one time I actually felt peaceful and safe, and James never came into my thoughts until he brought it up.

"Why did you do that!" I asked, getting a bit emotional.

"Do what?"

"Bring him up!"

"Who? Your boyfriend? I'm sorry. I didn't mean to upset you."

"But you did! Tonight was goin' so good with you, Casey. I was laughin' and not thinkin' about him at all." I said. "I don't wanna think about him."

"I'm sorry."

"I just wanna think about you."

He smiled. "A'ight, it's about us tonight . . . and no one else."

I sighed.

We stayed at Chantell's for an hour. And Casey never brought up the situation. He saw how touchy I became and let it be. After I calmed down, and went back into a positive mood, Casey had me laughing all night. He was funny. I like that. I haven't laughed around a man in so long.

Around one thirty, Casey volunteered to drive me home. He asked me if I was still on for spending Thanksgiving with him. I told him yes, I wouldn't dare miss it. Whatever James and I had planned, it flew the coop.

Casey pulled up in front of my building in his green '98 Honda Accord. His car was nice, with cream leather seats, a CD player, moonroof, and chromed rims. I joked and asked, "You sure you a cop? Because you lookin' like a baller right now."

He laughed it off.

When he parked in front of my building, I became nervous, thinking about James. I feared for my life. I knew he was out there, and dreaded that he might be watching me, and plotting to kill me. I sat frozen in the passenger seat, trying to get my nerves together.

"You okay?" Casey asked, looking at me.

"Yeah."

"Come on, I'll walk you up." I smiled, feeling a bit thankful.

He got out the car and, like a gentleman, walked around and opened the door for me, allowing for me to step out.

"It got cold out here," Casey said.

I glanced around. "Yeah, it did."

We headed for the lobby as the cold wind nipped at our skins. We were a few feet away from my building when I heard, "Yo, Jade . . . let me talk to you for a minute." It was James, and I felt my heart stop.

I turned around and saw James coming in my direction. He was accompanied by two other thuggish-looking men. He had on a black ski hat and a big winter coat. The look I saw in his eyes, I knew he wanted to fuck my ass up.

Casey stood next to me, quiet and staring at James as he

approached. I didn't say a word; I just stood with my feet planted to the concrete, like they were frozen there.

"Yo, what the fuck is wrong wit' you, Jade?" James asked. He talked to me like Casey wasn't even standing right next to me.

"James, please go away. I ain't got the time," I told him.

"Nah, bitch . . . You think you slick! That's my shit you threw out, bitch!"

"Yo, watch your mouth," Casey said, stepping up.

James glared at Casey with his face contorted with that thuggish attitude, like he was crazy. "Nigga, who the fuck is you?"

"James, please . . . ," I said.

"Nah, who the fuck is this cornball-ass nigga?" he shouted. I noticed his men glaring at Casey, like they wanted to jump in. But Casey held his cool and calmly replied, "Take a walk, yo."

"Nigga, what? That's my bitch you walkin' with! Fuck is wrong wit' you, bitch?"

"Yo, I'm warnin' you, please leave," Casey said again.

"Yo, y'all hear this nigga!" he shouted, referring to his boys. "Nigga, that's my word, you come out your mouth like that to me again, and I'll show you what's up!" James stepped up to Casey.

But Casey smoothly pulled out his badge and let known that he was a cop and watched a shocked James and his niggas halt in their tracks.

"Oh, it's like that, Officer?" James said, backing up.

"Yeah, it's like that. Now leave, before I take your ass in for disorderly conduct." I couldn't help but to smile.

"You laughin', bitch?" James said. "You think it's funny? A'ight . . . Fuck you! You still live here, Jade, remember that shit."

And he was right. I had my moment tonight, but when Casey leaves my side, I was going to be all alone again, and that terrified me.

James and his cronies strutted off back down the block and into the cold, going back to where they came from. It was scary—he just came out of nowhere.

"You okay?" Casey asked, putting his arm around me.

I nodded my head.

"You want to head up to your apartment, or do you want me to take you someplace else?" he asked.

"Walk wit' me up to my apartment," I told him.

We walked into my building, and Casey escorted me to my door. "So that was him?" he inquired.

"Yeah," I responded meekly.

"He a fuckin' asshole."

I smiled faintly.

"Listen—," he started.

"Please, let's not get into this."

"A'ight. But are you gonna be safe here?"

"Yeah. I changed the locks. He don't have a key."

"Good."

"Thank you."

"Jade, it's not a problem. If you need my help or someone to talk to, you have my number. Give me a call anytime. I'm a cop. I'm here to protect and serve."

"I will," I assured him.

Our speech became quiet. I looked into his beautiful hazel eyes and he peered into mines. I wanted to kiss him. I appreciated his help. If he wasn't around tonight, no telling what James would have done to me. I think Casey saved my life.

"Well," Casey said, breaking our lovely moment of silence, "I'm gonna let you be. I gotta work tomorrow afternoon."

"I understand," I said, with my voice sounding a tad disappointed.

He moved away from me slowly. I had my keys in the lock, but never took my eyes off him. All of a sudden, Casey became irresistible to me. He was funny, smart, cute, and he had heart. Not too many people would stand up to James for me, like Casey did tonight. He got respect for that. He handled the situation smoothly, but still being a little stern. I didn't want him to leave tonight. I couldn't. Casey was by the elevator when I turned around and called out, "Casey . . ."

He turned to me. And I quickly went up to him and jumped into his arms, and began kissing him passionately. He didn't resist. He followed me into my apartment, where our clothes quickly came off, and he carried me off into the bedroom.

I wanted him—physically. I fucked his brains out that night. He wasn't big like James, but he was decent, about seven and a half inches hard, and a sista was able to work wit' it. Casey made me feel like a woman. After the sex, I nestled in his arms, and he held me all night. He made me feel safe. He spent the night, and he definitely did protect and serve.

~ CHAPTER 18 ~

camille

The drama never ends around here, I swear. If you ain't having beef with a bitch, then it's a nigga. I started thinking that leaving for California would be the best thing for me to do. But if I do leave, I had to handle shit at home first. I wasn't trying to leave NY with turmoil behind me. Jade and Shy are my girls and I love 'em, but I had to straighten a few things out first. I started thinking about Shy, and for her to be fucking with James—that's trifling. But I wasn't sure. It looked like her from that day when I spotted them on L.I., but then again, maybe it wasn't. But I was gonna find out. I planned to speak to Shy personally about it.

I strutted around in my apartment in my soft terry cotton robe and peered out the window, holding a cup of tea. It was early afternoon, and the hood looked quiet. It was two days before Thanksgiving, and I'd made plans with Cream for the holidays. He wanted to take me out to the Poconos for the weekend. I was down for it. I was excited because I never been to the Poconos. I heard stories and was eager to go and spend the holidays with him.

I began to head into my bedroom and get dressed for the day when I heard the phone ring. I picked up the cordless from the cradle and said, "Hello."

"You have a collect call from . . . Roscoe Richardson . . . to accept, press one; if not, then please hang up," the operator instructed.

I was shocked. Why was he calling me? I accepted his collect call though. "Roscoe?"

"Camille, what's good?" Roscoe asked.

"What's up?" I asked, baffled. Roscoe and I were always cool. Before he got locked up, if Roscoe had a problem with Shy, or vice versa, they both would come to me about their problems. Roscoe trusted me somewhat, and he was good peoples.

"You know . . . city got me on hold for now . . . but I'm makin' good of my situation," he explained. "But I called to see how you were doin'."

I laughed. "Roscoe, cut the bullshit. What's up wit' this call? I know you, somethin's on your mind."

"Yo, what's up wit' your girl?" he asked, getting to the point.

"You mean Shy?"

"Yeah."

"Why don't you call her up and ask?" I asked.

"Nah . . . she ain't been coming around to see me lately. I called a few times, but I ain't been getting no answer. Last time we spoke, we had phone sex, but that night she answered the phone sayin' she naked and was waitin' for my call. Camille. Sumthin' funny about that."

"Fo' real?" I didn't want to blow up Shy's spot, because I wasn't 100 percent sure if her and James really did have something going on between them.

"Camille, be real wit' me. I'm gonna ask you sumthin', and no matter how crazy it sounds, be fo' real wit' me," Roscoe said. His voice sounded calm, but I knew he was kinda upset.

"What is it?"

"Yo, she fuckin' James?" he asked.

"What?"

"I'm askin' this because my niggas around there be putting me on about James being up in Shy's building a lot now. And he be up in there all night. I know he know peoples up in her building, but I hollered at them too, and they say he ain't been around like that. I got word that James came out of her apartment early one morning, after the nigga done spent the night."

"I don't know what to say," I blurted.

"Camille . . . I just wanna know. Do Shy and James got sumthin' goin' on?" he demanded. "I don't mean to put you in the middle of this, but you always been real wit' me and shit. And y'all tight like that. You good peoples, Camille."

I sighed. I didn't want to blow up Shy's spot like that, but then again, I didn't like James from the get-go. And I knew he was responsible for my attack the other night, and I became very vindictive—that nigga needed to be put down. He was a threat, a fucking nuisance to Jade and everyone else. He don't give a fuck about no one but himself. Selfish bastard. What kind of friend fucks his best friend's girl while his man is locked down, and knowing he's been dealing with Jade for four years now, and she was in love with his ass? James was cocky, ignorant, and I hated the muthafucka.

"Roscoe," I started. "I'm gonna keep it real wit' you. I think I saw the two of 'em gettin' a room out on L.I. But I'm not sure if it was Shy. I was too far away to tell," I told him.

"You think so?"

"James is disrespectful, Roscoe. He don't give a fuck about you. If he did, then he wouldn't be tryin' to play you behind your back like that. One night, I heard him talkin' mad shit about you, sayin' you was never shit to him, and he glad you locked down." I added fuel to his fire. "But don't blame Shy, Roscoe—"

"Why not? The bitch is fuckin' him!" he cursed.

"You don't know that fo' sure, but James is manipulative, Roscoe, and Shy . . . Let me talk to Shy."

"Do that, Camille. Let me know what's up. You know I love Shy, but if she playin' me out, I'll fuckin' kill that bitch."

"Roscoe, you're on a prison phone—calm down," I told him.

"I feel you, ma. But you know I hate to be disrespected. Her man locked down, and she out here gettin' buck-wild wit' my boy."

"She's young, Roscoe," I tried to explain in Shy's behalf.

"So what! She's supposed to be holdin' it down. And James, I'm gonna see that nigga! He supposed to be my boy! I trust him to bring Shy some money once in a while, and the nigga doin' me wrong like that—"

"Roscoe, let me see what's up!" I told him.

"Do that, Camille. You always been real—fuckin' talk to her," he said.

"A'ight."

"Let me get the fuck off this jack. I'm gonna holla at you, Camille."

I hung up. Drama. It never stops.

I was setting up James by fabricating stories about him talking disrespectful about Roscoe while he was locked down. I was lying about him—but who knows, what I said might turn out to be true. James is a fucking snake. I wanted James out of Jade's life, my life, and Shy's life. I wanted him gone. He was nothing but trouble. I never saw how Roscoe and James became so tight—yeah, they were thugs and hustle together, but they were different. Roscoe, he would look out for you if he liked you. He'd pass around money, give out free shit, and sometimes played ball in the park with the neighborhood kids. People loved and respected him. And him and Shy, they were a cute couple.

But James, he never did a damn thing for anyone but put fear on the block and terrorize niggas. He would get a crew to jump you if you even looked at him wrong. He was a dirty-dick nigga, fucking this bitch and that bitch, and then sleeping up with Jade every fucking night like everything was good. The nigga was nasty. Yeah, he was eye candy, I'll admit, but after meeting him, you'll confirm he's a straight fucking dickhead. The nigga tried to get at me one night while Jade's back was turned. We were at a party, and he tried sliding me his number on the low and trying to kick game, acting like he was Casanova or something. I gave him the screw face, tore his number up in front of him, and told him to fuck off. He's lucky I didn't toss a drink in his face. I tried to put Jade on about how grimy her man was, but the bitch was too hardheaded to listen, thinking James was her fucking soul mate or something. Now, she fucking knows the truth. It took her like four fucking years to open her damn eyes.

Today, my agenda was Shy. She was young, twenty years old and shit, and James, being an old head, probably manipulated her gullible ass somehow. I don't know how he did it, but it had to stop. When Roscoe is calling me up, beefing about what he heard throughout the grapevine about Shy and James, and he's locked up, then there was a problem. Shy must forgotten that Roscoe still got eyes and ears on the streets. I knew the bitch was lonely and missing her man, but come on, you don't fuck your best friend's man—I don't care if they're together or not—and she knows how James gets down. I wondered what the fuck was going through her head.

Another problem I thought about was Jade getting wind of this information. We're tight like sistas, and I'll be damn if I let an asshole like James tear our friendship apart. We've been friends for too long.

I threw on my gray sweats, a gray hoodie, and my white Reeboks, with my winter coat on top, and I trotted the few blocks down to Shy's building. It wasn't as cold like yesterday, but the wind still nipped at your skin.

I dashed into the lobby, catching the elevator as it was about to close. And stood next to an old man and his dog. I stepped off before the old man did and scurried toward Shy's apartment. I banged on her door, shouting, "Shy, open up the door. It's Camille. . . . Shy."

I waited for a few minutes. I knew she was home because I heard the stereo playing loudly in her apartment. And then I began to hear movement behind the door, and hearing the locks. Shy finally opened the door, and she wasn't even dressed for the day. She still had on a blue robe, house slippers, and looking like she just woke up.

"Oh . . . hey, Camille," she said, sounding tired. "Why you ain't call first?"

"Because we need to talk," I uttered, stepping into her apartment by pushing by her.

She closed the door and walked behind me. I glanced around her apartment, looking for any indication that there was a man staying up in her place with her.

"I was about to get dressed," she stated as she turned down the volume to the stereo.

I looked at her. "You a'ight?" She looked sluggish. Her eyes looked a little watery, and she didn't seem like herself.

"I'm okay. I'm just tired," she explained.

"Tired," I repeated. "What you been doin'?"

"Busy. Roscoe haven't called me recently, and I've been a little worried about him," she said.

I sighed. "Really?"

"Yeah. I talked to him a few days ago, and he hasn't called me back yet. He calls me every other night to talk and see if I'm okay. I don't know what's goin' on."

I didn't say anything to her. I just stood there and observed her. Her actions were funny.

"You want sumthin', Camille? I'll make breakfast," she offered.

"Nah, I'm good," I replied, still standing and looking around.

"So, you haven't talked to Roscoe in a while," I added.

"No. I miss him."

I was never the type to delay or drag shit out, so I got straight to the point with her. "How long, Shy?" I asked with a stern look on my face.

"How long what?" she returned.

"You gonna stand here and play me like this, huh, Shy? I saw you the other day with James."

"What? James? You saw the wrong bitch, then. I don't know what the fuck you're talkin' about!" she replied, catching an attitude.

"You fo' real, Shy. You gonna stand here and lie to my face so easily? I saw you that evenin' on L.I., gettin' out of his Hummer. It was you—don't fake it, Shy."

"I ain't fakin' shit. I'm not fuckin' him!" she angrily countered, screwing her face up at me. "That's what the fuck you came here for, to tell me some bullshit about me fuckin' James! You can get the fuck out then, bitch!"

"Don't curse at me like that, bitch. I'm in here lookin' out fo' your ass! And don't fuckin' disrespect me, because I'll wipe the floor wit' your skinny ass!" I said, with my face screwed up like hers.

This bitch. I'm at her apartment looking out for her, and she won't admit it and come clean. Roscoe's ready to beat her ass, and she being naïve about this shit.

"How I'm gonna do Jade like that, Camille? We friends. I got Roscoe. I know he locked down right now, but I'm gettin' used to it. I don't need James." That was a fucking bald-faced lie.

"Bitch! Roscoe called me earlier."

"What?" she said, shocked.

"He knows about you and James. So be real wit' me, Shy. You fuckin' him, and don't fuckin' lie to me."

"Why is he callin' you? Y'all got sumthin' goin' on? What you talked to him about? What did you tell him?" she barked.

"Shy, are you that fuckin' stupid and naïve? Niggas talk—people see. I know he be spendin' the night at your place."

"Please, niggas can believe whatever. They need to stay the fuck out my business!"

"Shy," I said, trying to be real calm. "We've been friends fo' a long time now, since high school. You know you're my girl. You know I always look out fo' you. This is me you're talkin' to. Roscoe called me earlier asking about you. He's been callin', and says you ain't been pickin' up lately, and he feels you ain't been actin' right lately. You're missin' visits. He hasn't gotten a letter from you lately. Niggas out here are tellin' him that they've been seeing James in and out of your place recently. He suspects, but I tried to tell him different. Now, be real wit' me, do you and James got sumthin' goin' on?"

Shy just stood there. She had her arms folded across her chest, and she never looked me directly in the eye. I backed off her and gave her time to explain herself. She peered up at the ceiling, and probably coming to reality. Her eyes diverted back to me, and she asked, "Does Jade know?"

"I don't think so," I answered.

"Camille . . . it just happened," she started. "He came by, dropped some money off fo' me, and volunteered to drop me off to work. I got into a beef at my job later on, and James handled that fo' me. Next thing I know, I'm in his truck, we got dinner, and then we got a room. I'm sorry, Camille. I didn't mean to. I'm so fuckin' lonely. I'm weak, Camille. I'm sorry." She started to cry.

I sighed. "Damn, girl."

"I don't wanna lose Roscoe! He means so much to me," she blurted.

"You should have thought about that before you fucked his best friend."

"I know. But he ain't here. He locked up over some dumb shit. And I needed company. You know how I am, Camille."

"So that don't give you the right to fuck his man. Any nigga woulda done, Shy . . . and you choose that one asshole to mess around with. *James,* Shy." I said his name like it was the Antichrist. "You know he a grimy nigga."

"I know."

"Damn, Shy . . . what were you thinkin'?" I asked lightly.

She exploded at me. "I'm not like you, Camille! I need a man in my life. I need someone to be wit' at nights. . . . Fuck, you happy. I need dick. I get stressed. I get fuckin' scared! I hate being alone! It may be cool wit' you, but it ain't wit' me."

"Calm down, Shy!" I said. "What's up wit' you? And you're not alone."

"Whatever. You gonna tell Jade?" she asked.

I thought about it. But Jade had enough problems to worry about. I didn't want to spring this on her so sudden. And then again, I didn't want her to find out through the streets, and have muthafuckas blowing it up in her face just to be spiteful.

"I don't know. But you need to go wash up and get your ass dressed. It's getting late," I told her.

She went into the bedroom, and I followed her. I was upset, because I told her to do her while Roscoe was locked down. But damn, when I meant do her, I meant do it subtle and shit, not fuck the one asshole that lives in the same hood with you and knows everybody you know.

I heard Shy bustling around in the bathroom. Her bedroom was a bit messy; her floor and bed were swamped with clothing. The bed was unmade. The television was on, but the sound muted. She had old bags of potato chips lying around on top of the television, and the garbage bin was filled to the rim with trash.

"Damn, Shy," I muttered to myself. "You need to keep yourself together." Roscoe ain't been gone that long, only about two months now.

Being her girl, I was going to help her tidy up. I started picking up clothing from off the bed and folding stuff neatly. I threw the empty potato chips bag in the trash and made the bed. I then continued with the clothing, arranging them neatly. I heard Shy in the shower, so I started attacking her floors. She had so many clothes out, like it was a holiday sale at Macy's.

I picked up a pair of her jeans and caught the bombshell when a long clear crack pipe fell from her clothing. I was bug-eyed. I picked up the drug paraphernalia and examined it like it was an alien object. But I clearly knew what the fuck it was.

"Nah . . . nah . . . ," I muttered, being in disbelief. "Shy, tell me you ain't fuckin' wit' this shit," I said to myself.

I found myself becoming really fucking angry. *Drugs, Shy!* I began rummaging through the rest of her clothing and searching her bedroom. I found more fucking drugs and knew she was probably smoking crack and whatever else.

I heard the shower stop running, and I waited by the bathroom door gripping the crack pipe and the rest of the drugs I found in her bedroom.

Shy opened the door, stepping out of the bathroom wrapped in a big blue towel. She instantly spotted the shit I found in the bedroom in my hands and cried, "Where you get that from?"

"Shy, you fuckin' crazy! You fuckin' wit' this shit now?" I barked.

"Camille, it ain't none of your fuckin' business!" She barked back. "Give me my shit." She tried to grab it from my hands, but I pulled back.

"Shy," I started, but she went reaching for the pipe like it was gold again. "Shy, what the fuck is wrong wit' you?"

"Ain't shit wrong wit' me. You need to mind your fuckin' business and stop bein' nosy and goin' through people's shit."

"I was helping you clean up your bedroom and found it. . . . Is you stupid!"

"Camille, please . . . it's my fuckin' life, I do what I wanna do."

"You ready to just fuck yourself up like this? You know what this shit will do to you!" I shouted. "How long, Shy?"

She ignored the question as she stood there in a towel, dripping wet. I peered at her with so much disgust at that moment; I just wanted to smack some sense into her, like I could never do with my mother.

I didn't want Shy to go down that hard road that my mother and so many before her had traveled when fuckin' with crack.

"Who got you hooked on this. James?" I asked.

"Don't worry about it."

"Shy, James got you hooked on this shit, right? What the fuck is goin' on wit' you?"

"Nothin'! You ain't goin' through the same shit I'm goin' through. I'm missin' my man. He locked up. I'm stressed, Camille. I need sumthin' to help take my mind off Roscoe."

"I'm tired of you usin' Roscoe's incarceration as an excuse. That's bullshit, bitch! I thought you were stronger than this, Shy. This shit ain't gonna help your situation any better. It's gonna stress you out even more. And James . . . I'm gonna see that nigga. Shy, you stay away from him."

"You ain't my mother."

"You need help, Shy," I tried to explain.

"I don't need nuthin'. I need you to stay the fuck out my business and let me do me."

"I'm not goin' anywhere. We've been friends for too fuckin' long, Shy, fo' me to watch you start slippin' and have you throw your life away."

"I know what I'm doin'. It's just temporary, until I get shit back in order wit' my life."

"This shit ain't temporary," I said, holding up the pipe. "You start fuckin' wit' this, and ain't nuthin' gonna ever get back on track wit' you."

"Camille, you don't know everythin'. You think you're so smart—Miss Fuckin' Know-it-all—always tryin' to play big sister . . . treatin' me like I'm stupid—"

"I never called you stupid—"

"You act like I am."

"You're stupid now fo' even beginnin' to mess wit' this."

"Bitch, just give me my shit and leave. Get out my fuckin' life! I don't need you anymore. I don't need you or Jade. Fuck y'all. Fuck Roscoe—he made a promise to me, and he never held up to his promise. He left me alone."

"Shy, you were never alone. I'm here."

"Whatever! You have Cream. Jade got James."

"And you think she's happy wit' James," I uttered. "You think James is a god or sumthin'? James is a fuckin' asshole, Shy. He's poison. I know he got you hooked on this shit. And you let him take advantage of you like this, Shy."

"I know what I'm doin'. I can handle myself. I'm not fifteen anymore, Camille."

I sighed. "Please, let me help you, Shy," I begged. "Don't do this to yourself. Roscoe needs you strong right now."

"I am strong!"

"If you think this shit makes you strong, and being wit' James, then you got it twisted," I stated loudly.

I was done talking and holding this poison in my hand. I threw the pipe against the bedroom wall, smashing it.

"Bitch! What the fuck!" Shy shouted, rushing up to me, but I subdued her down to the floor as she carried on, cursing and screaming. "Camille, fuck you! Fuck you! Why you always gotta come and ruin everything? Why can't you stay the fuck away from me! I don't fuckin' need you! I don't need nobody!"

Seeing Shy like this made me cry. Shy is my sista. Her, Jade, and I done been through everything together. And I'd die for my sistas. They the only family I ever known, and the only family I feel I got left on this earth. There's nothing I wouldn't do for them.

"I hate you, Camille. I fuckin' hate you! Get off me!" Shy shouted, trying to free herself from my grip.

I had the crack still clutched in my hand. I quickly got up and went into the bathroom, locking the door behind me.

"I'm not gonna let you do this to yourself, Shy," I shouted. "I got too much love fo' you to let you fuck your life up like this."

"Camille, don't flush my shit. . . . Camille!" Shy shouted, banging on the bathroom door.

I lifted up the toilet seat and dumped everything into the toilet bowl. I then flushed it.

"Bitch . . . Why you do that! Fuck you, Camille. Fuck you!" Shy continued to yell and bang loudly against the bathroom door. "Leave me the fuck alone. You ain't me. I ain't you!"

As I heard her scream, I thought about Cali. *Can I leave now?* I asked myself. Shy and Jade still needed me. There was too much shit going on for me to just break out and leave my friends behind, especially with the chaos that was happening.

Maybe I better put Cali on hold, I thought. I can't fly thousands of miles away, and leave Shy here like this. I couldn't. I knew Cream was going to be upset, but my friends come first. I knew he'd understand.

Two days had passed. I was afraid to leave Shy alone, but I couldn't watch over her twenty-four seven. I had my own life, and my own needs, too.

Sierra had called earlier, saying she missed me and wanted to link up. I hadn't heard or seen her in two weeks. Cream was out of town on business, and I needed to release my sexual frustration. I was stressed and horny. I told Sierra to come over to my place, not even thinking about her husband.

Seven p.m., Sierra was at my door, dressed in a business suit and heels. She looked exceptional. It was obvious that she had come here straight from work. She's a receptionist at some downtown Manhattan law firm.

I smiled, and she kissed and hugged me tightly in the doorway.

"Camille, I missed you," she said.

I hugged her back. Her body was so soft and inviting. She was wearing Christian Dior perfume, and it turned me on.

"I'm so sorry I got careless with my husband. I don't know how he found out about us," she said.

"Fuck him!" I said. "You're mines for da night."

We grabbed each other passionately and her hands were all over me. She grabbed my breasts, kissed me, and quickly removed my purple satin slip. Then she undressed herself, and followed me to the bedroom, where I had all sorts of toys laid out across the bed.

Sierra walked into my bedroom in her bra and panties. I was completely naked.

"I like," she said, referring to the nine-inch dildo and other sex toys I had spread out.

She came up to me again, embracing me, and I felt her hand move up my thigh and rest on my pussy. She then pushed me down on the bed and climbed on top of me, licking and kissing me from the waist up. I pulled off her panties and she removed her bra. We committed foreplay for several moments. I sucked and licked on her hard nipples, and she fondled my breasts and kissed me between my thighs. Sierra had a body like mine, petite, but firm and thick in the right places. I knew she took care of herself. She probably worked out three times a week at a Bally's. Her brown skin was flawless. No tattoos or scars. She gave birth to three kids, and her body still looked like that of a fit eighteen-year-old girl. Sierra lay across her back and gestured for me to get on top. I straddled her face and felt her tongue penetrate me down below.

"Aaaaaahhh," I moaned, gripping the headboard. Her tongue action was intense and it made my legs quiver with each stroke. We continued our strong sexual encounter without a care in the world. Sierra wasn't thinking about her husband, and I wasn't thinking about Cream.

Suddenly, there was a loud and disturbing knock at my front door. I was startled, and so was Sierra. I quickly jumped off her face and reached for my robe. I looked at Sierra, and she was just as clueless about the disturbance at my apartment door.

I approached the door with caution. I grabbed the nearest

weapon I could find, a broomstick. Sierra followed me out. She had my bedsheet wrapped around her.

The banging continued, louder and louder. "Open this door, you fuckin' bitch!" I heard him yell. "I'm tired of this shit!"

"Danny!" Sierra said, shocked. I turned to look at her, and she had this frightened look plastered across her face.

"Your husband?" I mouthed.

"Ohmygod!" she said.

"I know you're in there with that bitch! I told you to stay away from her!" he yelled. He banged on my door so loud and hard that I thought he was going to knock it down.

"Open this fuckin' door, you bitch! I wanna talk."

I had to do something. He was causing a scene in the hallway. I slowly unlocked my door. I shouted, "You need to calm down!"

"Fuck that! That's my wife in there!" he yelled back.

"If you calm down, I'll let you in," I said.

"Open the door!"

I took my chances and opened the door. I then took a few steps back, holding up the broomstick, prepared to whack him against his fuckin' head if he came charging in at me.

He pushed the door back violently. He was big, about six-foot-three, and dark-skinned. To my surprise, Danny was a very handsome man. He had a bald head and a trimmed goatee, and was clad in a blue three-piece business suit. I could see he had style and class.

Sierra was speechless.

"What the fuck is going on here, Sierra?" Danny asked. He was a few feet from me and Sierra. He never charged at us.

"You're my wife," he continued. "My fuckin' wife! And I catch you in bed with another fuckin' woman!"

"Baby, let me explain," Sierra managed to say.

"Explain what? How can you explain this?" he shouted.

I just stood there. Still gripping the broomstick in my hand in case he wanted to act stupid. I was letting them two talk it out. I kept my mouth shut.

"How did you find me?" Sierra asked.

"I hired a private detective. He led me here," Danny told her.

"You had me followed?" Sierra said, looking taken aback.

"I trusted you, and this is what I get? Who is this bitch?" he yelled. He looked at me with ice-cold eyes.

"Excuse me!" I said.

"You fuckin' heard me, you fuckin' cunt!"

"Oh, baby, don't get fucked up in here. You don't fuckin' know me, nigga," I said angrily. I gripped the broomstick even tighter.

"You're tearing apart my family!" he screamed, glaring at me.

I thought he was about to wild out in my place, and it was going to get ugly. But the unthinkable happened. He suddenly started to cry—tears trickled down his cheeks and everything.

"We have a family, Sierra . . . three beautiful kids. And you're willing to throw it all away to be with her. I thought you loved us," he cried out.

"Baby, I do," Sierra said.

"Then why do you wanna tear us apart?" her husband asked. "I love you more than I love myself. The kids are at your mother's. I didn't tell her what was going on."

"Danny—" Sierra started to speak, but shut up.

"Why are you doing this to us?" Danny asked. He looked at me. That tough, macho attitude went straight out the door, and he looked like a straight-up, soft teddy bear. "This is my family you're tearing apart."

I saw that he wasn't a threat anymore, so I dropped the broomstick. It was clear to me that he was deeply hurt by Sierra's infidelity, and all he could do was cry and confess his love to her.

Sierra went up to her husband, who was now seated on my couch, crying his eyes out. She consoled him by throwing her arms around him and telling him, "Danny, I love you so much. I'm sorry. I never meant to hurt you."

Sierra never looked up at me. My conscience began to eat away at me. Sierra did have a beautiful family. She once showed me pictures of her kids, and they were lovely. *Family,* I thought. Here I was, breaking up and destroying her happy home. Sierra was wrecking her home with infidelity, and drugs tore mine apart. I never thought about her kids or her husband. I just wanted to please myself, being self-centered. The only family I ever had was my grandmother, and my friends Jade and Shy.

I remained quiet, and felt a bit jealous of Sierra. I never knew how much her husband truly loved her until now. He came to the ghetto from his suburban home to seek his wife. I had some respect for him. It was nice to know that there was still a good black man around, who cared about his wife and held down a decent job.

"Do you still love us?" her husband asked.

"Baby, I always loved you, and I still do," Sierra proclaimed. She then looked up at me with this empty stare. I didn't return the gaze. I thought about my life and Cream. I never had a good man in my life, and I began wondering if Cream was the right one for me. We had an open relationship. *Was I really cool with that?* I asked myself. Everything seemed perfect for me now, but in the future, what if Cream began to fall in love with someone else. *How would I feel?* I love him.

Sierra got up off the couch, and walked into the bedroom. She didn't say a word to me as she passed. Danny remained on the couch. I stared at him. I told myself that I should apologize for my actions. But I stopped myself. We were strangers. I didn't mean to hurt him intentionally.

Sierra stepped out my bedroom five minutes later, half decent. I let her be. She gazed at me, and then said, "Bye, Camille."

Her husband got off my couch, and they both walked out my door. I knew that it would probably be the last time I would ever see her again. Our relationship was over.

When they left, this surge of sorrow and grief came over me. My knees buckled and I collapsed on my living floor, crying. I no longer felt like a strong, vibrant woman. I felt alone. My deceased baby brother came to mind; then I thought about my quick attack on the elevator. I never told anyone about it. Then I thought about Shy and her sudden crack addiction. The three of us, we never had strong families when growing up—Shy had an abusive father, and her mother was killed when she was young. Jade's mother dated drug dealers and hustlers since Jade was eight, and now her whole life was turned upside down by one man. And myself, I always distanced myself from serious relationships. I never knew my father, and my mother, I don't know if she's alive or dead. Last I heard from her, she had cancer, and was still serving her time in a woman's prison upstate.

It's like everything hits you all at once, and the pain can cause you to break down. I think the last time I cried was when they buried my brother. I always felt sympathy and sorrow for my friends throughout the years, but I never cried. I never let all my emotions out. I was scared to. I was scared to be looked on as weak. To everyone, I had it all together. But tonight, I cried for hours.

~ CHAPTER 19 ~

jade

It was Thursday, Thanksgiving morning, and Casey promised to pick me up around noon so we could head out to Long Island and spend the day with his family. For the past two days, every day before and after his shift, Casey would come by to check up on me. It made me feel better. He'd come by to talk and watch some TV with me for a few hours and then head home.

As far as my situation with James, he stopped coming by the apartment, but that didn't mean he wasn't still out there, and still a threat to me. He made a threat to get at me, and I still feared him. His relationship with Tasha was definitely out in the open. Everybody in the hood knew that they were fucking for sure now. I'll admit it hurts a little, seeing James fucking with that bitch Tasha. But I tried not to think about it. James made it his personal business to tell folks around the way that I was fucking with a cop, and calling me a fucking snitch. I hated that. Some folks sneered at me like I was trash and was doing something wrong, while others let me be and didn't give a fuck who I dated.

I was getting ready for the day, trying to get dressed and be ready before Casey came by. I wanted to look nice for his family. I was in the bedroom going over my outfit for the day when I heard the doorbell. It caught my attention. My nerves jumped because I knew it wasn't Casey. It was too early. I looked at the time and it was ten fifteen. *Please, don't let it be James,* I prayed.

I went to the door cautiously and looked through the peephole—and sighed in relief when I saw Camille at the door. I quickly opened the door for her.

"Happy Thanksgiving, Jade," Camille greeted, giving me a hug.

"Same to you too, Camille," I returned. "You up and out here early, what's up?"

"Cream is taking me to the Poconos today."

"Really? That's great. Have a good time."

"I'll try." She didn't sound so lively about it.

"Sumthin' on your mind, Camille?" I asked.

"We need to talk," she said, stepping into my apartment.

I locked the door and wondered what she wanted to talk about. Camille took a seat on my couch and proclaimed, "It's about Shy."

"She okay? I haven't seen or heard from her in a while. She called me one night, talking to me 'bout Roscoe, and saying they might drop the murder case. But since then, she's been like a ghost."

"Jade, she's hittin' the pipe," Camille said.

"What? Shy? You sure, Camille?" I asked, shocked into disbelief.

"I went by there the other day to confront her about some

news I got wind of, and I found drugs and other shit in her bedroom."

"Shy . . . Shy?" I said. "How the fuck that happened? Shy . . . Nah, she ain't like that." Shy was too pretty and loved her image so damn much. For her to be getting hooked on that crack, it was unbelievable. "You sure it was hers you found? Maybe she had some nigga up in her apartment and he left it behind."

"It was hers, Jade. If you woulda seen the way she was actin' when I went by there, you woulda knew she was on something."

"Who got her on that shit? It's probably some nigga she fuckin' wit'. Shit, I knew she was takin' Roscoe incarceration hard, but damn . . . *drugs?*"

"Jade, I'm gonna be real wit' you—this ain't the only thing we need to talk about. I don't want you to find this out through the streets, because people are already talkin' 'bout it, and I don't want you to find out no other way, but fo' me to say it to you. And there ain't any other way in sayin' it."

"What's that?"

"James and Shy had sumthin' goin' on."

"What? My James? . . . Camille, you're lying. Shy and James?" I said. I didn't believe it. "Who told you about this?"

"Shy broke it down to me, when I went to her apartment to confront her."

"That fuckin' bitch, yo!" I shouted.

"Jade, she knows she did wrong, but—"

"Ain't no fuckin' buts, Camille! How she gonna fuck my man behind my back like that?"

"Jade, she made a mistake," Camille said.

"So would it be a mistake to go over to her apartment right now and whip her ass?" I shouted.

"I'm not sayin' you shouldn't. I know the feelin', but c'mon, we've been friends fo' too long fo' us to let some dickhead nigga like James break our friendship."

"Fuck him too. Ohmygod, I'm so done wit' him. And fuck Shy. She's triflin' too. I don't give a fuck about that bitch right now!"

I was heated. It was Thanksgiving Day, and here was Camille breaking me off with the fucked-up news. Shy supposed to be my girl. I stay looking out for her, and this is how she repays me, by fucking James behind my back. I swear, I wanted to snatch Shy by her fucking hair and punch the bitch in her face.

"James got her hooked on that crack?" I asked.

"What you think, Jade? She's losin' it. She ain't herself," Camille proclaimed.

I sucked my teeth, trying to control my anger. *It's Thanksgiving,* I thought. I had Casey picking me up in a few. I wanted to enjoy today, but damn, why drama always up in my fucking face? Hearing about Shy and James put a fucking lump in my day, I swear. I tried to be reasonable, saying to myself that James and I are not together anymore, so why should I care. But I still did. It was bad enough to hear about James and that stank bitch Tasha. Now, I had to hear about him fucking my best friend too. And I didn't know who to blame more: Shy for fucking this nigga, knowing he's my man, and hearing me beef about his fucking cheating to her continually. Or James, taking it to the next level, and not caring about morals or boundaries, and fucking my best friend, and Roscoe shorty. I thought, *What that say about a man, where he ain't got no respect for me, himself, and his boy?*

Camille talked to me and tried to persuade me not to beef with Shy, saying she was sick and needed help. But my mind was like, *Fuck that bitch—let her be on her fucking own!* I've been there enough for her. Over ten years of friendship, and this is how she does me—fucked up.

Camille and I continued to talk throughout the morning while I was getting dressed. She told me that Shy was home at the moment, but I wasn't going by there. I wasn't in the mood to see or speak to her. I might come off and slap the shit out of her for being so stupid and disrespectful. I noticed that Camille seemed aloof since she came to my door. Something else besides Shy's crack addiction and James was bothering her.

"Camille, you okay? You seem worried." I said.

"Can I tell you something," she asked.

"Of course. We peoples."

"Cream asked me to move to California with him," she said. I was stunned.

"California, you serious?"

"Yes. He asked me a few weeks ago. I've been contemplating if I should go or not."

"Ohmygod! Go, Camille, that's your man, right?" I asked, because she never confirmed if they were together or not.

"Yes. Kind of," she answered incredulously.

"What's holding you back?"

"Y'all. You and Shy always been family to me," she said. "And I don't wanna leave for California knowing shit ain't right between you two. I love the both of y'all like sistas." I noticed

Camille tearing up, which was a first. Camille was always the strong one. I've seen her get emotional, but I never saw her actually cry.

"Camille, I'm good. We've been friends for over six years now, and been at each other's throats longer. And you know what, I never saw you cry. You're human," I joked.

A quick smile appeared from her.

I went over to Camille and sat next to her. "You love Cream, right?"

"You know I do."

"So what's holding you back? I know it's not us, Camille."

She let out a faint laugh, then confessed, "I've been having an affair with a married woman."

"Excuse me?" I was bowled over by that. "You're serious?"

She nodded.

"I never knew, Camille. I mean, how long?"

"It was only for a few months. But it's over now. Her husband came to my home, flipping, and then he started crying like a baby. That made me think, Jade. I was tearing this family apart, and I didn't even think twice about it. She has three kids, and they have something that I never had, a loving and caring mother," Camille said.

"Damn!" I uttered. "What about Cream? He knows about this?"

"He knows I'm bi. But I've been thinking, Jade. I want a family."

"Only you can make that happen," I said.

"I know Cream would be a perfect father, but what if I'm making a mistake? What if that life isn't for me? I've been playing it safe all my life, not getting too attached to men or women.

But I want something different now. I'm in love with Cream. I wanna be happy with him. But I'm scared."

The only thing I could tell her was to take a chance. "You'll never know unless you try, Camille," I told her. "I know that there is someone out there for each of us. But you'll never find your soul mate until you've sorted out the bad ones first. Go to Cali with Cream, Camille. Be happy. Please. I know Cream is a good dude."

When she confessed to me that she was bi, and I had no idea, at first it felt a little awkward. But that was her life and her choice. She never came on to me, and I was glad for that. We reminisced about the night we became friends. It was the night Raheem was killed, Shy's boyfriend. Camille stayed with us the entire night. We actually had had a decent conversation without cursing at each other for once. Raheem's death brought a friendship together, three sisters. I told Camille about my life, and Casey. She noticed me beam with joy whenever I spoke about Casey.

"So far, he's great, Camille. We talk. He makes me laugh, and today he's taking me to meet his entire family."

"Dats wassup," Camille said. "I'm glad to see you smiling again."

I smiled. I wasn't even thinking about Shy or asshole James anymore. I was thinking about Casey and a new future for myself.

It's been awhile since we talked like this. I was happy for this moment we shared together in my apartment. The only girl missing was Shy. We all had our problems, but we had each other to help work things out. I was glad to have Camille as a friend. When we first met, we were enemies and couldn't stand each other. I always thought she was fake. But she proved me wrong. Camille is the realest woman out there.

It was 12:25 when I heard the doorbell.

"That's him?" Camille inquired.

"Yeah." I said, leaving the bedroom. Camille never met Casey, and honestly, I wanted her approval. She knew Casey was a cop; I told her that much, and she didn't care. She said as long as I was happy with him, and he was treating me right, then she was cool. Shit, I think Camille would have been happy with anybody as long as it wasn't James. She hated him.

I tried to clear my mind and answer the door with a smile across my face. I was determined not to let the troubling news Camille told me ruin my day. Nah, fuck that, it was a holiday and I was going to enjoy this day stress-free—or try, at least.

I was looking good. I answered the door in an off-the-shoulder silk charmeuse blouse and black modern evening pants. My shoes were satin sling-backs with rhinestone trim.

I opened my door and greeted Casey with a smile plastered across my face. "Happy Thanksgiving."

"Happy Thanksgiving. You look beautiful, Jade." Casey returned.

"Thank you."

Casey stepped into my apartment looking fine himself. He wore a Rocawear shirt with Vokal jeans and a green Vokal jacket and a pair of white Adidas.

"You're so cute," I told him.

He smiled.

Camille came out my bedroom the minute Casey entered my apartment.

"Casey, this is my best friend, Camille. Camille, this is Casey."

"Nice to meet you," Casey said, extending out his arm for a handshake.

"Same here," Camille returned, gripping Casey's hand. "Jade, I gotta go. Cream is picking me up soon."

"Okay, girl. Have fun."

"I'll try."

I walked her to the door, and before Camille left, she looked at me and said, "He's cute."

I smiled.

"Thanks for listening and being my friend, Jade. You're my sista, and I'm happy for you. He's going to be around for a while. I like him already," she said.

"Thank you. You and Cream go and paint the town red, and don't get pregnant too soon," I joked.

Camille laughed. "I'm gonna take it slow with him. We'll see what's up."

"I love you, Camille. You be safe out there," I proclaimed.

"I love you, too, girl. Happy Thanksgiving."

"You, too."

We gave each other one last hug. I watched Camille get into the elevator, and then went back into my apartment to finish getting ready.

"I mean it, Jade. . . . You look really nice today. I know my family is going to love you," Casey stated.

"I hope so. I'm so nervous right now."

"Don't be," he said.

I went into my bedroom and picked up a few things to place in my purse, including my blade. I probably didn't need it, but it was a habit for me to carry it around.

I came out the bedroom throwing on my light brown leather jacket and headed for the door. Casey and I had small talk on the way out.

When we walked out my building, my face instantly twisted up with anger and rage when I noticed James standing across the street in front of the bodega with a few of his peoples. A bitch just snapped. I said nothing to Casey as I quickly strutted across the street in my heels to confront him. Him and Shy together—fucking, it disgusted me that he would even do that to me. He saw me coming, and a smirk appeared on his face.

I said nothing, just marched up to him, and as I came close, extended my arm out as far possible and smacked the shit out of him.

"Ooohhh," I heard one of his friends mutter.

"Bitch, you fuckin' crazy!" James barked, looking like he was about to come at me, but noticed Casey behind me. "Don't you ever put your fuckin' hands on me again. I'll kill you, bitch!"

"Fuck you, James. How dare you! . . . You're dead wrong, James. You're wrong fo' that. Shy, James. You were fuckin' my best friend behind my back like that!" I barked.

His anger turned into a devilish smirk when I brought up the subject. "You know, huh?" he said mockingly. "Don't hate, bitch!"

Before I could react again, Casey held me in his arms, preventing me from lunging at James.

"She fucks better than you, bitch!" James said loudly. "Pussy all good."

"Fuck you, nigga. You a bitch-ass nigga! I swear, you gonna get yours. . . . Watch, nigga!" I shouted, wishing I could tear his dick off with my bare hands.

"Officer, you better do sumthin' about that bitch. . . . She causin' a scene. . . . Do sumthin', arrest her ass for disorderly conduct!" James mocked.

"Shut up, and step back." Casey scolded James.

"I hate you, nigga. I fuckin' hate you," I yelled.

"Bitch, be easy wit' that. You was already on my dick fo' the longest. You know you was lovin' Daddy long fo' a long time. He's been good to you." He ridiculed me, grabbing his crotch in a very sexual gesture.

Casey carried me off to his car with me yelling and screaming at James, causing a scene on a holiday.

"Bitch, watch your back from now on!" I heard James shout.

"Get in the car!" Casey demanded.

I didn't argue. I got in on the passenger side and slammed his door. Casey jumped in afterwards, looked at me, and asked, "Can you tell me what that was all about?"

I looked at him. A few tears escaped from my eyes. "I'm sorry," I apologized.

"You okay?"

I nodded.

"Listen, we can't be going to see my family with you being so upset right now. So calm down and talk to me," he said evenly.

I took in a deep breath and said, "Everything is so fucked up, Casey. I just found out that that son of a bitch was fuckin' my best friend on the low."

"Damn," he muttered.

"Can we just leave? I don't wanna be here anymore," I said, staring out the passenger window.

"A'ight. But calm down. We'll go for a ride," he said, starting up the car, putting it in drive, and pulling off my block.

I was quiet for the next ten minutes. My mind was everywhere; I was feeling really incoherent at that moment. Casey continued to drive, not uttering a single word to me. I guess he was waiting for me to collect myself and have me speak first on it. I did have an attitude, but as we drove and traveled farther away from my buildings, my mood became more relaxed, and I listened in on the radio. I glanced at Casey. He drove with his seat reclined back, gripping the steering wheel with one hand and looking like a hustler right now. I noticed his jeweled hand on the wheel and thought to myself, he acts more like a homeboy than 5.0. His attitude, I loved it.

"I'm sorry," I blurted out, breaking the silence between us in the car.

"You calm now?"

"Yeah."

He flashed a quick smile. "No more drama fo' the afternoon, right?"

I smiled. "I'll try."

"I'm serious, Jade. Today, you're wit' me. So I want you to free your mind and enjoy the day. Forget about all that bullshit back there. I understand you're upset, but when you get that turkey in your system and you meet my family, everythin' is going to be all good."

"Promise?" I smiled.

"Yo, you ain't got nothin' to worry about when you're with me," he guaranteed.

"I'll take your word fo' it."

He hit the Southern State, and we were on our way to L.I. to meet his family.

It took us about twenty minutes to reach his destination: Brentwood. He pulled up to a beautiful sprawling colonial home with the shrubberies lining the driveway, manicured lawns that were covered with autumn leaves, and the block so tranquil that it felt like the day was on pause.

Casey spoke, putting the car in park and smiling. "This is it."

"It's beautiful out here." I said, looking out at the home and property somewhat in awe.

"Come on, I think everybody is inside already," Casey said, excited.

"Casey . . . ," I started to say, feeling nervous, with butterflies swimming around in my stomach. "Ohmygod, I'm so nervous."

"Don't be. My family is cool, Jade. We won't bite. We'll be too busy eatin' on turkey and yams."

This was new to me. I never had Thanksgiving with family—probably once with Shana and my aunt, but holidays always ended up in drama, with one of us fighting and leaving the crib with a black eye or a busted lip.

Casey coached me out of the car and promised to be by my side the whole time. Cars of all makes and models were parked in the driveway and on the streets. I knew there had to be a lot of people up in the house. And here I was, a complete stranger to everyone—even to Casey, to some extent—and I had to play nice and act like everything's all good.

As we approached, I asked, "Okay, and these are the people on your father's side?"

"Yeah. My younger brother, my aunt, my cousins, and my uncles. My father's side is where I have most of the family. Randy is spending the holiday with his mother." He looked a little bummed about that.

"Okay."

We went up to the door, and Casey pushed the doorbell with

me standing by his side. It looked like we've been a couple for years. He held my hand gently, with his shoulders broad and standing over me about nine inches.

The front door came open, and out came this hefty-looking female with long black hair, big hoop earrings, and the reddest lipstick spread across her thick lips. She had on a wide-neck thermal-knit top and a denim skirt with knee-high leather boots.

"Wassup, cuz," she hollered, startling me. She rushed up to Casey, gripping him a serious bear hug.

"Hey, Tracy," Casey groaned, as his cousin squeezed him into a loving hug. She finally placed him down on his feet, still smiling.

"It's been a long time," she stated.

"Yeah, I know."

His stout cousin then noticed me. As she stared at me, she asked, "Who you brought wit' you?"

"Tracy, this is Jade."

"Hey, nice to meet you," I greeted graciously, extending out my arm in a handshake.

"There ain't no handshakes in this home," she proclaimed. "We give out nothin' but hugs. You family to us if you wit' my cuz." She scooping me up into her full-size arms and hugged me like I was family. I was shocked. I looked over at Casey, and he shrugged his shoulders.

"Come inside—everyone is almost here," his cousin said. I was overwhelmed already. I never met a woman so lively. Tracy walked in first, followed by Casey, and then myself. When I walked in, we were greeted with a house full of folks—and not to be funny, but it looked like the Klumps up in here. I swear I never felt so small. I was only five-two, petite, and looking at Casey's family, I felt like a mouse trapped in an elephant exhibit. *Whew!*

"Casey, hey."

"You've made it."

"Ohmygod, who's your friend?"

"You got the day off from policin' huh, cuz?"

"Sit down."

"We're about to eat in an hour or two."

Everyone was joyous and exuberant about his arrival. Shit, Casey was the only slim person in the place. He and I were greeted with hugs and kisses. I was shocked. These people don't even know me, but they already were treating me like I was family.

"Jade, huh? That's a beautiful name," one lady complimented. She was beautiful in the face, but thick all around. She had on a gray turtleneck and a long plaid skirt. "I'm Aunt Jerry."

"Hello."

"Girl, you're beautiful. But damn, you need some meat on them bones. . . . Casey, you ain't been feedin' your girlfriend. She about to pass out bein' so thin," Aunt Jerry said, being humble about it.

"You know how y'all ladies are about food and diets. I try not to get involved," Casey hollered from the other side of the room.

"Don't worry, Jade. Before you leave here, we gonna have you fittin' into some plus sizes," Aunt Jerry said.

I smiled.

"She don't need no meat on her skin, Aunt Jerry. Homegirl fine just the way she is. . . . Hey, there, beautiful—I'm Travis,

Casey's older and more handsome and charmin' cousin. If you ever get tired of him, I'll treat you right," he said, taking my hand into his and kissing the back of it.

I giggled.

"Travis, ain't nobody tryin' to hear your corny lines," Casey joked. "Go help in the kitchen."

"He think just because he carries a gun around, he can boss me around now. . . . Boy, I'll still whip your ass like we were kids," Travis countered.

I chuckled.

Travis was big too, but he was cute, with curly hair and light skin. He wore a Sean John velour suit and brand-new Air Force Ones. He did have style. I'll give him that.

"So Jade, where are you from?" another one of his relatives asked. She looked older than the rest, with slight wrinkles in her face and a short 'fro. She had thick framed glasses and clutched a cane in her hand.

"I'm from Queens. Born and raised out there," I informed.

"Queens, huh? I know a few ex-girlfriends out there," Travis chimed in. "Not as fine as you, though—but hey, I'm workin' on it."

I laughed again. I liked Travis—he was cool.

"Boy, hush your mouth," the lady clutching the cane hissed.

"Sorry, Big Ma," he apologized.

"Serves him right," Tracy butted in. "Travis always actin' a fool around company. Can't bring the boy around nowhere."

"Hey, you can take your big ass into the kitchen and put your head in the oven fo' Thanksgivin'," Travis quipped back.

I tittered.

"Y'all behave around company," Big Ma snapped. "Casey

brought his new girlfriend home, and y'all acting like y'all don't have no home trainin'."

"Sorry, Big Ma," Travis apologized.

"Hey, Big Ma," Casey greeted, giving her a hug and kiss on her cheek.

"Hey, baby. I'm glad you came."

"You know I couldn't miss spendin' Thanksgivin' with you and my family for the world," Casey proclaimed.

For the next hour, I was introduced to family and friends, and they all made me feel at home. I'll admit: Being with Casey's family, for sure made me forget about my problems at home. I never had a Thanksgiving like this. It felt like the *Brady Bunch* up in here.

The aroma coming from the kitchen made my mouth water. I couldn't wait to eat. That soul Thanksgiving dinner was calling me, and I hadn't eaten anything all day.

"Okay, everybody—dinner is ready," Tracy broadcast to the family.

"A'ight, that's what I'm talking about. About time we get to eat. I done lost twenty pounds waiting fo' y'all to serve us," Travis uttered.

"Boy . . . you be quiet," another family member spat at him.

The table was set up beautiful and superb. We began to take our seats in the family room, where I sat next to Casey. The long dining room table seated ten and was draped in a long white cloth with Thanksgiving dinner spread out across it. I stared at macaroni and cheese, yams, greens, mashed potatoes, rice, stuffing, sweet potato pies, and the main meal—a giant brown turkey that sat in the middle of it all. The children sat at a nearby table and was just as hungry.

"Okay, before we eat, grace must be said. So I want everyone to stand up and say what they're thankful for," Big Ma said. She sat at the head of the table, looking at everyone including me.

Big Ma began first, as she went into being thankful for being able to spend another year with her family, and how the Lord blessed her with her health for so long and beautiful and loving children, and grandchildren. She also thanked Casey for coming, and then she peered at me, and said, "Also, I'm thankful fo' him bringin' home such a beautiful young woman. Jade, welcome to our family, and may you have many more holidays with us."

I blushed and damn near choked up. "Thank you," I returned.

After Big Ma, Tracy spoke, and then they continued around the table until they came to Casey. Casey stood up, cleared his throat, and began his quick speech.

"First of all, I'm thankful fo' my lovin' and crazy family. Wit'out y'all, I don't know where I'd be right now. I'm thankful fo' my career in law enforcement. My health. My son. My good looks," he joked, causing quick titters around the table. He then looked down at me and continued with, "I'm also thankful fo' meeting such a lovely young woman. Welcome to the family, Jade."

I was so caught up and stunned. I smiled, looking up at Casey, and thought he was something else.

"Your turn, miss." Big Ma was referring to me.

I was nervous—these people had so many kind words to say about me, and they accepted me so easily into their home that I was lost for words. But I stood up, peered around the room, and began with, "I'm so glad to be here right now, y'all are truly a blessin'. I mean, I never had a Thanksgiving like this; my family is not as tight as y'all. But I love this, and I want to definitely be a part of this. So I'm very thankful fo' spendin' some time wit' y'all right now."

"We're glad to have you here," Big Ma proclaimed, and everyone else agreed.

I took my seat, and Casey took my hand into his. He peered at me and smiled. "You did nice," he whispered in my ear.

After me, the children spoke, and then it was time to eat.

"It's about time," Travis said. "Y'all took so long that I thought the turkey was goin' to get bored, wake up, and bounce."

There were a few quick laughs, and then everyone dug in at the table fixing themselves a quick plate. Oh, God, the food was delicious. The mac and cheese, the yams, and the stuffing were the best. I had seconds and thirds.

"So," Aunt Jerry began, interrupting our meal, "tell me, Jade, how did the two of y'all meet?"

The question caught me by surprise. I looked at Casey, not knowing how to answer. But Casey looked at his aunt Jerry and replied, "I met Jade durin' my shift. There was an incident in her buildin' which I had to take care of. Before I left, Jade and I locked eyes, and let's just say, we took it from there."

"Ah, that's nice," another one of Casey's cousins uttered out.

"So, Jade, what do you do fo' a livin'?" Big Ma asked.

Another question I wasn't prepared to answer. I didn't want to be honest and say I lived off my man, or now my drug-dealing ex-boyfriend. So I lied and told them, "I'm in school now."

"Oh, that's nice. What school?" Big Ma continued to pry.

"York."

"Oh. Tracy, you went there. What semester?"

"Big Ma . . . ," Casey chimed in, "these yams are great."

"I know, baby. Tracy made them."

"Fo' real? Tracy, you startin' to burn in the kitchen like Big Ma now."

"You ain't tried nothin' yet. Wait till y'all get a whiff of my dessert," Tracy said. "I got cheesecake in the fridge."

"Cheesecake—girl, you better bring that bad boy out here," Travis said. "You know I love me some cheesecake."

And like that, Casey managed to get the subject off me and had his whole family hyped up over some cheesecake. Casey glanced at me and winked his left eye, assuring me that I was in good hands. I smiled and continued with my meal.

By evening, I had a full belly and didn't want to leave. Most of the guys were crowded around the TV, watching football, and the women chatted it up in the kitchen as they cleared the table and began washing dishes, with the children running around the house.

"You okay?" Casey asked.

"Yeah, I'm good."

"I'm goin' outside fo' some fresh air. You wanna join me?" he asked.

"Yeah, that sounds good." I retrieved my leather jacket from the closet and followed Casey out the front door.

I zipped up my leather as the cold air pinched at my skin. "Damn, it got kinda cold out here."

"It's a'ight," Casey said. "This that manly weather. Get your skin rough and shit."

"Please, I'm a tropical sista. I ain't fo' the cold. All the cold does fo' you is make your skin ashy."

"You wanna go back inside?" he asked.

"No. I'm okay fo' now. We can walk. Beside, gives me some time to spend alone wit' you."

We walked down the quiet suburban block and continued talking under the canopy of stars. "Thank you for that inside," I mentioned.

"Nah, it ain't a problem. My peoples can sometimes become a little nosy. But they will look out fo' you if they like you."

"I wish I grew up around a family like yours. Maybe things would have been different fo' me," I mentioned.

"Why you say that?"

"I don't know. I feel my life is so fucked up. My mother, she's down south, and she don't come to New York anymore. Shit, we hardly talk. The last time I saw her, I was nineteen. And my father never been around. I don't know the bastard, and I don't care to know him now. I've been on my own since I was seventeen, Casey. I don't have any siblings, but I got a few cousins. And my family ain't tight like yours."

"How did you meet that asshole?" Casey asked, and I know he was referring to James.

"When I was seventeen, when I was on Jones Beach during Greek Fest, and I thought I was so in love with him. I moved in with him a year after we met. I thought I was so in love at the time. James couldn't do no wrong," I admitted.

"That's how it be sometimes. . . . Cowards like him, they so smooth, so charmin', and always quick to flash money and cars to catch a woman's attention. But soon when they hook you, that's when things change. Jade, I've been around many men like James, and I see the terrible things men like James do to women. And we can't lock 'em all up. And when we do, the women don't wanna press charges, or try to forget that the abuse ever happened.

"Jade, promise me, if things don't work out wit' you and I, that you will never go back to him. Stay away from him," Casey advised. "All he's gonna do is cause you more trouble, and it will get worse."

"Oh, believe me, I'm so done wit' him," I said.

"Yeah, I heard a few women say that 'bout their abusive mate . . . that they were never goin' back, but eventually, more than a few do end up goin' back, thinkin' things are gonna be different the next time around, and feelin' their mate has changed. But most of these men never do, and these women more than often find out the hard way, sometimes endin' up in the morgue," Casey stated.

We walked a few blocks down, and I continued to listen to Casey. He had a lot to say. It was so beautiful on Long Island that I wanted a home out here for myself. It was away from everything, and it felt like a whole new world from Jamaica, Queens—quiet and away from the bullshit that saturated my projects at home. The moon shimmered down on us, and it felt like we were the only ones on earth.

"Jade, I'm gonna be honest. When we got that domestic call and you opened the door fo' my partner and I, it was like déjà vu."

"What you mean?"

"You look and remind me of a similar female."

I smiled. "Who?"

"Three years ago, my partner and I received a similar call when I worked at the Seventy-fifth Precinct in Brooklyn. She was a young woman—about nineteen, twenty—and her husband was beatin' on her. When we got there, her face was bruised and battered, so we arrested the son of a bitch. The next day she bailed him out, talkin' about she didn't want to see the father of her kids end up in jail. I tried reasonin' with her, sayin' she didn't have to be scared and to press charges, but her husband had her naïve mind brainwashed. He got bailed out. Two weeks later, she's callin' the cops on his ass again. We responded to the call, but her husband wasn't home that time, and her face looked bashed in, much worse off than before. I went searching for that asshole, but unfortunately the case got dropped, and he was free to go again.

"A few months passed, and we got another call from the same address. I remember it was cold and raining out, and the day seemed to drag by so slow. When we arrived to the projects where she lived, I noticed her four-year-old daughter wanderin' around in the lobby. I asked her, 'Where's Mommy?' and she told me that her mommy was hurt. My partner and I rushed up to her apartment, and saw the victim lyin' dead in her apartment. Her husband stabbed her ten times in the neck and chest, in front of the children, and he left her to die."

"Ohmygod," I uttered.

"It fucked wit' me fo' a minute. I remember thinkin' I could have done more fo' her. I shouldn't have given up on her so easily. Maybe she'd still be alive today. We caught and arrested her husband a month later. He was shacked up wit' his mistress in Staten Island."

"You did everything you could for her. If she didn't want to press charges or leave him, then that's on her," I said.

"I know, but sometimes I wish it woulda turned out different. Now, when I see you, I swear y'all could have been sistas. . . . That's the scary part about it."

"I see, so you're lookin' out fo' me because you feel guilty about not savin' her."

"Somewhat. When you closed the door in our faces wit' that attitude that day, I knew I just couldn't walk away from you so easily. But I like you, Jade. I'm serious. And I know you're used to the finer things in life, like Gucci, Fendi—and with me being a cop and on a budget, I can't do fo' you like these hustlers can."

"You already did enough fo' me, Casey," I said. We stopped, and I peered into his lovely hazel eyes. "I've been around the hustlers, pimps, pretty thugged-out boys who pushed the fancy cars and always flashed a wad of bills all my life. I grew up around them and dated a few. But what you did fo' me tonight, lettin' me have Thanksgivin' wit' your family—I will never forget this. I love this, Casey. I never had family. It was mostly my mother and myself. And my homegirls, Camille and Shy." My mind thought about Shy. I wanted to hear her side of the story, but then thought, *Fuck that bitch*.

"Well, you're family now, Jade. See, I told you my people would love you."

I smiled. "Thank you."

"I wanna see you turn out a'ight."

"I am now. And what you mean when you said, 'If things don't work out between you and me?' They are already workin' out." I softly affirmed. Casey took both my hands into his and gazed at me gracefully. He smiled and then leaned forward for a kiss. I accepted him, wrapping my arms around his neck and taking in his warm embrace. The cold no longer bothered me, and for a moment, I felt like an entirely new woman.

We kissed for a moment, until a gust of wind picked up and smacked across our faces. "Wow!" I exclaimed, catching the chills again.

"I think it's time to head back," Casey said.

"I agree."

We rushed back to the house hand in hand, and I was thinking, if this is how it's going to be like with him, then fuck James and every other thugged nigga I dated before him. Casey was different, nice and cute. I could get used to him and definitely his family.

I said to myself that it was definitely time for a change. A change in scenery, my lifestyle, the men I've dated, and reluctantly, friends too.

~ CHAPTER 20 ~

shy

By now, I'm sure everyone knew, because don't nothing stay a secret in the projects for long—nothing. But fuck 'em, I thought. I didn't need 'em. And Camille—fuck her too, trying to be up in my business and running things like she the muthafucking government, and thinking her shit don't stink.

But I was concerned about Roscoe; he hasn't called me collect in over a week. So I figure word got back to him about James and myself. But why should he be pissed off at me? I wasn't the one who made the promises and then broke them by getting himself locked up. I should be the one fuming. I was alone, I was horny, and fucked up as it sounds, James was there for me. I thought Jade probably didn't know how to hold his sexy ass down at nights, so the nigga had to creep.

I wrote Roscoe a few letters but never got a return. Thanksgiving Day, I spent in the crib getting high. James came by later on in the day and put the dick down on me. I remember him being upset when he walked through my door, but he never said anything to me. He just literally tore my clothes off, threw me down on the bed facedown, and rammed his big, hard, phat dick into my shit—froggy-style doggy-style.

I got high again and chilled for the remainder of the day. Fuck a turkey—my meal was the pipe. I tried to keep it a secret, but nosy-ass Camille had to go sneaking through my shit. I told the bitch that I had this shit under control. I was doing it just to free my mind from Roscoe and everything else. I wasn't hooked. I knew I could stop smoking crack if I wanted to. I was alone with James most of the time, so Camille and Jade had no idea that I got high. No one knew. And if I did leave my crib, it was hours after I finished getting high. Camille didn't know how stressed I was, she got her life, and she coming to my place playin' mother hen and shit.

I knew I had everything in order. I'm too cute to start slipping.

It was one in the afternoon on a Saturday, and James promised that he would be at my place by noon. I sat in my crib, getting frustrated and bored. I called his cell phone a few times, but no answer—just straight voice mail. I wasn't going to wait a second longer. So I went out to look for him.

I quickly got dressed in some tight jeans, a pair of stilettos, and my butter-soft leather and walked out my door. I hate when niggas don't keep their promises. It pisses me off.

I strutted out my building and was reluctantly greeted by two known hoodlums. "Hey, Shy. What's good, love?" one greeted. He gently tugged at my jacket, staring at me like I owed him a favor.

"What you want, nigga?" I spat, looking at him like *Why you touching me?*

"I wanna holla at you fo' a minute, ma," he said, dressed in a black hoodie, baggy jeans, and construction Timbs.

His friend stood off on the sideline, watching me. "You seen James?" I asked.

"Yeah, he in front of the store," he informed. "But come here."

"Damn, nigga, what you want?" I barked.

"I wanna talk."

"Later. I got somewhere to go," I spat.

"I'm sayin' . . . this shit ain't gonna take but a minute. You get high now, right?" he asked.

"Why is it your business?"

"Because I'm tryin' to look out for you, love. . . . I got that fo' you, if you wanna cop," he explained, gripping my jacket again and trying to pull me back into the lobby.

"Nigga, get the fuck off me!" I jerked my arm free from his soft grip. "I don't know what you think this is, but you need to step the fuck off, yo! Before I let Roscoe know you tryin' get at me."

His eyes flared up as anger appeared, and through clenched teeth he let known, "Bitch, Roscoe don't run things around here no more! You better talk to your boy! You in a different world, bitch! Start getting wit' the fuckin' program, and maybe I'll look out fo' you."

Him and his boy laughed and then proceeded into the lobby. I didn't have a clue to what he was talking about. But my main concern was catching up to James and copping a few rocks for free from him as usual. And I also wanted some dick too. The nigga promised to come by the crib, and he doesn't show.

I walked off down the block, and there was James standing in front of a black Escalade, paying attention to his niggas and his money. By now, I knew people around the way knew we were fucking, so I didn't bother to keep it a secret anymore. At this point, I didn't care who saw. James made me feel good. Good enough I risked friendship and my man for that feeling.

I strutted up to him being in all smiles and shit. He had a wad of cash gripped in one hand and passed a burning L to his man next to him.

"James," I called out.

He turned to look at me, and I noticed an attitude appear on his face. "What you want, Shy?" he asked, looking at me with the irate look.

"Why the attitude?" I asked, trying to be humble.

"Because I'm busy. Yo, what you need?"

"I need you to come over, and I also need that thang," I stated. He knew what I was talking about.

He snickered, "Yo, Shy, slow your ass down. You've been hittin' my shit fo' free fo' too long now. I'm gonna start chargin' you fo' it."

"Charge?" I responded, getting upset. "Fuck you mean charge? I'm sayin' you promised me you'll come by and bless me wit' a lil' sumthin'. Why you actin' up in front of your niggas?"

"You hear this bitch!" James mocked. "Shy, ain't shit free in this world. You gotta pay fo' my shit just like everyone else. You ain't wifey. You got the bomb pussy, but it ain't platinum."

"What?"

"Bitch, you heard me. You got cash? Twenty dollars, love," he proclaimed.

"Nigga, you serious? I had you stayin' up in my crib and fuckin' me, and you dissin' me like this!"

"Shy, stop wastin' my fuckin' time. You either pay up or

fuckin' bounce, you dumb bitch. I ain't got time to be fuckin' around wit' you right now," he said.

His niggas starting laughing while I stood there looking stupid. Then I heard one of 'em say, "Damn, James—you got Roscoe's bitch strung out like that! Oh, shit!"

James laughed and gave his man dap. "Nigga, you know how I do. Bitches be on my dick like that."

I felt so stupid. All I could do was look at him. He played me. He fucked me, got me high, and now the nigga was playing me. I cheated on Roscoe for his dumb ass, and now my business was all out in the streets, and now these niggas were looking at me like I was some bird-bitch. I remember niggas respected me when Roscoe was home. They all wanted to holla, but knew Roscoe would bash their fucking heads in if they attempted. But now, they looked at me like some plain druggie bitch.

I suddenly became belligerent toward him and shouted, "Nigga, fuck you! I'm gonna tell Roscoe, and he gonna get someone to fuck your ass up. . . . Watch, bitch!"

"Fuck Roscoe, bitch! That nigga ain't runnin' shop out here no more. Fuck that nigga. This my shit—what he gonna do? Fuck him and you! Cunt bitch!" he shouted as he stepped up in my face and towered over me with rage and his fist clenched.

I tried to hold my ground, being in heels and shit. But there wasn't shit I could do.

"Step the fuck off, Shy," James said.

A few tears began trickling down my face. I was hurt. I felt I had nothing. I betrayed my man for this asshole and lost friendship because I fucked this asshole.

I didn't even expect it, or see it coming. But James cursed me when I turned around to leave, and he kicked me dead in my ass, knocking me down to the floor and scraping my leather.

They all laughed as I kissed the concrete.

"Yo, that's fucked up, James. How you gonna do that to shorty," one of his friends said, but laughing as he said it.

"That's where she belongs—on her knees, right, Shy? You good on your knees, bitch," James spat.

"Fuck you!" I cried out.

"Been there, done that," he quipped back.

I picked myself up and left in a hurry. I still heard them laughing at me from a distance. I scurried back to my building, with the most anguished look on my face. I was hurt. My reputation, ruined. At that point, I felt like killing myself.

~ CHAPTER 21 ~

camille

I hated coming to Rikers Island, but I had to. Roscoe called me and requested to see and speak to me. He had some information for me. But he didn't want to say over the phone. I understood. You can't say too much on a prison phone.

So the following week, I jumped on the bus to Rikers. It was crowded with women. Christmas was only a few days away. I had on a pair of tight Baby Phat jeans, a sweater, and a brown leather coat. I knew Roscoe had to know about Shy already. The whole hood knew Shy was on crack and fuckin' James. And the news would reach Roscoe shortly. I knew Roscoe wanted to hear from me personally about his woman being a druggy.

I was nervous when the bus pulled up to the visiting center. I was the last one to get off the bus. I knew the routine, it was well-known to me, I dated men who had been behind these walls one too many times. And Cream was one of 'em. It took me about forty minutes to actually see Roscoe. I sat in the visiting hall, quiet as a mouse, my legs crossed, waiting patiently. I caught a few eyes looking at me, mostly men, who were probably fantasizing about me being naked.

Roscoe finally came out. He was in line with three other men, all who were wearing gray prison jumpsuits with DOC printed on the back. He had on white tube socks with brown sandals. He had changed a bit. He had a scruffy beard and his braids needed to be done. He gave me a faint smile as he walked toward me. I flashed a quick smile back.

"Hey, Camille," he greeted me.

I stood up and gave him a hug. "Hey, Roscoe. I came like you asked. What's on your mind?"

He took a seat across from me and glanced around the room. He gave an inmate a head nod, then turned back and looked at me.

"I got a lot of shit on my mind, Camille. I heard about my baby, Shy—" He paused; I guess he started thinking about Shy's fucked-up predicament. He then rubbed his scruffy beard and continued. "You know, you trust niggas to handle shit for you while you locked down. But dis game is grimy. You can't trust anyone. I thought Shy had my back, and my boy turned her out."

"Roscoe, I can help Shy. She's not herself," I said.

"She's dead to me, Camille. Fuck her! What's done is done. In here, you see who your real friends are. You're good peoples, Camille. Thanks for coming down here," he said.

"What's so important that you made me come here to see you in person?"

"I've done a lot of fucked-up shit in my life, yo. A lot of crazy shit. I know who set me up, Camille. He a hating-ass nigga. Yo, I should have seen it coming," he said in a low tone.

"James, right?"

"He kept telling me about this new connect for a minute

now. But I wasn't buying it. I was comfortable wit' the niggas I was dealing with. But James kept coming at me, sayin' we ain't gotta fuck wit' the Dominicans anymore. He wanted to scratch them out, and put me on to these Haitians that could get us a better price. I'm a loyal client to my connect. But James, he a greedy fuck. He don't give a fuck about nothin'. He knew he couldn't deal wit' the Haitians unless I approved, and he knew it wasn't happenin'. So the nigga tried to have me killed the night I got arrested for murder. He had to cut a deal with the Haitians, and I don't trust them niggas."

I was definitely listening, but I knew that there was more to the story. Roscoe didn't just call me up here to tell me about how grimy James was. He had something planned.

"Camille, in Jade's crib, under her bed you'll find a .357 hidden under a loose floorboard," he told me.

"A .357?"

"It's James's gun, and it got bodies on it. He's too stupid to get rid of it because it was his brother's gun, and his first gun. He loves that gun," he whispered to me. I knew he had to be careful, because I knew where he was going with this. And if I was right, he was about to snitch.

He continued: "But one particular body on that gun you'll be interested in hearing about. It happened six years ago at a party. We had beef wit' this nigga on the block. Yo, he wouldn't stop running his mouth about him being on the come up and getting down with Kahlil and his crew. He thought he was a badass. He robbed James and me one day of five large, and thought he couldn't be touched. So one night, we followed him to Kahlil's party. He came out wit' his girl; they were hugged up on each other tight and didn't even notice us watching them.

They went up into this Explorer to fuck, so that's when we made our move."

Ohmygod, I thought. I started to remember what he was telling me. It was the night Raheem was killed. I was there.

"We pulled Raheem and his girl out of the truck and beat on him. His girl came charging at us, so I punched her in her jaw and dropped her to the ground. Then James fired two shots into her boyfriend. We didn't even stick around. We bounced."

"Roscoe, ohmygod—"

He continued, "Yo, I didn't even know it was Shy when I met her. When I first saw her, I kept telling myself, 'Yo, home-gurl look so fuckin' familiar.' But I couldn't place her face. She was young back then. She was beautiful. I found out it was her when I saw a picture of her and Raheem. I felt bad for her, so I promised myself that I would look out for her and take care of her. But I ended up in here. Camille, I love Shy; don't get me wrong. I wanted the best for her. I owe it to her. I helped take her boyfriend's life right in front of her. I knew that fucked her up. So I'm giving you the gun. It got James's prints on it and everything. He don't move the gun. It stays hidden under Jade's bed. You do what you gotta do, Camille. I'm sorry that I had to tell you this. And tell Shy I'm sorry," he said. He then got up and instructed the CO that his visit was over.

I was shocked. I watched Roscoe leave. He never looked back at me. I guess he figured that this chapter of his life was over, why look back.

Two days later, Cream and I went out to eat. I had to reluctantly break the news to Cream that I couldn't make it out to Cali with him. What Roscoe had told me was a bombshell. I didn't know if I should tell Cream about it first, or just go straight to the police with the information. I knew that if I went to the police, it would implicate Roscoe. Maybe he wanted to implicate himself, but why? Maybe it was his debt being paid to Shy for helping take Raheem's life. I figured if he was going down, then he was going to bring James down with him. I wanted James to go down though, that's for sure.

"What you mean, you're not comin' out to Cali wit' me?" Cream barked. We were at BBQ's on Long Island, and I talked to him about not being able to leave with him.

"There's so much goin' on right now, Cream. I don't know where to begin," I tried to explain.

"So you gonna sit here and worry about other people problems, Camille. What about you? I'm leavin' in a few weeks."

"Cream, I'm sorry," I humbly said to him.

"Nah, I'm the one sorry. Here I am, tryin' to look out fo' you, and you're dissin' me fo' what, Camille? I thought you were ready to move on wit' your life. Obviously, I was wrong."

"Baby . . . listen—," I began to say, but Cream cut me short.

"Nah, I wanna be wit' you and spend some time in Cali wit' you by my side. I wanna help build your career out there, and get you away from the bullshit out here. But clearly, your fuckin' friends and the drama they get themselves into comes first, right?"

"It's not even like that," I countered.

"Whatever, Camille," Cream said, rising from his seat. He reached into his pocket, pulled out a wad of cash, and peeled off a C-note for the bill, dropping the cash on the table. "I'm out. You can stay if you want."

He began walking off as I continued to sit there. *He took that well,* I thought, trying to lighten my mood. On the real, if

Cream was some next nigga, I would have told him to go fuck himself. But Cream lucky he was Cream, and he didn't hear my mouth, and I ain't embarrass him in this bitch. It was sad to admit, but I love that nigga. I loved him more than anyone else I ever dated—male or female. He had attitude, charm, looks, and money. And he didn't hesitate to put me in my place when he knew I was wrong, or let me know what he felt was best for me. A lot of niggas are intimidated by me—but Cream, if I got loud and tried to embarrass him, he'll get loud and return the same attitude toward me. I like that. I need a nigga who's able to hold me down, and knows how to handle shit. But he never took it too far when he got loud, like being disrespectful and trying to put his hands on me. He had respect for me since the day we met.

I sat there for a few more seconds, thinking this nigga actually just walked out on me, on some attitude shit. Yo, I had to chuckle. Muthafucka. He really wanted me out in Cali with him. I knew he wasn't pussy-whipped. I've been around a lot of niggas who got strung up on my pussy, but Cream, I didn't know if I wanted to choke him or fuck him.

Eventually, I got up out of my seat and followed Cream out. "Keep the change," I told our waitress as I brushed by her.

When I stepped outside, Cream was already in his ride with the lights on and the engine idling. I dashed up to the passenger side, jumped in, and spat, "Nigga, you was goin' to leave me out here!"

He shouted, "Hurry your ass up, then!"

"Fuck you!" I said softly.

"Camille, listen. I never said this to any woman in my life, but I'm sayin' it now." He stared into my eyes. "On the real, I love you, and I wanna be with you. So what do I gotta do to help you change your mind? What's preventin' you from comin' to Cali wit' me?"

I thought about it, and my major concern that was keeping me rooted in NY was James and his beef with Jade and having my girl Shy strung out on the pipe. I wanted my revenge on that nigga. I was spiteful. He had someone attack me while I was in the elevator, and I couldn't leave for California without that nigga getting what was owed to him. I didn't tell Cream about my attack, or Jade and Shy. I let it be for now, but I knew something had to be done about him.

"Cream, I got unfinished business to take care of before I leave," I stated.

"Like what? You got beef wit' someone?"

I knew if I told Cream, he was going to handle it. And I knew his way of handling things. But I love Cream, and I didn't want him getting into trouble over me, and risk getting himself locked up, and losing everything he'd worked so hard to build. I couldn't have that on my conscience. He had his career, his future to look forward to. Cream still did dirt, but putting down that murder game, his hands been clean for years now, I think.

"Talk to me, Camille. Let me know what's up. Don't shut me out. You know I hate that shit," he said. He pulled out of the parking lot and headed home.

My cell started ringing, and I picked up. "Hello." But no one answered. "Hello," I repeated. For a minute, I thought I heard someone crying, but then the caller hung up.

"Who was that? Cream asked.

"Don't know. No one said a word."

Cream glanced at me. I knew he was still upset. "I'm not leaving without you, Camille," he said.

"What? Nah, Cream, this is your future. This is what you looked forward to. This is what you always wanted. You can't throw that away. You know I'm gonna love you regardless if you live in Cali or live on the edge of the fuckin' earth. Do you, Cream?"

"Camille, if you don't tell me what's up, then I'm stayin'. I'm gonna tell you right now: I ain't gonna be able to function out in Cali, 'cause I'm gonna be worryin' about your ass out here in NY. . . . If you were just some next ho, fine. But this is you, Camille. I got too much love fo' you to leave you behind so easily."

I sighed. Damn.

I knew I had to say something. He wasn't going to fuck up his career because of my bullshit and my problems. I wasn't having that. So I looked over at Cream, and said, "I got beef wit' this one nigga."

~ CHAPTER 22 ~

shy

Fuck this, I said to myself, hanging up on Camille. I wanted to say something—but nah, I got too much pride to be calling up Camille and crying to her after I told her to get the fuck out of my life. I wasn't going to cry and invite her back in. That shit made me look weak. And I refused to be weak.

James, he's an asshole. I wanted to spit in his fucking face—but that's a'ight. Watch, I'm gonna tell Roscoe what James did, and Roscoe is going to have him fucked up. My baby gonna call, I'm gonna tell him how disrespectful these niggas were to me out here, and he's gonna handle them. My baby going to take care of me.

I was too stressed with shit, and I needed something to free my mind. So I met up with one of these hustling niggas on the corner, Lil' Rome I think they call him, and he hooked me up with that free shit, but after I done told him he could come by to chill at my place later on. He was cute, young though, like seventeen. But he had the pull for that product.

It was 8:25 in the evening when the phone rang. I was about

to spark up, but the ringing of the phone stopped me from pressing the pipe against my lips and getting my high on.

"You have a collect call from . . . Roscoe Richardson . . . to accept—"

I immediately accepted his call.

"Roscoe—hey, baby. . . . Why haven't you called lately?" I asked, sounding sincere. "I've been missin' you."

I heard him snicker. "Shy, you know what? . . . Fuck you!" he snapped. "You a grimy-ass bitch!"

"What? Baby, why are you so mad? What's goin' on?"

"You fo' real, Shy? You gonna talk to me on this phone like it's love like that, when you was out fuckin' my man."

"Roscoe, that's a lie . . . I . . ."

"Bitch, stop your fuckin' lying. 'I—I' *what?* You're dead to me, ho. I don't wanna hear nuthin' from you!"

"Roscoe, no, please! Nuthin' happened, I swear! James . . . James, he came by, but I don't love him. Baby, it wasn't even like that, I swear," I cried out.

"Shy, you wanna know why I'm up in here? . . . James set me up. Word got out. That nigga I killed—he was meant to kill me, but I got the shot off faster. He got me off the streets one way or the other, and now you fuckin' this nigga. He had someone pick up the gun and had it hidden somewhere. Now he runnin' shop and talkin' shit about me. He got the best of both worlds now, right, Shy? He fuckin' my bitch, and runnin' my hood."

"Oh, God, Roscoe . . . I didn't know!" I sobbed. "He tricked me, Roscoe. You gotta believe me."

"Fuck you! Bitch, you're naïve right now."

"I love you, baby. I love you. . . . Please don't do this!" I continued to cry out, not believing what I was hearing.

"I was goin' to get at you on some one-eighty-seven shit, but your homegirl Camille talked me out of it. So I'm gonna let you die slow, you junkie bitch! I ain't gotta touch you. You're fuckin' killing yourself anyway. I already paid my debt to you. I'm sorry, Shy. And I bet you don't even know what I'm sorry for. You figure it out, bitch," he said, then hung up.

"Roscoe . . . no, please . . . don't leave me," I shouted. "Roscoe, it was a mistake! I'm so sorry . . . Baby."

I dropped to the floor, clutching my sheets. *This ain't happening—this is not fucking happening. I can't lose him. I can't.* It wasn't meant to end like this. Roscoe and I, we were supposed to move out the projects, have kids, and be a family. We were supposed to do us. And one man, he fucked all that up for me. He ruined my life. He destroyed me so quickly. Foolish, Shy—why you had to be so fucking foolish?

~ CHAPTER 23 ~

jade

Today, I start a new life. Today, I become a brand-new woman. Today, I free my mind from the foolishness and drama that plagued me for twenty-one years. Today, I become reborn and change my life around. I promised myself these things as I stared at my reflection in the bathroom mirror. I was tired of the BS, and I definitely wanted a new beginning. Casey instilled that in me, that I was able to escape the poverty and the ghetto. The Forty Ps wasn't my home forever, and I'll be damn if I would let it be. I knew that there was more out there for me. Spending Thanksgiving with Casey and his family opened my eyes to a lot of things, and I definitely wanted a family of my own. And I know having a family with James—fuck out of here, never that. I wanted to be with Casey. He was my beginning; he was my head start. He became my inspiration.

I called up my mother last night and had a two-hour talk with her. I told her about Casey and explained how we met. I told her that it was definitely over with James, and she wished me the best. She said being with James and moving in with him was the worst choice I'd ever made. She'd been there and done that with men. And I watched these different types of men come in and out of my mother's life since I was eight. And she warned me that it's not healthy, and it is also dangerous. But she told me that she wanted to meet Casey. So I promised her that we'd try to make it down there for Christmas, which was three weeks away. I haven't had a mother-to-daughter talk with my moms in so long that when I hung up, I cried for a few moments.

I wanted to get my life back on track, and that including having constant contact with my mother. I wanted to see her and spend some time with her. It's been too long now.

I woke up this morning, and I was feeling great. I called up Camille and told her that I wasn't upset with Shy any longer. Fuck it, what's done is done, and I wasn't going to continue to beef about this shit. You can forgive, but sometimes it's hard to forget.

I knew Shy needed our help, so fuck it, I knew that I had to be the better woman about it. So I planned to take care of my business early in the morning and then confront Shy about everything later on, and let her know that I was still a bit upset about it, but I was willing to work things out with her. Like Camille said, we've all been friends for too long to let one grimy nigga come in between us.

Missing Casey a bit, I decided to call him on his phone while he was at work. I just wanted to hear his voice.

"Hey, baby," Casey happily greeted, knowing it was me calling.

"We still on fo' the night, right?" I asked, referring to our dinner date at Tavern on the Green.

"Of course. I'm gettin' off early. I don't wanna upset you by being late," he said.

I chuckled. "As long as you don't break our date, I'm good."

"I'll be at your place around ten, so you be ready, baby. Okay?"

"I got the bomb dress to put on. I can't wait for you to see me in it," I mentioned.

"I'm picturin' it now."

"The dress?"

"Nah, takin' it off later on tonight," he joked.

"Casey," I tittered, "behave."

"I will. Promise."

"Go back to work, and lock up some criminals."

He laughed. "I'll see you tonight, okay?"

"Okay. And Casey . . ."

"Yeah."

"Love you."

"Love you too, Jade."

After our brief conversation, I started to clean my place up a little. I vacuumed the floor, mopped the kitchen, and straightened up my bedroom. After that, I called up Camille and told her that I was going over to Shy's place, and I wanted her to come along. We all needed to talk. We all needed to be together. She told me she'd be there soon after, and to call her when I got there.

It was a little past noon when my phone rang. When I picked up, there wasn't any answer. That was the second time today somebody called my crib and no one spoke. I paid it no mind; I thought it was just niggas being stupid.

I quickly got dressed, throwing on some jeans, sneakers, a light sweater, and my leather, and strutted out my door, heading to see Shy.

The day was clear, and being forty-five degrees outside. It felt like a great day. The skies were blue, and Christmas was coming.

And I had plans—not just for the holidays, but for my future. I was going to enroll in school in the fall and probably take up nursing. It was something that I always had an interest in doing. After that, I wanted to have kids, move out of Jamaica housing, and start doing me. I wanted a life. I wanted a career. I was tired of being a drug dealer's girl, who he sported around under his arms only for show and a piece of pussy. I was tired of depending on niggas for money and to pay my bills and rent. A bitch needed to start being more independent. And Camille was my role model. She's been doing her for years, without having a man around all the time. And I needed to follow in her footsteps.

I started down the block with a smile on my face, and for the first time, I wasn't worried about James, Tasha, or bumping into some drama. Yo, I was so done with that, that I wanted to put it behind me and start my new day right. *Today, I begin a completely new life for myself,* I thought.

As I was walking down 160th Street with my destination on my mind, I noticed Tasha up the block. I thought nothing about it. I wasn't even going to start beefing with her. In fact, I was willing to let shit be and tell her that I wasn't stressing her and James anymore. She can have the nigga. Let her deal with the bullshit, abuse, and his fucked-up attitude. I was doing me, and I ain't got the time for it anymore.

Tasha continued to approach me, dressed down in a black puffy Sean John coat and, as usual, her face scowling at me. My smile faded, but I wasn't starting nothing. I was just being cautious, and I wasn't going to say a word to her. I was just going to quickly walk by her, and keep my mouth shut, not acknowledging her at all. I figured it would be better that way. I didn't want to utter something and have her take it the wrong way.

She was a few feet away from me when I noticed her pull something from her coat, and I saw a black object gripped in her hand. She took a few more steps toward me and raised her arm up at me, and that's when I noticed she had a gun in her hand. I became bug-eyed, and before I could react, a loud shot went off.

Pop!

"What now, bitch! You ain't talkin' that shit out your mouth, now, huh!" Tasha shouted.

I fell back, smashing against the cold concrete and landing on my side. I knew I was hit, but didn't know where at. Majority of my body suddenly felt numb. I tried to get up, but—*pop*—I was hit again.

I screamed out in agony as my body lay limp against the concrete. I became scared as I stared up at Tasha—looking up at death. I heard people screaming around me, and wished I could wake up from this horrible nightmare.

"Fuck you, ho! Don't you ever fuckin' disrespect me again," she chided, with no remorse for her sudden action. I watched her take off running as she left me there to die.

"Oh, God!" I cried out.

After Tasha fled, people slowly started to gather around me, peering down at me like I was some science project. I didn't want to die. I couldn't die. Casey. Shy. Camille. I thought to myself, *Today, I begin a completely new life. Today, I become a brand-new woman. Today, I—*

~ CHAPTER 24 ~

camille

The loud *bang, bang, bang,* at my door was followed by the constant ringing of my fucking doorbell. I swear, whoever was at my door acting a fool was about to hear my mouth go off at them.

I hurried to my door, ready to curse some fool out. I opened it and saw Melinda, this seventeen-year-old high-school student who lived up the block by Shy and Jade. She looked like she'd been running as she stood in front of me, breathing heavily, with this gloomy look plastered across her face.

"Camille—yo—"

"What you want, Melinda?" I asked, a bit annoyed that she was banging on my door like she ain't had no damn sense.

"Jade got shot!" she blurted.

"What?" I was shocked. "Jade? What you talkin' about?" I swear it felt like I was having a panic attack. My chest tightened, and it felt like I was about to pass out. Not Jade. Melinda got it twisted, I thought.

"Tasha. She shot Jade, Camille. I think she's dead."

I heard nothing else as I rushed by Melinda dressed only in

some jeans, slippers, and a light T-shirt. It had to be forty-something degrees outside. But the weather had no effect on me as I dashed out the lobby with no coat, no hat, nothing, and rushed up the block where I saw flashing police lights, an ambulance, and a crowd of people gathered around.

I ran like a madwoman to the scene. I didn't want to believe it. Not Jade. Nah, I know this bitch Tasha ain't take it this far—nah, nah, nah.

When I arrived, I peered over where the sprawled body lay covered in a white sheet against the cold ground. I stared at the scene. My eyes trickling tears down my face. I didn't believe it. Not until I saw her, it wasn't true. My girl ain't dead.

I noticed some of the local residents peering at me with the saddest gaze across their face. The way they looked at me, and when Mrs. Robinson came over and threw her arm around me and gave her condolences, saying, "Camille, I'm sorry," I fucking lost it.

"Nooo! fuck! . . . Nah, nah! She ain't dead! Jade! Fuck this! Fuck, yo! What the fuck!"

I felt Mrs. Robinson arms tighten around me as I cried out. I collapsed down to the floor, and Mrs. Robinson still gripped me tightly in her arms.

"Where that bitch at?" I demanded to know, with fury and vengeance embedded in my eyes.

No one answered me. I became so enraged that I sprung myself from Mrs. Robinson arms and was about ready to hunt Tasha the fuck down.

My homegirl was dead and gone, and I swear to her death, James, Tasha, and whoever else was involved were going to feel my wrath.

I glanced across the street and noticed Casey slumped over the hood of a police car, and it looked like he was crying. I didn't go over to him; I was hurting my damn self. I knew I had to call her cousin Shana and let her know what happened. And Shy, I didn't see her around. I had to break the news to her too. I wanted to be strong and hold myself together, but the pain was too much for me to bear. Seeing Jade's body covered in a white sheet and spread out on the ground like that almost made me go fucking crazy out this bitch. I was ready to flip on anyone, even Mrs. Robinson—I wanted payback.

Two hours later, Shana and her friends Sasha and Naja came around beefing and ready to wild the fuck out. I was with them, and whatever went down, I was in 100 percent.

"Camille, who shot my fuckin' cousin?" she snapped, looking at me with tear-streaked eyes. Her head was wrapped in a blue scarf, and she wore a heavy blue coat and gripped a small knife in her hand.

"That bitch, Tasha!" I told her.

"Where that bitch at?"

"I don't know, but her dyke cousin live over on Union Hall Street," I mentioned.

"Fuck that! We gonna see that bitch!" Shana shouted, and her and her posse marched over to Union Hall Street to see Dee. I know Dee knew where Tasha was at. They were cousins, and they were close. If Tasha had any beef, she would instantly go check her cousin.

I followed behind Shana and them, and we got to Dee's crib shortly, and already the drama was about to pop off. Tasha and Dee's people were outside, because they knew we were coming. There were about six of 'em—male and female—and when we approached, this older-looking lady shouted, "Y'all bitches better leave from my crib! I ain't fuckin' joking, Tasha ain't here!"

"Fuck that—let me see that bitch!" Shana shouted. "I know y'all hiding that bitch! She shot my fuckin' cousin!"

"Fuck you, bitch. . . . Don't be comin' up to my grandmother's crib beefin'!" Dee barked.

"What, bitch?" I heard Sasha snap back. "You better step the fuck back, you Big Bird–lookin' bitch!"

"Fuck you!"

"Yo, tell Tasha to stop fuckin' hiding. Let me see that bitch!" I shouted, getting in the mix of things.

"Yo, y'all bitches better move!" this one cornball-looking nigga shouted, wearing tight sweats and a tight hoodie.

"Nigga, what!"

"Fuck y'all."

Everyone was shouting at each other, and I knew that at any moment, somebody was going to take it to the next level. I was boiling mad and glared at everyone on Dee's porch. If looks could kill, they all would be dead.

A crowd started to assemble around on the block, watching Shana, myself, and her clique beefing with Tasha's fuckin' family. But no one intervene, because they knew what went down earlier with my girl Jade, and I guess they knew payback was coming sooner or later.

When I suddenly heard Dee shout, "Fuck that bitch, Jade," I abruptly snapped and picked up a brick, rushed over to Dee, and smashed her across the fucking head with it, dropping that bitch to the ground. Fuck that—it was on.

Shana and everyone else rushed at the family, and we all started brawling. Tasha's grandma hurried in the house while the rest of her family tried to stand ground and fight us. I grabbed another cousin and tore into her like I was a fucking savage. She fell to the floor, and I stomped, kicked, and beat the shit outta her, turning her face into a crimson color.

"Y'all disrespect my girl like dat, huh. . . . Y'all fuckin' crazy!" I screamed.

"Ahhhh, that fuckin' bitch stabbed me!" I looked over, and it was Dee clutching her gut as blood seeped through her clothing.

"Fuck that, bitch!" Shana shouted.

Moments later, police began swarming the block, with their lights blaring and flashing. They rushed from their cars and quickly began trying to regain order out this bitch.

I went nowhere. I just stood there with my clothes torn, my anger still seething, and still mourning from the lost of Jade.

An hour later, I sat in the 103rd Precinct next to Shana and Naja. We all were handcuffed to a chair. We all were quiet. I guess after all the drama and our adrenaline faded away, we finally came to the realization that Jade was gone. She was no longer with us. And I started tearing up as I started reminiscing about her. Tears ran down my cheeks when I thought why it had to end this way. She was happy. She was moving on.

Casey entered the room and he stared at me. He had a somber look on his face. I didn't say a word to him. I just continued to sit there being lost in my thoughts.

"Camille, right?" he asked incredulously.

"Yeah," I muttered back.

"Can we talk?" he asked.

I shrugged my shoulders. "I guess so. I'm cuffed to this chair, though."

He came over, pulled out a set of keys, and quickly unlocked the cuffs. I stood up, soothing my wrist a bit, because the dick-head cop that put them on clamped them on too tight.

I followed him to a back room, where he shut the door and sat on a desk. I remained standing, peering around, and wondered what he wanted me for.

His eyes watched me and then he began with, "You knew her fo' a long time, right?"

"Yeah. We grew up together."

"I never fell in love with a woman so quickly. But Jade, she was different," he admitted. "I just wanted to talk to her best friend. We met briefly at her apartment. I'm sorry," he uttered, his voice trailing off in sorrow.

"What about Tasha? Y'all lookin' for that bitch, right?"

"We got cops knockin' down doors fo' her killer," he said.

"She really liked you," I told him. "And I liked you. You were definitely an improvement from her last boyfriend. She was happy wit' you."

A faint smile loomed on his face, and then it quickly disappeared as he broke down into tears. "Oh, God!" he cried. "I was supposed to protect her. I was supposed to be there fo' her. I promised her that she was safe with me. I feel like I let her down."

"You were there fo' her. You gave her happiness. You made her smile again. If it means anything to you, it's good to know that she spent her last days happy and knowin' you were there fo' her."

He nodded.

"What's goin' to happen to her cousin, and the rest?" I asked.

"Shana, they might charge her wit' assault and attempted murder. But you're free to go. Go home and get some rest."

"I'll try."

I walked out the room, leaving Casey behind to ponder about Jade and his relationship. He knew her fo' a short while, and already he missed her as much as I was missing her now.

I passed by Shana, Naja, and Sasha and never uttered a word. Shana glanced up at me with her tearstained face and nodded her head slightly at me.

I walked out of the 103rd Precinct and never looked back.

I caught up with Shy at her apartment earlier that evening, and when she answered her door, I already knew she heard about Jade's death. She broke down, collapsing in my arms, howling loudly.

"What happened?" she muttered.

I didn't even respond to her. I was just quiet. The day felt gray, and I felt so empty. It felt like a part of me was missing. A part of me had died. I remained with Shy throughout the day. My eyes stayed watery, and I still couldn't grasp that Jade was gone—taken away from us so abruptly. These projects, all they do is cause pain and suffering. No life came from here, just hurt, constant drama, and those who envy and hate.

aftermath: cream

The night was quiet as Cream sat patiently in his parked burgundy Denali peering out at the projects—looking at stillness on a cold December night. Camille had called him the day Jade was murdered, and she was distraught. He came by that night to console her. He met Jade a few times, and she was a cool shorty. Pretty too. It was fucked up what happened to her. Camille told Cream about everything that went down and what was going on. She broke down to him and brought up the attack in the elevator after he done dropped her off. She brought up Shy, and how James got her girl hooked on crack, fucked over his best friend, setting his ass up, and she also mentioned how James had Jade killed. If it wasn't for him and his infidelity, Jade would have still been alive.

Cream thought, *Damn, how one nigga can cause so much drama and turmoil in the hood?* He thought if he didn't have to kill him, maybe he could have some use for him. But he disregarded the sickening thought from his mind and focused back to business. He knew a nigga like James had to go. He had no respect, no morals for himself and the game they played. And plus, he had gone after Camille, put his hands on his woman, and was preventing her from leaving for Cali with him. So the nigga had to go.

He sat in his Denali, holding a chrome nine-millimeter Beretta, and listening to his 2Pac CD. He could have gotten someone else to do the job for him, but he wanted to do it himself. Cream hadn't caught a body in over four years—and to him, this was personal. He saw the hurt that James put into these three women lives. And the one thing Cream had some respect for was women. Even though he was a player and did him over the years, he respected women and always been straight up with them. He never laid a hand on any woman, and he never mislead a bitch, promising her one thing and then doing totally the opposite. He really did love Camille. Over the many years they knew each other, his heart grew fonder and fonder for her so strongly, that his plan was when they got to California, he was going to ask Camille to marry him. He let Camille slip from his grip once. He wasn't going to let it happen again.

Cream had resources. He had clout, and he knew people—occasionally the wrong people, and sometimes the right people. He got word that James be staying in one particular building where he was hiding out in Brooklyn. His name became mud in Jamaica, Queens. The cops were after him, and Roscoe wanted him dead. Things didn't quite turn out the way James expected them to turn out. After Jade's death, everything went to shit for him. They arrested Tasha a day after she shot Jade, and she snitched him out, telling police that James made her do it. He promised her that if she killed Jade, getting her out the way, then he'd pay her and hook her up. Tasha was in love with James, and she was the type of bitch, if he said jump, she'd ask how high.

James became jealous and was raging that Jade was dating a cop. And when he knew she was happy with him, his ego couldn't handle that Jade was finally happy without him around. He wanted Jade to become miserable and come crawling back to him, begging for him to take her back and wanting the dick again. But Jade moved on, and James couldn't stomach that.

Now he was on the run, trying to escape prison. He knew if caught, his fate was sealed. Because he would be transported to Rikers Island, and Roscoe was in Rikers. And he knew Roscoe had the right niggas to get at him—and he knew Roscoe was undeniably going to try and get at him. He done talked shit, fucked his woman, and set him up—James was fucked.

Cream got wind through niggas he knew from way back in the day that the man he was looking for was staying up in a particular building on the seventh floor, and he crept out only at nights. James stayed with his baby mother Gloria, who he had a two-year-old son by. No one knew but him and Gloria.

Cream glanced at the time, and it was eleven fifteen; and the wind picked up dramatically.

"Bingo," he uttered, spotting James coming from a twenty-four-hour bodega, gripping a black plastic bag and trying to look inconspicuous.

Cream shook his head. Niggas like him—fucking cornballs. They don't know how to stick it out. Shit get rough, and they go out and run, shacking up with some gullible bitch. Cream did five years for murder. He never got someone to do his dirty work; he always pulled the trigger on someone himself. Cream was the real gangsta. James, the nigga, hid behind bitches and naïve muthafuckas that believed his hype. But tonight, he knew James's hype was about to come to an end.

He stepped out the truck, concealing the nine-millimeter. He subtly followed James to his destination, and placed the silencer on the tip of the barrel quickly. He didn't need the attention on himself, having muthafuckas in the hood hear the loud shots. Cream wanted to be in and out—body the nigga and catch a 7:20 flight to LAX the next morning.

James never turned around as he strutted to his building. He had the hood to his large black coat draped over his head and munched on some chips.

James entered the lobby, and soon after, Cream stepped in right behind him, playing the nonchalant role—pretending to be a local resident. He knew James was new to the hood, and he didn't know faces on the regular. So Cream had an advantage.

"What up?" Cream nodded.

James nodded back, giving Cream a quick glance and not being intimidated by Cream's presence. James stood over him a few inches, gripping his bag and kept his mouth shut. The elevator came down, and the black metal door slid back into the wall, allowing for the two men to step in.

Cream stepped in first, and James next. Cream pushed for the sixth floor and James pushed for the seventh. The elevator door came to a close, and both men stood in silence as the elevator began to ascend.

Cream slowly reached into his coat and began pulling out his weapon. His eyes looked forward the entire time. James seemed to be in his own little world.

They passed the third floor, and then the fourth, and suddenly Cream was smacked across the head with the plastic shopping bag, the contents inside dazing him a bit. James began pounding on Cream.

"Nigga, you lookin' fo' me!" James shouted, his fist striking Cream. The gun dropped, and the two men struggled in the elevator.

James slammed Cream against the wall; his grip was strong against Cream. "Who the fuck is you, nigga? You think I'm stupid? I'll fuckin' kill you. Roscoe sent you, right?"

But what James didn't know was that the gun Cream dropped was a .45. Cream casually reached into his other pocket while trying to fight off James with his one free arm, and pulled out the loaded nine-millimeter, and had it pointed at James abdomen on the low.

Poot!

A single shot went off, causing James to jerk suddenly. His eyes widened with shock. And his grip against Cream loosened. He stumbled back, clutching his wound, his hand covered in blood.

Poot! Poot! Poot! Poot!

Cream fired four more times at James, dropping him. Shockingly to Cream, James was still alive, lying on his back, sprawled out on the floor and clutching his stomach. His breathing was sparse. James peered up at Cream, seeing his attacker breathing down soft on him.

"This is for Jade, Shy, and Camille, you dumb son of a bitch!" Cream said as he pointed the gun down at James's head.

James had it mistaken. He thought Roscoe had sent him. He was surprised that those bitches had the nerve to send a hit man to finish him off.

He let out a quick chuckle. "Fuck 'em! Fuck those bitches!" he mumbled.

Poot!

The last and final shot struck James in his front lobe—killing him instantly.

Cream picked up the .45 that was dropped and darted off the elevator and went for the stairs. His job was done. The one nigga who had caused so many so much pain and suffering was shot down. Because of James, Shy was now a junkie, suckin' on that glass dick everyday, and she lost two boyfriends, one to the streets and one to prison. Jade was dead. And Camille, she lost both her sisters and had seen enough drama for a lifetime.

Like a thief in the night, Cream ran back to his truck and took off. His luggage was packed, and he was ready to catch his flight with Camille in a few short hours.

New York would be nothing but a memory for him and Camille.

acknowledgments

First, I thank God for the talents He blessed me with. It's my gift from Him. Now what I do with it, is my gift back to Him. I'm blessed with this. With every book I'm getting better at it.

Second, I got to give love to my daughter, my true love, heart, and soul. Emari Gray I love you, girl. You know Daddy is in this to win.

Third, I thank God for the parents He blessed me with, Alinda and Spencer Gray; they keep me standing strong with the courage to carry on. They watched me grow, and when I was about to buckle and fold, they were the ones who came along, prayed for me, and unfolded the one they love.

Before I go on, Lauren Hamilton, thank you for your love and support.

I can't forget, got to show love to my sisters and brothers, Tanya, Terry, Pat, and Vincent. We recently lost one—rest in peace, Corey L. Gray—but as a family we're still strong, and our younger brother still lives on through us, as we continue to carry on the family name.

Also, I thank Mark Anthony for all he's done for me, and the Q-Boro family. You're blessed with Q-Boro, a company meant for great things. You inspire me and others to keep reaching for their dreams.

Danielle Stallings, my home girl from Connecticut, I love your honesty and assertiveness; keep that fire in you beautiful. I had to show you love, too.

Special thanks to Monique Patterson, Emily Drum, and the people at St. Martin's Press for helping me put this book together.

Nakea, my home girl from Philly—city of brotherly love—thanks for being a friend, a listener, and a great publicist to us all. You, Mark, and the rest all make up an excellent team.

My peoples who I've known forever, David Beaumont, K.T., Ryan, Sean, Hasheem, Jamel Rice, my cousin Jamel Johnson, Lovey, Michael Thompson, Jerry A.K.A. Law, James, Bryant, Lanise, Tania, Kay, and Gregory G. Goff (rest in peace). Thanks for holding it down.

Okay, this next statement is going to take a minute, so bear with me as I shout out, Linda Williams, Tasha, Herman, K'wan, Jay, Anthony Whyte, Brandon McCalla, Tracy Brown, August, Ebony Stroman, Denise Campbell, T.N. Baker, Kashamba Williams, Ed Mcnair, Hickson, Asante, Thomas Long, Mo Shines, Dejon, Kiniesha Gayle, K. Elliott, Anna J., Joe-Joe, Al-Saadiq Banks, Crystal Lacey, Jihad, Treasure E. Blue, Vonetta Pierce, Danielle Santiago, C. Rene West, Azarel, Shannon Holmes, Ike Capone, Carl Weber, T.L. Gardner, Gerald K. Malcom, Gayle Jackson Sloan, Dynah Zale, Tu-Shonda Whitaker, Zane, Brenda L. Thomas, S.A. Sabuur, Deborah, and many more in this game. Let us continued to blow up this genre. If I missed you, I didn't forget about you.

I got to thank Coast 2 Coast and the ARC book club for them online chats. Y'all know I'm always looking forward to them. But thank you for helping put us authors out there in the market and keeping us on the map.

And last, I'm shouting out myself, for getting things done. I'm thankful for everything, even for my downs, because it all made me a stronger and better person today. And I thank my fans and readers for showing me love and support. Thank you.

If y'all wish to get at me, you can reach me at Bootycall2099 @yahoo.com or Writeone04@yahoo.com. Peace.

Erick S. Gray

ERICK S. GRAY's climb to success in the literary genre has been fortunate, but also nothing but trials and tribulations for this talented, forty-four-year-old writer from Jamaica, Queens. Since his debut in 2003 with *Booty Call,* he's been consistent, with over sixteen books published, participating in many anthologies and novellas, and helping to cowrite the Streets of New York trilogy within the span of twenty years. His style of writing has been known to be raunchy, but also fruitful. His diversity in storytelling makes him one of the most prolific writers of the genre. His characters are memorable and true to life, and Mr. Gray has the drive to become an icon in a growing genre.